MADE
OF
Steel

MADE
OF
Steel

MADE OF STEEL SERIES – BOOK 1
IVY SMOAK

CHAPTER 1

8 Years Old

It had already been fifteen minutes s
Julie, had arrived. Why were my paren
very strict schedule to stick to if I was
Miles tonight. Just thinking about him r

"The pizza should arrive any min
for what had to be the tenth time. "Th
counter. And there's juice and soda in t

"I got it, Mrs. Brooks," Julie said w

My mom always went on and or
Dad had a date night. Julie had wa
times, though. She already knew all thi
old for a babysitter. I sighed and fol
my chest.

My dad turned his head and saw n

A smile spread over his face as h
"What's the matter, Summer? You ne
upside down."

Whenever he said that, I couldr
don't need a babysitter, Dad. I can ta
would have been more convincing
him. "I'm almost two whole hands." I
to prove my very valid point.

He ruffled my hair. "Well, I kno
how your mom worries. Besides," h

e, "you're not quite two whole hands yet. You still
a couple of years."

'm rounding up."

le laughed.

Isn't your movie at 6:30? You're going to be late. You
should get going." I loved my parents to death, but
were being ridiculous. Nothing bad ever happened on
il-de-sac. It was probably the safest place to live in
orld.

And why is it that you're so eager to get rid of us?
vouldn't have anything to do with sneaking over to
house, would it?"

y eyes got huge.

hich just made his smile grow. "It's okay. Just don't
ur mother," he said with a wink. "You're right, the
re brighter after your bedtime. It can be our little
"

ou ready to go, sweetie?" my mom called from the

lake sure you're back in your bed by 11 when we get
though," my dad whispered as he gave me a hug
kiss on the forehead.

at wouldn't be a problem. Since Miles lived at the
the cul-de-sac, it was easy to see my driveway and
orch from his tree house. Even if I was still out
ny parents got home, I'd be able to see them pull up
eak back just in time. If I ran really fast, I could be
in bed before my parents came to check on me to
ure I was asleep. And I was an expert fake snorer. I
y dad an innocent smile.

To Ryan. Because...love.

He smiled, as if he knew what I was thinking. "And go say goodbye to your mother."

I ran over to the door. "Bye, Mom," I said and gave her a swift hug.

"Behave yourself."

I shrugged my shoulders in what I thought was an innocent way. But I wasn't planning on behaving. I was planning on annoying Julie to no end and getting sent to bed early. I had this babysitter thing all worked out. It was the same every time.

My dad ruffled my hair once more, and then they both walked out the front door.

Finally. I closed the door behind them. Phase 1 was complete.

"Hey, kiddo," Julie said as I turned around.

I hated when she called me that. I wasn't a kid anymore. *Time for phase 2.*

***

"And he bought me these," Julie said and stuck her foot out from under the table so I could see her new Converses. "Aren't they awesome?"

"Mhm." But they weren't really. They just looked like any other pair of shoes. My bunny slippers that my dad had bought me were much more awesome. I glanced under the table at my fuzzy slippers. My feet didn't reach the floor, so the bunnies' ears sagged slightly forward, which made the slippers look even cuter.

"Jacob is seriously the best boyfriend ever. I'm so lucky. We already got our tickets for homecoming and it's not even until the end of the month. He bought a tie to match my dress. I can't wait to show you pictures."

"What color is your dress?"

"It's this really deep purple."

"What color shoes did you get?"

"Silver. They're really pretty. They have these little gems on the straps."

"Is he going to buy you a corsage?"

"I think so."

"Do you love him?"

She laughed. "What? I don't know. We haven't really talked about that yet."

"Really? How long have you been dating?"

"Just a few weeks." She took a huge bite of her pizza. It looked like she was thinking.

"So how long does it usually take to know if you love someone?" I was purposely trying to push her buttons, but it didn't mean I wasn't curious about the answer.

She swallowed her mouthful of pizza and gave me a stern look. "At least a few weeks longer than that."

Hmm. I wasn't sure that was true. I had fallen in love with Miles Young the first time I ever saw him. My family had moved here two years ago. The first time I saw Miles, he was riding a bike without a helmet. Just the thought of it was thrilling. I loved him before I ever even spoke to him. "What about love at first sight?"

"That's only in fairy tales, Summer. What Jacob and I have is real."

"But how do you know?"

"I can feel it."

"So are you getting married?"

"I'm only 17. Of course I'm not getting married."

"Then it probably isn't love."

"Summer Brooks, what on earth do you know about love?"

Everything. I shrugged my shoulders. "I've seen a lot of Disney movies. All of them I think."

"Well this is real life. We're not in some movie."

"Are you saying you don't like Cinderella? Or Beauty and the Beast? Or The Little Mermaid?"

"I liked them when I was a kid."

"It sounds like being a grown up is no fun at all."

She laughed. "Trust me, it's fun."

"Well, did Jacob at least ask you out in a really grand way?"

"Actually, I asked him out."

"That's really stupid."

"Summer!"

"Well it is, Julie! That's not how it's supposed to go at all. He's supposed to realize he loves you and then ask you to be with him forever. He should have proposed by now."

"That's not how life works anymore. We're not in the dark ages. Women are empowered and independent now."

"You're only 17. How would you know?"

She raised her eyebrow at me.

That's when I knew I had her just where I wanted her. She only ever raised her eyebrow when she was getting mad at me.

"Clear the dishes, kiddo. And your mom mentioned that you were reading a book. Do you want to read that for a bit?"

"Definitely. It's a big book of fairy tales."

She sighed and shook her head. "I have to study anyway. How about you just read that in your room and then get to bed?"

I glanced at the clock on the kitchen wall. It was almost 8 pm. The timing couldn't have been any more perfect.

Phase 2 complete.

CHAPTER 2

I tiptoed down the hallway and peered around the corner into the living room. Julie was asleep in front of the TV. Her notes were strewn across the coffee table and she was snoring from the couch. Phase 3 was definitely complete. I tried to stifle my excitement as I ran back to my room. I pushed the window open while I slid my feet back into my bunny slippers. For just a moment, I thought about changing them. Bunny slippers were for children. I thought about Julie's new Converses that she couldn't stop talking about at dinner. I wanted Miles to think I was sophisticated. He was two years older than me. Maybe he liked Converses too. I bit my lip. But I loved bunnies. There was no better footwear than the slippers I was currently wearing. I climbed out the window without another thought.

With one last look at my house to make sure the coast was clear, I ran across my lawn. I opened up the gate to Miles' backyard and closed it as quietly as possible. The light was already on in his tree house. I climbed up the rickety ladder and knocked twice on the boards above my head.

"Secret password?" Miles said from the other side.

The password was different every month. It was always a constellation that was easy to see in the sky during whatever month it was. It had taken me a long time to memorize them. But I preferred this method over what his password always was a couple of years ago: boys rule and girls drool. When I first moved in next door, I was pretty sure he hated me. I had worn him down though. Now we were best friends.

"Lyra," I said. He had a habit of choosing the smallest constellations that were the hardest to see. It just so happened that I liked those ones the most. The ones that he had to point out in order to show me where they were hiding.

"Access denied. It's September first, Summer. New month, new secret password."

I laughed. "It's Sagitta then." It was one of my favorites. It looked like an arrow in the sky and reminded me of cupid's arrow. I had been waiting for it to hit Miles for two years.

The board lifted above my head. I climbed up into the tree house and he closed the floorboard door behind me.

"Nice slippers, Summer."

I smiled up at him. Yes, he used to hate me. Yes, we were friends now. But what Miles didn't realize was that I was hopelessly in love with him. Every time I thought about him, my heart raced. Every time I saw him, I was momentarily speechless. I loved the way he smiled out of the corner of his mouth. And the way his brown eyes lit up when he talked about the stars. For me, it was love at first sight. It was like all the fairy tales I read about. Despite what Julie said, it was real. Now I just had to wait for him to realize he loved me back. It would happen one day. There wasn't a doubt in my mind. That arrow was coming his way.

"What are you staring at?" He pushed his shaggy brown hair off his forehead.

"Nothing." I laughed awkwardly and looked down at my slippers. Bunny slippers were always a good choice. *I knew it.* "How was soccer practice?"

"Fantastic." He lay down on the blanket in the center of the tree house and put his hands underneath his head. "I get to be a striker in the first game tomorrow."

"That's awesome." I really had no idea what it meant, but I knew he had been wanting it, and therefore I was just as happy as he was. I lay down on the blanket next to him and looked up at the stars. That was the coolest thing about Miles' tree house. It had no roof. Every night that the sky was clear, I'd sneak out of my room and meet him in his tree house. We never had a set plan or anything. It's just how it was.

"You're coming to my game tomorrow after school, right?" he asked, breaking the silence.

He wants me at his games. I smiled up at the stars. "Of course. I'll ask my parents if it's okay once they get home."

"I thought I saw Julie's car. Did you annoy her to no end tonight?"

"Not to no end. Just until she fell asleep."

He laughed.

The sound made my insides flip over.

"My parents can drive you home after. We'll probably get dinner somewhere if we win."

It wasn't a date. But he technically had kind of asked me to dinner. Maybe he reciprocated my unspoken feelings. I thought about what Julie said about her new boyfriend. She had asked him out. It wasn't exactly how fairy tales went. But she certainly seemed happy.

"I got you something," Miles said as he sat up.

He bought me a present too?

He pulled something out of his pocket and then put both his hands behind his back. "I got it from that quarter machine at the grocery store. I thought you might like it." He put both his hands out in front of him with both his fists closed. "You have to guess which hand it's in, though."

So he hadn't actually bought me a present. He probably tried to get something for himself and failed. But he thought of me when he opened it. That counted for something.

I looked into his eyes. He had always been really hard to read.

A smile spread over his face, like he already knew I was going to choose wrong.

I slapped his left hand. He opened it up. It was just an empty palm.

"You're lucky that we're friends." He opened up his other hand and tossed a small object at me.

I caught it and opened my hand. It was a small keychain with an arrow on it. *Sagitta.* "I love it."

"Thought you might." He lay back down, not reading into my words at all. "Can you see it tonight?"

"See what?" *How much you love me back?* My eyes were glued to the arrow keychain. It was the perfect present.

"Sagitta." He pointed to the stars.

I lay back down and looked past his index finger at the arrow in the sky. The constellation was as bright as could be. I nodded.

It was like he knew my response even though he couldn't hear it. He dropped his hand on the blanket between us. Without thinking, I slipped my hand into his.

And then I held my breath. For one second. *My heart is going to beat out of my chest.* For two. *What did I just do?* For three. *Should I say it was an accident?* For four. *He's never going to speak to me again.* For five.

His fingers tightened around mine.

I exhaled slowly. Miles Young was holding my hand. It felt like I was dreaming, because I had dreamed of this exact moment for years. *Miles Young is holding my hand!*

Neither one of us said a word. We just looked at the stars in the sky.

Thank you, Sagitta.

"Summer?"

"Yes?"

"I like this."

I swallowed hard. "Me too." My life was complete. I could already picture the wedding. My dad would walk me down the aisle. Miles would wear a blue tie to match my bridesmaids' dresses. It would be the best day of my life. Besides for this one. It would definitely be hard to compete with this one.

"Maybe we could do this more often?" Miles said.

I nodded.

He squeezed my hand, hearing my nod even though he couldn't see it. Miles could read me much easier than I could read him. Maybe he knew I was in love with him for the past two years. I was glad he finally got hit by that arrow.

He really was perfect, because he never made me feel like I was one of the smallest constellations in the sky. That's how I knew it was true love. I stared up at Sagitta. Suddenly the sky turned red and blue.

Miles' hand fell from mine as he sat up. "What is that?" He looked out the window of the tree house. "Summer..."

His voice sounded strange. I sat up and looked out the window too.

There was a police car. The officer walked to my door and knocked. Why was he knocking on my door? Why was Julie's hand covering her mouth? Why did it look like he was trying to comfort her?

My feet started moving before my mind could even process what was happening.

"Summer!" Miles called after me as I climbed down the rickety ladder and started running back toward my house.

Once I was through the gate into my yard, I kicked off my bunny slippers so I could run even faster.

Julie turned toward me. The police officer turned toward me. And then I froze. Because he started walking toward me. He wasn't there to tell Julie something. He was there to tell me something.

The officer crouched down in front of me and I held my breath for one second.

"Your parents were in an accident."

For two seconds.

"We rushed them to the hospital."

For three seconds.

"I'm so sorry, Summer."

For four seconds.

"They didn't make it."

It took five seconds for me to realize that my whole world had suddenly changed. Five seconds to realize that my life was no longer complete. Five seconds to realize that everything was broken.

CHAPTER 3

Summer,

I know your grandmother said you could come visit sometime soon. My soccer team made it into the playoffs. If you could come to our next game, that would be amazing. I know it's a long drive, but you're my good luck charm.

Hope you're doing well. How is your new school? I'm trying to convince my mom to move to Colorado. She's not thrilled with the idea. Give me all the highlights and maybe I can sway her.

-Miles

***

Dear Miles,

I would love to come to your game. But my grandmother isn't up to driving so far. Apparently my nagging annoys her as much as it always annoyed Julie. Thank you for thinking of me though.

Your mom's got the right idea. You don't want to come to Colorado. It's lonely here. I just started a new school and everyone looks at me in this way I can't quite explain. Like I don't belong here. Or maybe it's because I want to come home.

I miss you,

-Summer

***

Summer,

I do want to come to Colorado. You're there. That's all that matters. I'm still going to try to convince my mom. But you shouldn't feel lonely. You have me. And I'm sure you're going to make lots of friends at your new school.

My soccer team is going to the finals! I still can't even believe it. Once my season is over, I'm going to come visit.

I miss you more,

-Miles

***

Miles,

Congratulations! I'm sure you were amazing all season. Good luck in the finals, although I know you won't need it.

Sculptor is in the sky tonight. Have you seen it? I'm assuming that's your new secret password.

I miss you the most,

-Summer

CHAPTER 4
9 Years Old

The porch door slammed behind me as I ran down the front steps.

"Summer!" my grandmother called. "What have I told you about slamming that door!"

Miles' car had just pulled into our driveway, though. If there was ever a time for letting a door slam, it was today. This was the first time we had gotten to see each other since I had moved. Getting his parents or my grandmother to drive the four hours that separated us had proved to be almost impossible. His mom was going to visit a few of her friends in Santa Fe for the weekend, though, and my grandmother's house was basically on the way. How he convinced his mom to let him come here instead of going with her, I'd never know. But I had been looking forward to it all summer.

As soon as Miles stepped out of the car, I tackled him in a hug.

We both laughed as we fell into the grass.

"Summer!" my grandmother called from the porch. "Get out of the grass!"

I smiled down at the boy I loved. "She hates it when I get grass stains on my clothes."

He laughed.

God, I missed his laugh.

"What's the point of living if you can't get your clothes dirty?"

I smiled. No one had ever understood me as well as Miles Young. I stood up just so that my grandmother would stop yelling.

"Hi, Summer," Miles' mother said as she stepped out of the car.

"Hi, Mrs. Young."

She embraced me in a hug. "It's so good to see you, dear. You look well."

People said that to me a lot. That I looked well. At first I wasn't sure exactly what it meant. But after hearing it so many times, I had figured it out. They were only saying half of what they were thinking whenever they said it, especially when it was combined with the expression on Mrs. Young's face right now. The one that was kind of sad but hopeful at the same time. What she meant was, "You look well despite everything that's happened."

I wasn't sure it was true. Some days it was hard not to cry when I was alone in my room. I wanted to remember but at the same time I wanted to forget. But for some reason, when people said it, it made me want it to be true. I had become good at smiling even when I hurt. I had become impeccable at make-believe.

"Thanks, Mrs. Young."

She gave me a kind smile and then walked up to the front porch to talk to my grandmother.

"You're it," Miles whispered in my ear before sprinting off to the backyard.

He didn't need to tell me to follow him. I'd follow that boy to the ends of the earth. I quickly ran after him despite my grandmother yelling at me to slow down.

***

I opened up my bedroom window and climbed out onto the roof. Today had been perfect. Miles and I had spent the whole day running around outside. Nothing had felt the same without him. But now that he was here, I felt like my old self again. He made me smile like no one else could. Somehow he reminded me of the way things used to be without making me feel sad. Really, he made me feel whole again.

I heard the squeak of another window opening. I smiled to myself. Miles and I never talked about it. We were always just great at meeting at the right time.

He lay down beside me and slipped his hand into mine.

A year ago, that had been the happiest moment of my life. It mirrored my feelings today. Yes, we wrote to each other all the time. But it was never really romantic. I closed my eyes for a second. It was nice to know that his feelings hadn't changed. Miles Young was the only constant in my life.

"Do you come out here a lot?" he asked.

"Every night that the sky is clear." I opened my eyes and stared up at the stars. "Do you still go out in your tree house?"

"All the same nights as you, I bet."

That made me smile. Whenever I was hurting, looking at the stars made me feel better, because I always knew he was looking at them too. It was the only way I could feel close to home.

"Are you happy?" His voice was quieter, like he was scared to hear my answer.

No one had asked me that in a long time. Was I happy? "I miss them. I miss them every day." The thing that hurt the most was how guilty I felt. That night, I had been so eager for my parents to leave. I didn't even tell them that I loved them. But I would never tell Miles that. He'd beat himself up because I had been eager to go see him. That was my own burden to carry. It weighed on me though. I'd do anything to go back. I'd do anything to see my parents' smiles one more time.

He squeezed my hand.

"But yeah, I think I'm happy." I blinked away the tears that were threatening to escape. "I love my grandmother. She yells at me a lot, but I think it's because I remind her so much of my mom, you know? She misses her too. I know it's been hard on her." I was quiet for a moment. "And I have you." I turned my head toward his. He was already staring at me instead of the stars.

"Yeah, you have me." He smiled out of the corner of his mouth.

I had never seen that look on his face before. He was different in a lot of ways. Taller. More handsome, if that was possible. But the look on his face right now was the main difference. I'm pretty sure it's the look I had always given him. "You look different," I whispered.

He laughed. "You look different too, Summer."

"A good different?"

He nodded his head and left it tilted slightly down toward mine. "A very good different."

I tilted my head up toward his until his lips were pressed to mine. We stayed completely still. It was better than holding his hand. It was better than anything I had ever experienced.

He smiled when our lips parted.

And I know I was smiling. I'm not sure I'd ever stop smiling again. He was my first love. My first kiss. My rock.

***

Summer,

I'm so sorry about your grandmother passing. How are you holding up? I'm sorry that I couldn't come to the funeral.

Sagitta is really bright right now. Do you still look up at the stars? It reminds me of you. You don't seem so far away whenever I look up.

What happens now? Where will you go?
-Miles

***

Miles,

Sometimes I feel like I look at the stars more than I look at what's around me. I still have that keychain you gave me of Sagitta. It reminds me of you too.

I'm moving again. I'm going to be part of a foster family. They seem nice.
-Summer

CHAPTER 5
11 Years Old

Summer,

Merry Christmas! We have about a foot of snow here. I know you just moved again. Does it snow in Colorado too?

What happened with your last foster family? I thought they might stick. I was rooting for you.

-Miles

***

Miles,

Happy New Year! Do you have any resolutions? My resolution this year is to make my new foster parents want me. Maybe this will be better. I feel like it's something I'm doing. Well, I know it is. The last family I was with adopted the other girl I was with instead of me. The social worker says I read too much. But I love reading. I'll try to do it a little less, though, just in case that's it.

Yes, it snows here. At least where I am. But it didn't snow for Christmas. I'm not sure it would have felt like Christmas even if it had. No Christmases have felt the same since I left home.

-Summer

CHAPTER 6
12 Years Old

Summer,

There was blood on your last message. I know it's not a nosebleed. I'm not an idiot. It's the second time it's happened. Tell me what's going on. Let me help you. I'll get on a bus and be there. Just tell me to come.

-Miles

***

Miles,

I'm fine. I've been getting nosebleeds because of the altitude I think. You don't have to come. I'm really okay. You don't have to worry about me. I can take care of myself. I'm not as small as you remember. I'm at least a foot taller, I swear.

-Summer

***

Summer,

I don't believe you. At all. But if you don't want me to come, I won't. You won't be able to stop me soon though. My parents said they're going to get me a car after I pass driver's ed.

Which reminds me. I started high school! I know how excited you are to go in a few years. It's not any different though. It's still school. But I made the varsity soccer team. I'm one of the only freshmen to do it.

Look up. Even though it's not September yet, Sagitta is pretty bright.

-Miles

***

Miles,

There's nothing to worry about. I promise. Is it as wild as Julie made me believe? I get that school is just school. But high school is high school. No matter what you say, I still can't wait to go.

-Summer

CHAPTER 7
13 Years Old

Miles,

Happy Birthday! I haven't heard from you recently. I know you're really busy with soccer and school, so I understand that you can't write as often.

I bet you're taking driver's ed now. I believe you promised me a visit.

I miss you,
-Summer

***

Miles,

It's been months since you've written. Are you okay? Even when I look at the stars, you feel so far away.
-Summer

***

Miles,

You were right. I can't take care of myself. I thought I could and I was wrong. Please help me. Please don't leave me alone.
-Summer

***

Miles,

It's getting worse and I don't know what to do. Where are you? You were right. You're always right.

-Summer

CHAPTER 8
14 Years Old

Miles,

I lied, is that what you want to hear? I just didn't want you to worry. But I'm sorry that I lied to you. It was never a nosebleed. He's been hurting me. I don't know what to do.

-Summer

***

Miles,

I don't understand what I did wrong. But whatever it was, I'm sorry. I'm so, so sorry. Please just tell me how to fix it. You're all that I have left, Miles. You're it. How am I supposed to keep going without you?

I'm sorry,

-Summer

CHAPTER 9
18 Years Old
Saturday

I looked outside the window of the coffee shop at the tall building across the street. In just a few minutes, I'd be stepping into my new life. I had started fifteen new schools in my lifetime. There was no one more used to this than me. But I didn't want to be here. For once in my life, I wanted to make my own choices. I just wanted to go home. I hadn't been back to the only place I had ever loved in ten years.

"Sadie?"

This city wasn't for me. I had been here less than ten minutes and had already been bumped into at least as many times. There was a buzz of excitement in the air, but it didn't quite reach me. Instead, my stomach was twisted in knots. I felt like I was going to be sick.

"Sadie," Mr. Crawford said again.

I blinked and continued to stare at the building. He thought I wasn't listening, but I was. I just didn't want to answer to that name. *I'm Summer Brooks.* I could feel myself disappearing. I didn't want to disappear. I never asked for this.

"Sadie." Mr. Crawford reached across the table and touched my hand.

I immediately pulled my hand onto my lap and stared at him. *Don't you dare touch me.* I clenched my hand into a fist.

His eyes softened. He pitied me. For the past week, I had gotten that look enough times to know what it meant. And it made me angry. I didn't need his pity.

"I'm sorry. I didn't mean to startle you," he said. "You read the papers, right? You're going to have to get better at answering to your new name."

I nodded and looked down at the folder in front of me. My new life was written on the pages before me. Once I walked out this door, I'd have to lie to everyone I met. But in a way I was used to that too. I had been lying about my home life for as long as I could remember. For some reason I had this stupid hope that this would be different though. I was tired of lying. I was just tired in general.

"Sadie?"

I looked up at him.

This time he smiled. "Good. Here's your new ID." He slid me the small piece of plastic. "You'll probably need it at check-in. Have you memorized your new identity?"

"Should we really be discussing this in a crowded cof- fee shop?"

"Welcome to New York, Sadie. No one cares what we're talking about." He gestured to the people around us.

They all seemed totally focused on their phones and computers, completely self absorbed. I wasn't sure what I was worried about. No one had taken an interest in my problems when I had actually needed help. No one would care now either. I was invisible.

"Have you memorized your new identity?" he asked again.

I knew it backwards and forwards. I had read it dozens of times. "Yes, I've memorized it." I picked up the ID and looked at the picture. My hair was brunette now instead of red. My eyes were brown instead of blue. I barely recognized myself. It's exactly what they wanted. *I'm disappearing.*

"There's a card with my number on it in one of your suitcases. If you see anyone from your past or anything suspicious at all, call me right away. If someone recognizes you, you'll be putting yourself and them in danger. So call and we'll relocate you immediately."

I nodded. I had heard all this before. "Are you sure I have to be here, though? I had been looking at a lot of schools. I even got into Dartmouth and I was really hoping..."

"Which is why you can't go there. Your friends knew you got in. You'd be easy to find. It'll be easy for you to blend in here. People come to New York City to start over. This is your chance, Sadie."

What friends? I had been invisible in school. Barely anyone had even talked to me. "I'm not starting over. I'm hiding."

"This is the best we could do. You'll be safe here."

I glanced out the window again at the immense building. I didn't want to be in a skyscraper in NYC. I wanted to be in a cute small town where everyone knew my name. I sighed. That was the problem. No one could know my name. But if he was right and I truly could be safe, then it was worth it. I hadn't felt safe in years. "Okay."

"You're looking at this all wrong, Sadie. You should embrace your new life. I know the past week has been hard." He stopped when he saw the expression on my face.

Because it wasn't the past week that had been hard. It was the past five years. When no one would help me. When no one was on my side.

"A fresh start will be good for you."

"You want me to just forget about my old life? I don't think..."

"That's exactly what you're supposed to do. You're here for your own safety. Anything that you do to jeopardize that will put you into danger."

"So what, I'm supposed to lie to everyone I meet? Never form real relationships again? How is that better than the way I was already living?" I would never be free. This was supposed to be different.

"You're a bright girl. Convince yourself that this is real." He tapped the folder in front of me. "We're asking you to blend in, but that doesn't mean you can't form relationships. You just have to form them around Sadie Davis. Not Summer Brooks."

I gave him a small smile.

"You get to find yourself here. Just don't forget to blend in while you do that." He grabbed the folder in front of me and tucked it into his briefcase. "Your suitcases are packed with new clothes. But try to keep your neck covered until the bruises go away. You don't want people asking any questions and drawing unwanted attention."

I put my hand on the side of my neck. He didn't need to tell me that. I was already wearing a hoodie even though it was 90 degrees in the city today. I was used to making sure no one had a reason to ask me questions.

"And if you need anything else, we transferred your money into a bank account under your new name. All the information for that is also in your suitcases. With the money that..."

"Thanks," I said, cutting him off. I felt guilty enough for getting handouts from the state. I didn't need him to tell me that I only had about a hundred dollars in my savings account. It wouldn't even be enough for the school books I needed. One of the first things I was going to do was get a job.

"Is there anything else you need to give me before I head out? Anything at all that would jeopardize the secrecy of your new identity?"

I thought about the arrow keychain I had hidden in my pocket. I had already handed over everything that belonged to me. Every memory I had of my old life. I needed this one thing. For some reason, it still meant the world to me, even though the boy that gave it to me meant nothing. It reminded me of home. It reminded me of being carefree. It reminded me of everything I lost. "No, there's nothing else."

He nodded. "I'll be reaching out to you as soon as the bail hearing takes place. But I have it under good authority that Roberts will be staying behind bars for a long time."

God, I hoped that was true. "Do you know when the trial will be?"

"One day at a time. We have to get through the bail hearing first." He glanced at his watch. "Check-in ends in about thirty minutes. I should leave you to it."

I nodded and stared into the coffee mug that I hadn't touched. I didn't even like coffee. Was I supposed to now?

"Well, good luck, Sadie. You have my number if you need to reach me. Don't be late for check-in."

"Right. I don't want to draw attention to myself."

"Exactly." He hesitated once he stood up. "And remember to smile, Sadie. This is going to be a good thing, I promise. If everything goes well, you won't be seeing me ever again."

"Thanks for all your help, Mr. Crawford."

He nodded and disappeared out the door of the coffee shop.

If everything went well, I'd never be Summer Brooks again. That may have sounded good to him. But it didn't sound good to me.

CHAPTER 10
Saturday

I stepped up onto the sidewalk in front of my dorm building. Even though there were tons of people around me, I felt alone. Never again would anyone truly know who I was. But maybe that was for the best. Maybe Summer Brooks needed to disappear. What was left of her anyway? Pain? Scars?

Yet another person bumped into me without an apology. I pulled my suitcases closer to my sides. I would have chosen absolutely anywhere else for college. But I hadn't gotten to make a single decision about my life since my parents had died. Just like everything else, I was forced to go here. It could have been worse, though. Mr. Crawford had said I was free to do whatever I wanted, free to be whoever I wanted, as long as I blended in. And I wanted to be different. I wanted to be brave and strong.

"Hey, do you need help with that?" a man in a bright yellow shirt asked me.

I shook my head and gripped the handles even tighter in my hand. Even though I had no idea what was inside, everything I owned was in these suitcases. I wasn't brave. I wasn't strong.

He pointed to his shirt. "I'm helping with move in. I can get that if..."

"I don't need any help."

He shrugged. "Suit yourself. Are you in Dorm B?" He gestured to the tall building in front of me.

I nodded.

"Check-in is on the first floor in the common room. Just go through the main doors and head left. There's a freshmen welcome shindig on the Green tonight. Make sure to come, it's going to be a blast." He left to go help someone else.

I exhaled slowly. He wasn't trying to mug me. He was just being nice. I glanced around at all the people once more. No one knew me here. It was a fact. Or else I would have been sent somewhere else. This was a new beginning. *I can do this.*

In ten years, I hadn't lost my optimism. I would have thought it would be one of the first things beaten out of me. But it wasn't. I still hoped. I still dreamed. What I had lost was my confidence. My voice. I was a shell of the person that I once was. I hid in the shadows, hoping not to be seen, hoping not to draw unwanted attention toward myself. Somewhere along the way I had become invisible.

Just because I needed to blend in, it didn't mean I needed to be invisible though. There was no reason to live that way. I wasn't Summer Brooks anymore. I barely recognized myself when I looked in the mirror. This was my fresh start. I could be whoever I wanted. *I really can do this.*

I took my first step toward my new life. And I held my breath for five seconds as I walked toward the front doors. For some reason, whenever I was nervous, I held my breath. And when I exhaled, I'd know if something good or bad was about to happen. In five seconds I'd know. I exhaled when I reached the front of the line at check in.

"Welcome to Eastern University," the girl sitting behind a folding table said with a huge smile. "We just need you to sign in and we can get you all set up. What's your name?"

This was going to be a good thing. I smiled back. "Sadie Davis." It sounded weird to say it out loud.

"Okay, Sadie." She glanced at the clipboard. "You're in room 1216. It's a double. I'm sure you've already been chatting with your roommate online, though."

I hadn't. I nodded instead of saying that, though. It had only been two days since I had been told I was coming here.

"Can I just see your ID real quick?"

I handed her the image of what I looked like now. The person I didn't recognize. This strange person that was suddenly me.

"Perfect. Just sign here." She handed me my ID back and slid the clipboard toward me.

I lifted up the pen and signed my name as quickly as I could. My signature looked strange. I'd have to practice it.

"And here's your room key and a fob to get into the building. Just wave it in front of the scanner outside the building in order to get in. And try not to let anyone in behind you. It's the main security precaution we have on campus."

"Got it." I'd definitely be following those instructions.

"Okay, you're all set. There's a freshmen welcome party on the Green tonight. I know there's a comedian and I think there's also a movie playing. It should be a lot of fun. Make sure to stop by and meet some of your fellow classmates."

I nodded. If everyone else was going to a party on the Green tonight, I would be going too. That was the first tip of Blending-In 101. Do what everyone else does. I said goodbye to the girl that was all smiles and made my way over to the elevators.

A group of girls were crowded by the doors laughing about something. I figured a lot of people would already know each other. In-state schools were always cheaper. Summer Brooks wouldn't have said hi to these girls. She wouldn't want them to ask her questions about where she lived. She wouldn't want them to ask her questions about the random bruises she always seemed to have. I wasn't Summer Brooks anymore, though. But I was also supposed to be blending in. I kept my head down as I stepped onto the elevator, keeping to my old ways.

They were chatting about some hot guy they had just run into. Dating was the absolute last thing on my mind. Is that what everyone was going to be talking about? What if I didn't have anything in common with anyone here? I stepped off the elevator once I reached my floor. The girls' laughter disappeared as soon as the doors shut again. There were a few people in the hall. I tried harder to smile at these strangers as I lugged my suitcases down the hallway. They'd be living near me all year. I might as well try to be friendly. Finally, I found room 1216.

For a moment I hesitated. *Should I knock? Would that be weird because I live here too?* Trying not to overthink it, I put my key into the lock and slowly opened the door.

"You must be Sadie!"

I didn't even get to take in the room before a bubbly girl appeared right in front of me. She looked like the girls from the elevator. Perfectly smooth blonde hair. Perfectly straight teeth. Perfectly tanned skin. But she was smiling at me. I instantly liked her. Especially because she had a book in her hand.

"Hi." I smiled back. "I actually don't know your name..."

"I'm Kinsley," she stuck her hand out to me. "But most of my friends call my Kins. Who am I kidding though, I literally know no one here. Well, except you. Most of my friends went to out-of-state schools. They couldn't wait to get away. I have no idea why though. I love it here."

I shook her hand. "What are you reading?"

"Oh." She laughed. "Don't make fun of me. I was feeling a little homesick and it's one of my favorites from when I was younger." She held up the book. It was a worn copy of Sisterhood of the Traveling Pants.

"That's actually one of my favorites." I had probably read it a dozen times. Reading had been an escape for me growing up. And when I could relate to the characters, I was more than happy to escape from my actual life.

Her smile grew. "It's great, right? Geez, when I saw you didn't have a Facebook, I thought you were going to be totally bizarre. I'm so glad you're normal."

Normal. I wouldn't describe myself as normal at all. But Sadie Davis could be normal. *I'm normal now.*

"I already put my stuff on this side," she gestured to her totally decked out side of the room. "But we can rearrange the furniture however you want. I was just trying to get my stuff organized."

"Everything looks great." I placed one of my suitcases on the empty bed and the other on the floor.

"Do you want some help unpacking?"

"No, that's okay. Really, I barely brought anything. I'm going to have to go shopping for some new clothes and stuff. Thanks for offering though." I didn't want her going through my suitcases when I had no idea what was in them yet.

"Well, welcome to New York City." She smiled. "That's one of the many things we're famous for. Maybe we can go shopping sometime this week? God, I'm so nervous to start class on Monday, aren't you? My schedule looks insanely hard."

"Mine too." I liked that she talked a lot. It meant I didn't have to. I sat down on the plastic lined mattress and pulled my hoodie up slightly around my neck. I couldn't go shopping with her until the bruises went away. "Shopping later this week would be great."

"Awesome. We're going to have a blast. So where ya from?"

A small town in Wyoming. I had lived in Colorado for longer than I had lived in Wyoming. But no matter how much time passed, Wyoming would always be home to me because it was the last place I had lived with my parents. I thought about what my new ID said. "North Dakota."

She whistled. "You came a long way. Did you live in a city out there? Is that why you wanted to come here?"

"The exact opposite actually. I've always wanted to live in a city." I opened up my suitcase and pulled out some of my clothes. I felt uncomfortable lying to her. She seemed so nice. I looked down at the jean shorts and tank top in my hand. They were the perfect size. I thought for sure the suitcases would be filled with horrible clothes in gray and tan, perfect for blending in. But most of the clothes actually looked a lot like the outfit Kins was wearing. They'd probably make me fit in even better than lame neutral colored clothing. I'd look like every other college student on campus. I didn't even want to think about how much money Mr. Crawford had spent to make this happen.

"Well, I can't imagine living anywhere else," Kins said. "You're going to love it here."

That will be a first.

CHAPTER 11

Saturday

"Aren't you hot? It's like a thousand degrees," Kins said as she spread out a blanket on the Green.

I pulled the side of my hoodie up slightly to cover my neck. "I'm cold all the time. It must be a North Dakota thing." I laughed awkwardly. I had changed into a pair of jean shorts, but I was still wearing a baggy hoodie.

"I guess. It would be awesome to visit sometime. I've never been farther west than Chicago. What's it like?"

Shit. "Well, the badlands are pretty cool, but I've seen them dozens of times." That was literally the only thing I knew about North Dakota. I had never been there in my life. "Honestly there isn't a ton to see." I needed to change the topic. "So did you grow up around here?"

"In Queens. Whenever you're missing a home cooked meal, you can come visit my parents with me."

"Thanks, I'd like that." I couldn't even remember the last time I had a home cooked meal.

"It's just like a thirty minute subway ride away. I'm actually super lucky they let me live on campus. Why do you keep looking over your shoulder?"

"What?" I turned back toward her. "Sorry, I thought I heard something." I should have felt safe surrounded by hundreds of new students. But I didn't. It felt like someone was watching me. A chill ran down my spine.

She laughed. "I'm a little jumpy too. It's a little weird that neither one of us knows anyone else here. Maybe we should change that. Hey, look," she said and lightly touched my shoulder.

I tried to hide my cringe.

"Those guys are totally checking us out."

I laughed. I highly doubted that they were checking me out in my huge hoodie. They were probably both staring at her. I didn't even bother looking at where she was pointing.

She started waving them over.

"What are you doing?"

"We have extra room on our blanket. They're about to sit in the grass. I'm just being nice."

"But you don't even know them."

"Exactly. I don't know them. But I want to." She winked at me and then laughed. "You should see your face. You're acting all stranger danger on me. It's our first night here. We're supposed to talk to strangers. That's the whole point of this mixer thing. We were strangers this morning. And now you're literally my best friend here."

I couldn't argue with that. Kinsley was now officially my only friend. I wasn't even allowed to contact anyone from my past. It probably wouldn't hurt to expand my circle a bit.

"Hey, is it okay if we join you?"

I looked up to see two very handsome guys standing next to our blanket. What I didn't expect was for one of them to be smiling at me.

"Is that okay?" he said, still looking directly at me. "We didn't think about bringing a towel or anything to sit on." He shrugged his shoulders.

"Of course you can sit with us," Kins said. "Right?" She nudged my shoulder.

Again I tried to hide my cringe. "That's fine. We can move over. There's plenty of room." I slid all the way to the end of the blanket and waited for Kins to slide over next to me.

But she didn't move over. Instead she smiled up at them and tapped both the spots beside her.

And now I know Kins is a ridiculous flirt. All I wanted to do was watch the movie. I tried to keep my eyes glued to the screen as the guy who had smiled at me sat down between Kins and me. I folded my arms across my chest and leaned slightly away from him. If I leaned over any farther I'd probably fall over in the grass. But I couldn't seem to stop trying to put more distance between us. It took all of a few seconds for it to actually happen. I placed my hand down on the wet grass just in time to not completely topple over.

The boy next to me laughed. "Um, you sure this is okay? I promise I'm not trying to ruin your night. I really did just forget to bring a blanket."

I knew I was being awkward. I just didn't know how to stop. "It's fine," I gave him a small smile and turned my head back toward the screen. It was only previews, but I had always enjoyed the whole experience. I had no idea what movie was about to play, but I hoped it was a good one. It would be nice to be able to take my mind off the script of my new life for just a few hours.

"I'm Eli." He put his hand out for me.

I lifted my hand out of the grass and shook his hand. *Oh God, I just got his hand all wet.*

His eyes twinkled like he was holding back more laughter. He wiped his hand off on his jeans as I leaned even farther away from him. "And you are?"

"Summer." I immediately coughed. "Summer is my favorite time of the year. And my name is Sadie." *What is wrong with me?* "Sadie," I said again. It still sounded strange coming out of my mouth.

He smiled. "Well, it's nice to meet you, Sadie. I'm a fan of summer myself."

Before he could ask me any questions, I asked one of my own. "Are you from New York?"

He laughed. "No. Actually, I'm from this super small town in Utah."

"Really? Where?" I had never been to Utah. But I had been to almost every state through the characters in the books I constantly read. It was almost like I had been there. The descriptions reminded me of home.

"Moab. I'm sure you've never heard of it."

I hadn't heard of it. But how different could it be from Wyoming and Colorado? I could picture mountains everywhere. I could almost smell the crisp air. "No, I haven't traveled much," I lied. "I had never even left North Dakota until moving here."

"North Dakota? So you couldn't wait to move to the big city either, huh?"

"Yeah. I guess we came here for the same reasons." I swallowed hard. I was forming a connection with him based solely on a lie. This was harder than I thought it was going to be. He seemed like such a nice guy. I wished he had sat down on any blanket other than mine. My lies weren't worth his time.

He smiled. "I guess so."

I turned back to the screen, but I kept glancing at him out of the corner of my eye. He was wearing a button down with the sleeves rolled up. There were earbuds hanging out of his front pocket. He had dirty blonde hair and a kind smile. And it seemed like he wore that smile almost all the time. There wasn't a single threatening thing about him. He actually looked like the classic boy-next-door. But he wasn't my boy-next-door. I pulled my knees up to my chest and hugged my legs.

I hated when my mind wandered to Miles. It had been five years since I had even talked to him. Things still reminded me of him, though. That's what sucked the most. That I remembered him when he had so blatantly forgotten about me.

"Ouch, that must have hurt." Eli lightly touched the side of my knee where there was a huge bruise.

Don't touch me. I shifted slightly away from him. For some reason, his gentle touch hurt almost as much as getting the bruise in the first place.

I hadn't even thought about hiding the bruise on my knee. In comparison to the one on my neck, it was so tiny. But it wasn't exactly small. Not to a normal person. I laughed awkwardly. "I'm ridiculously clumsy. It's nothing."

"What happened?" He sounded concerned.

"It really was nothing. I just fell. Up the stairs. Believe it or not, it's actually a lot easier to fall up the stairs than down." *What the hell am I saying?* Luckily the movie had just started. I shushed him before he even got a chance to respond.

The movie should have been a reprieve. But when I saw the Disney logo, I bit my lip. *Frozen*. Even though it had been out for years, I had never watched it. I had stopped watching Disney movies when I was a kid. I hated how the parents always died. How were these characters supposed to find their happily ever after when there was so much pain in their hearts? *Maybe this one will be different.*

After several minutes of happy images, I watched the parents' boat sink into the water. It felt like it was hard to breathe. I looked up at the sky. Seeing the stars always gave me strength. They reminded me that anything was possible. But I couldn't see a single star in the sky. The city lights were too bright. It felt like my throat was constricting.

"It's weird, right?" Eli whispered. "That you can't see the stars?"

I blinked hard, trying to keep my tears at bay. "I have to go."

"I'm sorry, I'll be quiet. I hate when people talk during movies too." He smiled.

"No, it's not that." My voice sounded strangled. "It was nice meeting you." I stood up before he could say anything else and weaved my way as quickly as possible between all the blankets filled with other freshmen.

I knew I wasn't blending in. I knew I wasn't being normal enough. Unlike the characters in Disney movies, my life didn't seem to keep going after bad things happened. It was like I was frozen in time. In pain. And I couldn't breathe in this city. How could I breathe if I couldn't see the stars?

CHAPTER 12

Sunday

I stood under the water until it started to get cold. And even once it had, I stood there for another few minutes.

I was grateful to Kins for not making a big deal out of me ditching her last night. Apparently she had a great time with Eli's friend, Patrick. And I was glad she had something to occupy her mind. It made her stop asking questions I didn't know how to answer.

When the water felt like ice on my skin, I finally turned it off and wrapped a towel around myself. Tomorrow was my first day of classes. I had done it more times than I could count. But my stomach was still twisted into knots. Usually I avoided talking about myself by choice. Being forced to not talk about myself seemed a lot harder. What if I let something slip? I wasn't sure I could do this.

It was tempting to call Mr. Crawford. I could just tell him that I saw someone I knew. He'd transfer me. But a new school wouldn't fix anything. I knew that.

I walked out of the shower stall and stopped at the mirror. Years ago I had transformed the Sagitta keychain into a necklace. I never went anywhere without it. It reminded me of my parents more than anything else. It reminded me of the night I lost them. I touched the arrow pendant on the center of my chest. It reminded me that they were the last people that truly thought I wasn't invisible. And for some reason, it made me feel hopeful that maybe I would be able to find myself again.

I pushed my hair behind my shoulder and stared at the bruises on my neck. It was like I could still feel his fingers. It was like I could feel my throat constricting. I closed my eyes and took a deep breath. If I could survive that, I could survive this. I didn't need to find myself. I needed to recreate myself. *I can do this.*

I opened my eyes and moved my hair back over my neck. This was the start of my new life. I could be whoever I wanted to be. And Sadie Davis was done living in the past. I nodded at my reflection in the mirror. Summer Brooks was gone. There was nothing left of her. I nodded once more before grabbing my things and walking out of the bathroom.

This time I kept my head held high as I walked through the hallway. No one was there to witness my sudden confidence level, but I was still proud of myself.

"You just missed our RA," Kins said as soon as I stepped into our room.

"I have no idea what an RA even is, so I guess I didn't miss much."

"It stands for Resident Assistant. It's basically just a college student a few years older than us that helps us adjust, you know? Keeps us in line." She winked at me.

I laughed. "What was she like?"

"First of all, it was a he, not a she. A very dreamy he." She jumped onto her bed.

"I thought you were already in love with Patrick?"

Kins laughed. "I never said I was in love with Patrick. And just because I like him doesn't mean I'm suddenly blind to hotness."

"Fair enough." Kins really was a huge flirt. "What's the dreamy RA's name?"

"Matt, I think he said. It doesn't matter." She waved her arm dismissively. "I'm going to call him Mr. RA. That's hot right? Anyway, he was just walking around meeting everyone. He's hosting this pizza party thing tomorrow for everyone on our floor. It sounded like fun. You'll come, right?"

"Actually, I was probably going to go try to apply to some more jobs tomorrow night." I had spent most of the day applying to jobs around campus. But most of them were already full or were work-study jobs for students with financial need. I wasn't exactly sure how I was paying for college. Mr. Crawford had said it was part of the program I was in or something. I hadn't really heard all the details. Either way, it probably meant I didn't have financial need even if my bank account said otherwise. I'd have to venture out into the city tomorrow. I was way more nervous about that than my classes.

"No." She gave me an exaggerated frown. "Please come with me? I need to see his hotness again. And it's a sin that your eyes haven't experienced him yet. Please?"

I laughed. "How about you show me some cool local places that I should apply to after classes tomorrow? Then we can go to the pizza party together after?"

"Deal." She slid under her covers and hit the switch on her bedside lamp. "Goodnight, Sadie."

"Goodnight." I quickly changed into my pajamas and climbed into bed too. The darkness settled in around us. Just because I told myself I could forget, it didn't mean it would just happen overnight. I needed to actively become Sadie Davis. I stared up at the ceiling. I wished I was staring at the stars. Apparently the new me had insomnia.

"Sadie?" Kins whispered. "Are you still awake?"

"Mhm."

"I know it's silly. I'm only like half an hour from home. But I'm really homesick."

"Me too." I had been homesick for the last ten years. "It gets easier, though." I realized my mistake as soon as it slipped out. Sadie Davis had lived in North Dakota her whole life. She had never moved. I held my breath until she responded.

"You've been away from home before?"

Crap. "Just for overnight summer camps and stuff. It does get easier, though. I promise." *Please let that be enough information.*

"Yeah. It doesn't help that I'm nervous about tomorrow. Like, really nervous."

I exhaled slowly, relief washing over me. I needed to be more careful. "Just remember that at the end of the day you get to hang out with our hot RA."

She laughed. "I am looking forward to that."

"Besides, we have our first class together. It's going to be fun."

"You're right. I don't know what I'm so worried about. At least I'll have someone to sit next to. Goodnight, Sadie."

"Night, Kins." I continued to stare at the ceiling. Maybe I had been lying to myself for years. It didn't feel easier tonight. All I wanted was to go home. I squeezed my eyes shut. I wanted another chance. I wanted to tell my parents I loved them one last time.

I touched my necklace. It was so painful to remember. So why couldn't I make myself forget?

CHAPTER 13

Monday

"But the back row is where all the fun is," Kins protested.

"And the front row is where all the learning is." I may have been a new person, but it didn't mean I couldn't still love school. I sat down before she could somehow manage to convince me to go to the very back of the huge lecture hall.

"You're ridiculous, you do realize that, right?" She sat down next to me. "We're the only people in the front row."

"That's because there's still fifteen minutes until class starts."

She laughed. "I don't even think I need an RA. You'll be the one keeping me in line."

"Is he really that handsome? You haven't stopped talking about him since last night."

"You'll see. He has this kind of bad boy vibe, which I am definitely into. I bet he rides a motorcycle. Wouldn't that be hot?"

"I guess."

"You guess? Have you ever ridden on a motorcycle? It's like the epitome of romance."

"No, I haven't. What kind of romances are you into, anyway?"

"The sexy kind."

I laughed. "And you thought I was the ridiculous one? Oh, shhh, here's the professor."

"I didn't even say anything."

But my mind was already tuned to my first college class. I had been dreaming of college for as long as I could remember. It had always been the ultimate escape from my life. No, this wasn't my first choice of schools. But I was definitely going to make the most of this opportunity.

The sociology professor introduced himself, handed out a syllabus, and immediately dismissed us with a reading assignment.

Kins leaned on the arm rest and whispered, "I'm glad we sat in the front row for that riveting lecture."

"It'll be better next time." I put my blank notebook back into my backpack and zipped it closed.

"Mhm. My last class ends at 2. Want to meet on the Green and then we can find a perfect place for your services?"

"You do realize that makes it sound weird, right? I just want a normal job. Like at a coffee shop or something."

"Right, right. I guess we'll see what happens. I will see you at 2. Don't be late because I hate standing alone."

"I won't be late. Have fun sitting in the back row of your next class."

She smiled. "I absolutely will."

***

I was one of the first people to my Psych 101 class. I was relieved to see that it wasn't a huge lecture hall. There were only about 30 desks. I made my way to the front of the room and took the seat right in front of the chalk-board.

Most of the rooms I had walked past had whiteboards and projectors. This professor definitely liked it old school, which I preferred anyway. I pulled out my notebook and placed it on my desk. A chill ran down my spine and I glanced toward the door. It was just a group of students walking in. None of them were even glancing in my direction. But it felt like someone was watching me. I couldn't really explain it. I stared for another moment at the empty doorway and then looked down at my blank notebook. It was just in my head. *I'm safe.*

In a few minutes the room was abuzz.

The seats around me quickly filled up as the professor walked in. He was younger than the sociology professor and had a warm smile.

"Welcome to Intro to Psychology. I'm Professor Bry-ant." He pulled out a stack of papers and handed them to the girl at the end of my row.

"Take one syllabus and pass them on."

Great, another class about syllabi.

"One of the things we're going to be focusing on this semester is a group project. No, you don't get to choose your partners, I do. And no, you cannot change your part-ners. Before you all groan, an important part of psychology is learning how to work well with others."

I didn't mind a group project at all. The professor picking my partner was fine too. I didn't know anyone in the class so it would have been awkward finding my own partner anyway.

"The project is going to be about understanding why people do the things they do. Their underlying motivations. It's about looking underneath the surface. Which is why it's so great to have the perspective of someone you don't know."

I had a feeling I was going to love this class.

"You'll just have to choose a well known figure and analyze something that he or she has done recently. Like everything in psychology, it's simple yet complex." He lifted up a sheet off his desk. "To make things easy, we're just going to go in alphabetical order. When I call your name, raise your hand so that you can find your partner.

I tuned out the beginning of roll call as I looked down at the syllabus. The group project was worth half of our grade. Hopefully I'd get a good partner.

"Sadie Davis," the professor said.

I continued to read my syllabus.

"Sadie Davis?" he said a little louder.

Oh, shit. I raised my hand as fast as I could. How many times had he called my name? It felt like my heart was beating loud enough for everyone to hear.

But the professor didn't seem to notice. He just looked back down at his paper. "You will be partnered with Eli Hayes." His eyes darted to a spot in the back of the room.

I turned my head in the direction he was looking. It was the same Eli I had met the other night. The one with the boy-next-door smile. The one I had almost cried in front of.

I turned to face the front of the room. This school was huge. What were the odds that we'd have a class together? I was kind of hoping I'd never see him again. Maybe he didn't remember me. We had only talked for a few minutes. I glanced over my shoulder.

He smiled his boy-next-door smile at me.

He definitely remembers.

"Don't bother asking, there is absolutely no switching partners. Exchange contact information with each other so you can start getting some ideas. Topics will be due on Friday. Class dismissed."

I shoved my notebook into my backpack.

"Hey, Sadie."

I almost jumped. Class had been dismissed just a few seconds ago. Had he run over to me? "Hey."

"Sorry, I didn't mean to startle you. I just wanted to catch you before you ran off again."

I laughed. "Oh, yeah, sorry about the other night."

"You owe me one, by the way. I had to third wheel with Patrick and Kins all night. It was incredibly awkward."

"I'm sure it wasn't that awkward."

"They started making out right next to me."

"Okay, fine. That's a little awkward." I stood up and pulled my backpack over my shoulder.

"Do you have another class right now?"

"Um...no."

He smiled. "Let's get lunch. We can talk about the project." He started walking toward the door, not bothering to wait for my response.

I quickly caught up to him. "Actually, could we just exchange numbers? I was hoping to get a little work done during lunch. So I don't really have time to hang out right now."

"I doubt you have any work." He pushed through the door leading outside and held it open for me to walk through.

"Thanks," I said as I walked through the door. "But I do actually have work. There's this reading assignment for my sociology class. And it looks like it's going to be pretty interesting. I'm excited to get started."

"Come on, you're the only person I've met that isn't from New York. Us non-locals have to stick together."

I laughed.

"It's just lunch. To discuss our project. It'll be fun." He smiled. "Plus, it's kind of work too."

Fair point. "Okay, yeah. Sure."

"Awesome. Let's go." He started walking in the opposite direction of the dining hall.

"Isn't the dining hall that way?" I asked and pointed down the walkway.

"Yeah." He turned around but continued to walk backwards. "But what's the point of coming all the way to New York if we're not going to explore it?"

He was right. What was the point of moving here and changing my identity if I wasn't going to try to embrace my new life? The same chill I felt earlier ran down my spine. I glanced over my shoulder. There were just a bunch of students walking to and from class. No one was watching me. I tried to shake off the eerie feeling. Maybe if I knew more people, I wouldn't feel like everyone here was out to get me. That could start with Eli. I ran to catch up to him and his smile seemed to grow.

"What are you in the mood for?" he asked.

"I would kill for a burger and fries."

He laughed. "Well you don't have to kill for it. I forced you to come with me, so I'll buy you lunch."

"Oh, no, that's not what I meant. I just meant that I'm hungry. You don't have to buy me lunch. I can pay for my own food."

He shrugged his shoulders. "That's okay. I want to buy you lunch."

CHAPTER 14
Monday

I should have been excited that a handsome boy wanted to buy me lunch. But I wasn't. For some reason I wanted to run in the opposite direction. I was about to protest him paying for my lunch, but he interrupted my train of thought.

"So, what's your story, Sadie?"

"My story?" I tried to focus on the buildings we were walking by while trying not to run into anyone. "I'm not that interesting."

"I highly doubt that."

I swallowed hard and glanced back over at him. "Well, what do you want to know specifically?"

He smiled. "For starters, why did you choose to come to Eastern University? I get that you wanted to get out of your small town. But this is a really big change."

"Maybe I needed a big change." I dodged someone who was walking straight at me.

Eli laughed. "Did you ever even visit the campus before choosing this school? You seriously have this deer in headlights thing going on right now. It doesn't even seem like you like it here."

"Of course I visited ahead of time," I lied. "I'm not one to make rash decisions. And I do like it here. It has a great...energy." I had heard someone say that about New

York on TV before. I internally rolled my eyes at myself. Honestly, I hated the energy. There were way too many people everywhere.

"Right," he said. He clearly didn't believe me at all.

I couldn't even defend myself. He was probably pretty accurate with the deer in headlights comment.

"Really, though. Was it an ex-boyfriend thing or something?" he asked. "Trying to move as far away from him as possible?"

I laughed. "No, not at all."

"Not at all? Hmm. I have no idea what you mean by that, but I accept that answer." He smiled. He really was handsome.

"What about you?" I asked. I didn't want to answer any more questions. Thinking about appropriate responses was exhausting. "Why did you choose here?"

"Because I was sick of seeing the same people every day of my life, you know? I think I was starting to feel claustrophobic. I guess I needed a big change too. My mom is not pleased that I chose a school so far away, though."

"What's she like?"

"My mom?" He shrugged. "She drives me crazy and I love her in spite of that."

"And your dad?"

"He drives me a little less crazy. They've been happily married for 20 years. They just had this huge anniversary party a few weeks before I came out here."

"That must be nice." I started studying the buildings again. Dingy skyscraper after dingy skyscraper. How long would my parents have been married? They had gotten married really young. I did the math in my head. They would have celebrated their 25th wedding anniversary this year.

"Well, what about your parents?"

They were the best. "Um, my parents are great but we're not really that close. And I'm an only child." I basically repeated verbatim what was in my new identity notebook. I wasn't close to my fake parents so that no one would wonder why they never called.

"Did you have a fight or something?"

"No, nothing like that. They both work fulltime and are way more into that than they are into me. I was much closer to my nanny than I was to either of them." I wasn't sure why I was supposed to say that. This part of my identity seemed flimsy at best. I couldn't even afford to buy all the books for my classes. No one would ever believe my parents had hired a nanny for me when I was growing up. But I repeated what the notebook said anyway.

"Sorry, that sucks."

Not as much as the truth. "Actually, I loved my childhood. I wouldn't have wanted it any other way." *I just wish my real childhood had lasted longer.*

"This looks like the kind of place that would have good burgers." He stopped outside of a diner on the corner. "Shall we try it?"

"If you promise to let me pay for myself."

"I'm not going to make you a promise I don't intend to keep."

"Look, Eli, you seem like a really great guy. But I'm not really ready to date anyone right now."

"Oh, you thought this was a date? Psh. No. It's work, remember?" He smiled and opened up the door for me.

I couldn't tell if he was joking or not. I'm sure my face was bright red. Had I really just assumed this was a date and it wasn't? What was wrong with me? I didn't say a word as I walked into the diner.

"Table for two?" the hostess said.

I just nodded my head.

"Right this way."

I followed her without looking back at Eli. Now I had embarrassed myself twice in front of him. I didn't usually lose my cool in front of good looking guys. Or maybe it was just that good looking guys had never even bothered talking to me before. Either way, apparently Sadie Davis was the freaking worst.

I slid into the booth and immediately lifted up the menu. I wanted to go back to being invisible again. The diner was busy and I was glad the noise helped drown out the thoughts in my head.

"Your waiter will be right with you," the hostess said and left us alone.

I stared at the menu without really seeing it. Now that he had turned me down, why did I suddenly wish he did like me? Yup, Sadie Davis was definitely the freaking worst.

Eli put his hand on top of my menu and lowered it down until I could see his face.

"Sadie Davis, I find you incredibly endearing. Even more so when you blush. But if you'd like to talk about our project, let's talk about our project."

I could feel my cheeks flushing even more. Every nerve in my body was telling me to flirt back. My brain was a different story altogether, though. I knew I wasn't ready for that. I wasn't sure if I'd ever be ready. "Do you have any ideas for it?"

He looked disappointed. "Yeah." He let go of my menu. "What if we just do it on that vigilante everyone's talking about?"

"What vigilante?"

"You haven't heard? This guy stopped a bank robbery the other day. Well, partially. Technically one of the robbers got away."

I laughed. "Oh, you're serious? You want a project that's worth half our grade to be about a vigilante who's not even that good?"

"He is good. He saved someone's life instead of running after the guy with the bag of money. Here, let me find the video." He typed something into his phone and held it out to me. There was a poor quality video playing. It appeared to be footage from someone's phone that was at the bank.

"What bank is this?"

"North Union."

My new bank. I was lucky I hadn't checked my account balance yesterday or I may have been there during the robbery.

Two men with black masks appeared on the screen waving guns in the air. One of them grabbed a bank teller and pressed the gun against the side of her head. Something flashed across the screen and whoever had been taping the scene dropped their phone. A second later the phone was being lifted back up. All I saw was the back of someone's hoodie. The robber who had been holding a gun to the woman's head was lying face down on the ground. The man with the hoodie touched the woman's shoulder who he had just saved, and then he ran away, seconds before the police showed up. Then the screen was blank.

"A few hours after this happened, the guy who got away turned up on the steps of the precinct with his hands and feet bound," Eli said. "The money was gone, though. He probably hid it somewhere. Street cameras verified that the vigilante dropped the guy off. He finished the job when the police couldn't."

"Maybe he should have just given the police more time. They probably could have found the criminal and the money." I wasn't sure that was true though. The cops had never helped me. And it wasn't like I didn't try. Especially at first. No one even gave me the time of day. I swallowed hard.

"Either way, he'd be fun to analyze," Eli said. "Clearly he's crazy." Eli took his phone out of my hand and slid it back into his pocket. "So now a few million dollars is missing. But what does it really matter? Both robbers are in jail and he saved that woman's life. He's a hero."

"Yeah. Maybe he's not so bad after all." Actually, I admired him. No one should be able to put a value on someone's life. So what if there was a few million dollars missing? That woman was alive because of him. Two criminals were in jail too.

Eli smiled. "Sounds like we got the topic for our project."

"It's going to be a little hard to analyze someone who we know nothing about. If we choose someone more famous, we could at least find some information online about what they're like."

"Or maybe we could just figure out who's behind the hoodie. It'll be fun. We can do a little investigation of our own."

"I don't know. Why should we make the project harder than it needs to be?"

He shifted his mouth slightly to the side while he considered my point. The action almost took my breath away. I could still picture Miles smiling at me out of the corner of his mouth. Even though it wasn't a smile, it reminded me of Miles. It reminded me of my past that I was supposed to be forgetting. And this small part of me wanted to cling to that.

"Yeah, okay. Let's do it," I said without even thinking.

"You sure?"

"Like you said, it'll be fun."

He nodded and looked down at his menu.

I knew he wasn't Miles. And honestly, I'd rather be sitting across from Eli anyway. Maybe I was thinking too hard about everything though. Eli made me smile. I watched him while he studied his menu. No, I wasn't ready to date anyone. But maybe Eli could teach me how to trust again. He made me feel safe, with his warm smile and his kind eyes. I needed that. I wanted that. Maybe I should be holding on to the one small town boy in this stupid big city.

"I find you endearing too," I said before I could stop myself.

He lifted his eyes from the menu.

"It's just that I'm trying to focus on school right now. But I could really use a friend. You're right about me. The move here has been a little harder than I thought and..."

"Me too."

I laughed.

He smiled.

And just like that, the awkward tension seemed to settle. "You really were right about me. I'm worried that I might hate New York. It's stifling. I really didn't realize that you couldn't see the stars here at night until I was looking for them."

"Is that why you ran away the other night?" He wasn't making fun of me. He was just asking.

Partially. "For some stupid reason, it's the only thing that makes me feel closer to home, you know?"

He put his elbows on the table and leaned forward slightly. "I guess we just need to find a spot where we can see them then. We can research that before we start stalking the vigilante."

His smile was so warm. I'm not sure I had ever seen anything so genuine. For the first time in a long time, I didn't feel scared. New York didn't seem so bad when I was with Eli. The smile he was giving me was just as bright as any star.

CHAPTER 15
Monday

I looked both ways and crossed the busy intersection. My last class had let out early. I wasn't supposed to meet Kins until 2, but I was pretty sure I already knew where I wanted to work.

Looking through the windows, I could see that the diner was just as busy as it was during lunch. It was exactly the kind of place I needed to work. I would have to focus on the present in a place like this. Plus the burger I had earlier was mouthwatering. I glanced over my shoulder as I opened up the door. Why did I keep doing that? No one was following me. My heart was pounding, but it was definitely just because I was nervous about applying here. That was it. I took a deep breath as the door closed behind me.

The same hostess from earlier today greeted me. This time I wasn't mortified and actually made eye contact with her. She had curly brown hair and looked like she was in her mid-forties or so.

"Hi, I was wondering if I could have a job application?"

She beamed at me. "Thank God. I was beginning to think that none of the new students were going to apply. We're still low on staff since the end of last semester. I haven't had a day off in weeks."

I laughed. "Well, I'd love to apply."

She handed me a sheet of paper and a pen. "Just fill this out. Do you have any experience in the food industry?"

"Actually, I was a waitress at a diner back home." I started to fill out the form.

"I'd say that's the perfect experience. Where are you from?"

My heart sank. They were going to want a reference. I wasn't going to be able to put any real ones down. "North Dakota."

"You're a long way from home."

"Yeah." I tucked a loose strand of hair behind my ear. The blank references section stared back at me. "I'm going to have to call my old boss to see if it's okay if I use him as a reference." I gave her a small smile and handed her the paper back. *So much for that.*

She glanced down at the sheet of paper. "Don't even worry about it. Luckily for you, I'm in charge of hiring. The owner is my husband," she said with a wink. "When can you start?"

Really? "Tomorrow. I have classes in the morning and afternoon. But I could be here by four. Mondays, Wednesdays, and Fridays I can be here even earlier though if you need me."

"Four is perfect. I'll put you down for the dinner shift tomorrow and we'll see how it goes. Wear comfortable shoes or your feet are going to be killing you by the end of the night."

"Thank you so much."

"Welcome to New York..." she glanced down at the paper, "Sadie. I'm Joan by the way." She shook my hand.

"It's nice to meet you, Joan."

"See you tomorrow." A customer just walked in, and she was back in hostess mode.

I quickly made my way outside before she had a chance to change her mind. Maybe New York wasn't so bad. I had made a new friend. My classes seemed really interesting. And I had just landed a great job. I stopped on the sidewalk and looked across the street. The best part was that it was only a few minutes from campus. I could actually see my dorm building from the windows inside the diner. Straying much farther than that made me feel a little nauseous. I was going to stick to the people Mr. Crawford knew I didn't know. That was the safest.

I took a deep breath and immediately regretted it. The air was stale. I noticed a pile of trash on the curb. Okay, New York wasn't perfect. But I was going to make the best of this.

***

"Ready to go find that super sexy job?" Kins said as she sat down next to me on the bench. I looked up from my phone. I was trying to memorize my number so that when people asked, I wouldn't have to look it up. Eli had already made fun of me for having to do that this afternoon.

"Actually, I found one already." I slid my phone into the front pouch of my backpack. "I just got hired at the Corner Diner." I pointed across the street.

"Well, congrats. That's like one of the most popular places to eat off campus. You didn't even need me." She looked slightly disappointed. "How'd you find it?"

"I went to lunch with Eli and..."

"Really?" she said, cutting me off. "Patrick's friend? I thought you kind of ruined that after you totally ditched him the other night."

"Well, it wasn't a date or anything like that. We got paired up for a psychology project. We were discussing our topic."

"That sounds hot."

I laughed. "How on earth is that hot?" *It was kinda hot.* "We're just friends."

"And there's a 70 percent chance it'll become friends with benefits. Fact."

I laughed. "That's not a fact."

"So how about we just go shopping instead?" she said, ignoring my comment.

"That's a great idea. I really do need to pick up my books. We have that reading assignment for sociology and..."

"No, not for books. For clothes. You mentioned that you wanted to go shopping the other day. That'll be more fun than a job search anyway." She stood up. "And I know the perfect place. I need to pick up a new dress too. Patrick asked me on a date later this week."

"That's great." I touched the side of my neck that my hoodie was covering. I couldn't go shopping today. She'd see it. "I'll definitely help you look. But really I just need a new pair of sneakers."

"Suit yourself."

I grabbed my backpack and followed her. "So, a date with Patrick? I thought you had the hots for our RA?"

"I like to keep my options open. Patrick is a really nice guy. But I don't drool when I see him."

"That's probably a good thing. Or else he wouldn't like you."

"Well tonight I'm going to try to get Mr. RA to like me. I have this master plan. I'm going to trip right next to him and surely he'll catch me."

"And if he doesn't?"

"Then I'll make a fool of myself. But you'll be there to calm me down afterwards. So no harm no foul." She shrugged her shoulders. "When are you seeing Eli again?"

"Probably in class on Wednesday. How were the rest of your classes today?"

"The same as sociology. Pretty much just a day of syllabi. I don't know why I was so worried last night. Oh, here we are."

I stopped in my tracks. A tall man in a dark gray suit had just stepped onto the sidewalk in front of me. All I could see was the back of him. But his stature was the same. The way his muscles bulged in his suit was the same. His buzzed head was the same. *It's him.* It felt like my body turned to ice. *He's here.* Fear gripped at my heart.

"Sadie?"

I could feel his fingers around my throat. I took a step back and bumped into someone.

"Watch where you're going," said a gruff voice.

The man in the suit turned his head at the commotion. It felt like I started to breathe again. I had seen Don Roberts' face when they were cuffing him. It was ruined, half scarred from the burns. His blue eyes had bore into mine with hatred and what I thought was a promise of revenge. But this man's face was perfectly smooth. And his brown eyes weren't looking at me with hatred. He was looking at me like I was a dumb girl, blocking everyone's path on the sidewalk. His eye color didn't prove anything. After all, my eye color had changed too. But there was no way he was going to be able to fix his face. At least not anytime soon. *It's not him. I'm safe.*

"Earth to Sadie." Kins stepped in front of me and waved her hand in my face. "Hey, you okay? You look like you just saw a ghost."

"Yeah, I'm okay." I touched the side of my neck and stepped out of the way of the people walking by. "I just thought I saw someone I knew."

"Geez, not someone you liked I'm guessing? You look so pale. Are you sure you're okay?"

"I'm fine." I plastered a smile to my face even though my heart was beating out of my chest.

She was looking at me like she was truly concerned. "We're here." She gestured to the building beside us. By the way she was staring at me, it didn't seem like it was the first time she had said it. "If you're still up for it?"

"No, I'm definitely still up for it. I'm sorry." I shook my head. *Act normal.* I had been so busy having a mini heart attack that I hadn't even realized Kinsley had been trying to get my attention. I looked in the window of the small boutique. I wasn't sure I was going to find comforta-ble shoes here, but I followed her in anyway. I didn't want to be outside. There were too many people in this city. How could I keep an eye out for someone I recognized if there were a million people every time I stepped outside? Nothing felt safe. I swallowed hard. *It wasn't him.* No matter how many times I told myself I was okay, my heart was still racing. I tried to focus on the racks of clothes. *I'm safe.*

"Aren't these clothes so cute?"

I appreciated Kins' distraction. I glanced at a price tag on the first dress I passed. $79.99. "Definitely cute." *And expensive.*

"This one's perfect. And this one." Kins already had a few dresses draped over her arm by the time I registered the fact that I couldn't afford anything here.

I walked through the rest of the displays until I came to the back of the store. The wall was lined with shoes. Most of them were ridiculously high stilettos. But along the bottom were some fashionable sneakers. I stopped when I saw a pair of light gray Converses.

I could still picture that night like it had happened yesterday. I imagined Julie sticking her foot out from underneath the table, showing me her new Converses. She thought they were the coolest things ever. In my mind, they weren't nearly as great as the bunny slippers my father had given me. I missed those slippers. I couldn't even remember what happened to them. But it didn't matter now anyway. I wouldn't have been allowed to bring them with me.

"I'm going to go try these on," Kins said. "You'll have to let me know which one is the best."

"Okay." I nodded and smiled as I picked up the pair of Converses. $50. I immediately placed them back down as Kins walked into the dressing room. I really needed to head to the bank to see exactly how much money I was working with.

"Did you want to try a pair on?" the sales associate asked. I hadn't even seen her approach me.

"Oh, no, that's okay. I was just looking."

She waved her hand dismissively. "Now's the time to get them if you want them. We're getting a new autumn line in. These are all half off."

That seemed like a pretty good deal. And I was starting a new job tomorrow. I'd have more money soon. "Could I try on a seven?"

"Sure thing. I'll go grab a pair from the back."

They were pretty much exactly what I needed for waitressing. If they reminded me just a little of home, all the better. I thanked the sales associate when she handed me the box, and then I sat down outside the dressing room.

"What do you think?" Kins asked as I pulled the lid off the box.

I looked up. I had learned three things about Kins since we had met. She was an incorrigible flirt. She was one of the sweetest people I had ever known. And she was gorgeous in absolutely anything she wore. I bet she'd look good in a trash bag. The dress did hug her in all the right places though. "It looks great. What look are you going for exactly?"

"Sexy but chic."

"Maybe you want something slightly longer then? That looks like..."

"I'd put out on the first date?"

We both laughed.

"Seriously, though. This is more of a dress for our RA than for Patrick then. I'll set it aside." She disappeared back into the dressing room.

Poor Patrick. I didn't have a doubt in my mind that she'd be dating our sexy RA by the end of the week. He was in serious trouble. I kicked off the flats I was wearing and slid my feet into the Converses. They were a perfect fit. I laced them up and stuck my feet out in front of me. They looked good with the jeans I'd have to keep wearing until the bruise on my knee faded. Hopefully they'd look good with shorts too. I couldn't wait until I could wear some of the clothes Mr. Crawford had given me. I set my feet back down on the ground.

For a long time I had wondered how Julie was. I wondered if she and Jacob ever said I love you to each other. Maybe they were still together. I'd never know. She had never contacted me after that night. She was right though. Love at first sight didn't exist. Whatever I had with Miles had been a lie. And I had never fallen in love again. For the longest time, I had been holding out hope that one day he would just appear back in my life. But I knew better than anyone that real life wasn't like that. Nothing was like a Disney movie.

I untied the shoes and put them back into the box. Even though I didn't really have the money to spend, the shoes made me smile. And they were comfortable. Apparently Sadie Davis didn't care if she was completely broke.

I tapped on the dressing room door. "How's it going in there, Kins?" She hadn't come out in a few minutes.

"Nothing that tops that dress yet. I'll be out in a few minutes."

Before I sat back down, I saw a dress on a hanger, waiting to go back out onto the floor. It was a royal blue sundress. There was no harm in trying it on as long as I didn't let Kins see me in it. I grabbed it and went into the dressing room next to hers.

I pulled off the sweatshirt that I was literally sweating in. The bruises on my neck did look a little more yellow than purple today. Maybe I'd be able to wear clothes I wasn't melting in by the end of the week. I shed my jeans and t-shirt too and stared at my reflection in the mirror. The scar on my stomach stood out on my pale skin. I ran my fingers across the uneven skin. Some things didn't fade as easily.

I quickly changed back into my clothes. There was no point in even trying on the dress. It would have matched my eyes if I wasn't wearing colored contact lenses. But I was. My eyes were brown now, not blue. And I shouldn't have wanted to draw attention to myself by wearing a nice dress in the first place. I was supposed to be blending in.

It wasn't like the scar on my stomach was the only one I had. I'd never be taking my clothes off for a boy without a serious conversation of what the hell I'd been through. And that could never happen. The fact that it had even crossed my mind was stupid anyway. Eli and I had agreed to just be friends. Yes, he was handsome and sweet. He had to remain off limits though. Besides, what would a relationship with him even be like? He'd never know the real me.

I walked out of the changing room and hung the dress back up where I had found it. Even though Mr. Crawford said this was my fresh start, it still felt a lot like hiding to me. No matter how much I embraced my new life, I could never escape the physical scars. I'd be lucky if I could escape the emotional ones. The Sagitta necklace wasn't the only thing I had kept from my old life. I sat down in one of the chairs outside the dressing room and closed my eyes. Maybe I could figure out a way to explain the scars away. A car accident. People wouldn't ask questions about that. I just needed to avoid questions.

"What about this one?" Kins said.

I opened my eyes as she emerged from the dressing room and twirled in a circle. The loose skirt was definitely more casual but still sexy. I gave her two thumbs up.

"Awesome. Did you find some shoes?"

I lifted up the box.

"Are you sure you don't want to try anything on?"

I smiled. "Positive."

CHAPTER 16
Monday

I finished reading the article and exhaled. The bail hearing still hadn't happened yet. Don Roberts was in prison. I had just been imagining things. He wasn't here. No one was following me. I had needed the validation of the article. I had started to wonder if my mind was slipping. I had become good at pretending I was okay. Now I was worried that I was too good at make-believe. I bit the inside of my cheek. I wasn't crazy. It was just taking me time to adjust. Which was normal. *Right?*

I exhaled slowly. Mr. Crawford had sent me to New York City for a reason. I clicked out of the article and closed my laptop. I just needed to focus on the present. Really, I needed to finish unpacking. The first suitcase Mr. Crawford had given me basically had everything I'd ever need in it. There were so many clothes, toiletries, sheets, and even a computer for my classes. I hadn't even gotten around to going through the second one because I hadn't needed anything else. But I needed to stop by the bank tomorrow and the documents weren't in the first suitcase. I'd have to get the information to Joan tomorrow so that they could pay me.

Kins had just gone to the bathroom, so I had a few minutes where she wasn't looking over my shoulder. I pulled the second suitcase out from under my bed and unzipped it. When I lifted the lid, I almost started crying. I lifted up the sociology textbook that I wasn't sure I could afford and glanced back down at the rest of the books I needed for class. I wasn't supposed to call Mr. Crawford unless it was an emergency, but I was tempted to call so that I could thank him. This was too much.

Underneath the textbooks were a few other books. No, not just any books. *My books.* I picked up the worn copy of Harry Potter and the Sorcerer's Stone and pulled it to my chest. He had told me I couldn't bring anything with me. But he had snuck in a few things of mine underneath everything else. Now I was crying. I wiped away my happy tears and quickly opened up the cover to see my father's inscription. There was a sticky note on top of it. "Anything is possible if you believe, Sadie," was scrawled across it in Mr. Crawford's handwriting.

I smiled as I lifted up the sticky note.

Summer,

I hope that I'm beginning to instill in you a joy of reading and a sense of adventure. Just remember that one day, your real life will become an adventure even greater than the stories you've read. When that time comes, I know you'll embrace it. You may not have a scar on your forehead, but I know you're destined for great things. Never stop believing in the impossible.

Love always,

Dad

I wiped my tears away again. Maybe my life right now wasn't how I'd dreamed it would be. But this was my adventure. I needed to embrace it.

I placed the sticky note back over my father's inscription and put the book on top of all my textbooks. No, my parents weren't here to see me experience life anymore. I could still make them proud, though. I was always determined to do well in school growing up. But there was more to life than textbooks and good grades. It was about experiences. If people asked a few questions along the way, so what? I was done hiding. I was Sadie Davis. And I was going to own it.

"Hey, you ready to get going?" Kins asked as she walked back into the room.

I grabbed a manila envelope labeled "bank documents," out of a pouch in the suitcase and closed the lid. "Yeah." I set the envelope down on my bed. Tonight I was going to be completely focused on getting to know the other people on my floor. It was going to be fun.

My phone started vibrating on my desk.

Kins was closer to it than me. A smile spread across her face as she lifted up my phone. "You have one new message from Eli." She tossed it at me. "What'd he say?"

I swiped my finger across the screen. "He said to meet him outside." I looked up at Kins.

"Now that's romantic."

"I'll just tell him I'm going to the floor party." I started typing out the text. But my stomach felt like it had flipped over. We had agreed to be friends. What was he doing standing outside my dorm building? I tried to hide my smile.

"Are you kidding? You should just go outside."

I shook my head. "I already told you I'd come with you, though."

"You can't shoot him down. It's probably some big romantic gesture."

"I'm sure it's not." I kind of hoped it was. It was like I was getting a second chance. At lunch today I felt like I'd stomped on any idea of us being more than friends. I wasn't so sure that's what I wanted though.

"Seriously, Sadie, I'm just going to be flirting with our RA all night. I'm not going to ask you to miss this opportunity for you to witness me embarrassing myself. You can always stop by later if you want. But Eli is clearly into you. It's definitely some romantic surprise."

"We're just friends." I smiled to myself.

"Did he say anything else except for 'meet me outside'?"

"No, that's it." I showed her the screen.

"Then go get your surprise. I'll vet our floor and introduce you to anyone worthwhile later. You won't be missing anything."

"Are you sure?"

"Mhm. You should definitely put on something...well, less. You've been living in that hoodie. It's 90 degrees outside."

"I like this hoodie."

"Suit yourself. It'll officially be the most comfortable first date in history."

"That's what I was going for. You look great, by the way." I had just noticed the extra makeup she was wearing. And she had changed into a crop top paired with the shortest shorts I had ever seen. Mr. RA would be the one drooling tonight.

"Thank you." She smiled. "Now I just have to try not to make a fool of myself. I have to go though. I want to be one of the first ones there so that I get a seat next to the RA. God, I'm getting all nervous just thinking about him." She opened up the door.

"You're going to knock him dead."

Kins laughed. "Same to you."

As soon as the door closed, I texted Eli to let him know I'd be right down. He was probably just here to talk about our project, but I glanced in the mirror anyway. It was still strange seeing myself with brown hair and brown eyes. I wondered if Eli would be attracted to what I really looked like. I quickly shook my head. *This is what I really look like.* I was done overthinking everything. I had originally planned to make new friends tonight. Instead, I'd be focusing on improving the one relationship I had already started. And seeing if it could be more.

It had been a long time since I had been this nervous to see a boy. I shook my head. It had probably been ten years. That was way too long. I smiled at my reflection in the mirror. *I can do this.*

Without another thought, I walked out of my dorm room and locked the door behind me. There were some people gathered at the elevator. But I was feeling too antsy to wait around. I pushed through the door to the stairwell and started walking down. I liked this feeling in my stomach. I was used to being nervous. Not in an excited way, though. Every day it seemed like I lived in fear. Terror danced around in my stomach. God, this type of excitement made me feel alive.

When I stepped outside, Eli was leaning against a lamppost staring down at his phone. He was wearing the same button up shirt with the sleeves rolled up as he was in class. He was even still sporting a backpack over one shoulder. But he had changed into a pair of pants that hugged him in all the right places. It actually made me like him even more for being sensible. It got cold at night here even though it was hot during the day.

A pair of earbuds were hanging out of the front pocket of his shirt again. I suddenly wanted to ask him a thousand questions. What was he listening to? Was he homesick too? Did he leave some heartbroken girl behind in Utah?

He put his phone in his pocket and slowly lifted up his head. His eyes seemed to light up when he saw me. I realized that I had been awkwardly standing there staring at him. I quickly walked over to where he was standing.

"Hi." My voice sounded strange in my throat. I needed to calm down. As far as he knew, I still just wanted to be friends. He was probably here to talk about the project or something.

He smiled and lifted up the plastic bag he was holding. "Have you eaten yet?"

"No. But you already bought me lunch."

"Well, now I've bought you dinner too. I hope you like Chinese food."

"I love Chinese food." I looked back over my shoulder. "Did you want to come in to eat?" The thought of being alone with him made me a little more nervous. I probably shouldn't have just invited him up to my room. That made it seem like I was putting out or something. Is that why he was smiling at me right now?

"As enticing as that is, no. I have a surprise for you. "

Thank God. I exhaled slowly. "What is it?"

"You better come find out." He nodded his head toward the far side of campus and we started walking together.

"You do realize that I have a dining meal plan that I should be taking advantage of?"

He laughed. "Yeah, me too. Maybe we can check that out a different day. The menu tonight looked really strange. I'm glad I caught you before you headed over."

"Oh, I wasn't going there tonight anyway. My floor was having this pizza party thing for everyone to meet."

"I'm sorry. If you want to go to that, we can always do this another night."

"No, I was happy that you texted me. Crowds aren't really my thing. I'd rather just slowly meet people as I run into them in the bathroom or something."

He smiled. "I never would have guessed that."

"Really?" I stepped closer to him on the sidewalk to avoid someone walking by. As soon as the person was out of the way, I could have stepped farther away from him, but I stayed where I was. I liked being close to him. I had that overwhelming feeling of how safe he made me feel. For the first time since I had moved here, I didn't have this creepy feeling that someone was watching me. Eli somehow calmed my nerves at the same time he was making my stomach do backflips.

He laughed. "Yeah, I was kidding. It takes all of five seconds walking with you on the sidewalk to see how bad you are at crowds. It's almost like you're scared of everyone."

I laughed. "I would have thought it was a small town thing. But you seem to be adjusting alright."

He shrugged his shoulders. "Honestly, besides for my roommate, you're one of the only friends I've made."

Friends. It was my own fault for being put in that category. "Same to you, buddy."

He laughed and shook his head. It almost seemed like he was annoyed by my comment. And that made me smile. Kins was right. He still wanted to be more than friends. We stopped at the edge of campus at the street light and he put his free hand in his pocket. He stared at the crosswalk that had a red hand telling us not to cross, not saying a word.

"What are you listening to?" I asked.

"What?" He tore his eyes away from the crosswalk and glanced down at me.

I touched the earbuds dangling from his shirt pocket.

"Oh." He laughed. "Nothing, actually. My iPod broke a few months ago. But I've found that I kind of like just looking like I'm listening to music. People tend not to bother you when you look like you don't want to talk to them."

"And here I thought you were a nice western gentleman."

"It's an adjustment for me to be here too. Sometimes I just need to feel...alone I guess? Maybe that sounds kind of weird. I kind of miss the silence, is what I mean."

"No, I get it. It's very loud here."

He laughed.

"But at the same time, I actually hate being alone. I like that there's always someone nearby." *Someone to hear me scream.* I shook away the thought as we crossed the street. I had a feeling I'd never need to scream if Eli was beside me.

"Is that why you're still hanging out with me even though I refuse to stop flirting with you?"

"Because I like having someone nearby?" I laughed. "No, that's not it."

"Ah, so it's because you're forced to be my psychology partner then?"

"No, that's definitely not it." I wasn't going to play games with him. That wasn't me. "It's because you remind me of home."

His eyes met mine. "You remind me of home too, Sadie."

I swallowed hard. "Why, did you leave some brunette back home or something?"

He laughed. "No. I don't really know how to explain it. But your smile seems warmer than other peoples'. No one else's smile reaches their eyes here."

I could feel myself blushing.

"We're almost there," he said and turned to walk down some steps.

I hadn't been paying attention to where we were going at all. My eyes hadn't left him since we stepped off campus. But I'm pretty sure we had just turned into Central Park. "Is this Central Park?"

"The one and only."

"I didn't realize how close it was to campus."

"Are you sure you visited here before deciding on this school?" He smiled at me.

"Yes, of course." I wasn't sure if I sounded convincing though, because all I could focus on was how amazing it felt to be surrounded by grass again. The farther we walked, the more and more it felt like we weren't in a city at all. "This is amazing."

"I thought you might like it."

I smiled up at him. "Thank you for my surprise."

"This isn't your whole surprise, Sadie. I want to show you something." He held his hand out for me.

CHAPTER 17
Monday

I hesitated. And he noticed. Of course he had noticed. I liked him, but I was still staring at his hand like it was the plague. I hated when people touched me. How could I have thought we could be more than friends if I was scared for him to touch me?

He immediately shoved his hand back into his pocket. "Um, it's just right over here."

I felt bad about the hurt look on his face. "Okay." My voice was quiet.

He stepped off the path and I followed him through the grass until he stopped at a pile of huge rocks. There were a few couples sitting on them eating dinner. Laughing. Looking normal. Why couldn't I just act normal for five seconds? I wanted to hold his hand. There was a lump in my throat that wouldn't seem to go away. I stuffed my hands into the front pocket of my hoodie.

Eli turned back around. "Yeah, so, I thought we could eat dinner here. If you still want to, I mean. And then..."

"I want to."

"Are you sure?" He pushed his mouth to the side like he had done at lunch earlier. It was the gesture that reminded me so much of Miles. It just drew me to him even more. He was probably thinking this was a bad idea. He was probably thinking he'd rather be with anyone else in the world right now instead of the awkward girl standing in front of him.

But I was trying. I didn't want to be awkward. I liked him. I really, really liked him. *Embrace your adventure.*

"I can walk you home if you want," he said. His hand was still stuffed in his pocket.

"No." I smiled. "Let's eat. I'm starving."

The smile returned to his face. "Okay." He glanced over his shoulder at the rocks and then back at me. "Just follow me to the top one."

Without a doubt in my mind, I knew that he had just wanted my hand so he could help me up. He was a perfect gentleman. I had to let go of this fear in my head.

I climbed up the pile of rocks behind him. When I reached the top he was unzipping his backpack.

"I remembered a blanket this time," he said as he pulled it out of his backpack and laid it down. He sat down on the very edge of the blanket.

As far away from me as possible. I sat down in the middle of it and picked up the Chinese food carton that he placed in front of me.

"I knew you weren't a vegetarian because of the burger you ate earlier. But I didn't know exactly what you'd like."

I opened up the lid and smiled. "Chicken Lo Mein is my favorite. Good guess."

He smiled.

We ate in silence for a few minutes. I didn't know what to say to fix the awkward tension. If I was going to reject him again, I shouldn't have been blatantly flirting with him. I told him he reminded me of home. No wonder he had tried to hold my hand. I needed to get a grip.

Eli cleared his throat. "So, I was actually doing some research. It's not quite dark enough yet, but I was reading that you can see the stars pretty well in Central Park. It's not as easy as it is in the middle of nowhere. But apparently it's still possible. You just have to look a little harder."

"Thank you." My voice was quiet. My favorite constellations were always the smallest and hardest to see. If you really could see the stars if you looked a little harder, that was okay. I'd be okay.

He smiled and looked back down at his food. "That's what friends are for."

God. I had completely ruined tonight. It was romantic and wonderful. And I had sabotaged it. All I wanted to do was fix it. "This is probably the nicest thing anyone has ever done for me." It was nice to be able to tell the truth. I hated lying to him. I wanted him to understand why I was so scared.

He looked back up at me. He did that thing with the corner of his mouth again. It felt like he was studying me. "How many boyfriends have you had, Sadie?"

I wasn't expecting him to ask me that. Did Miles count? Probably not. We had never given our relationship labels. But he had always counted in my mind. He was my first kiss. He was my first love, even though he had never loved me back. "Just one. What about you?"

"Three. Girlfriends though, not boyfriends."

I laughed. "I guess you were pretty popular in high school?"

"It was a really small school. What about you? Were you voted quietest or class clown?" The smile was back on his face.

"Geez, neither. I doubt many people even knew my name in order to nominate me. Quietest was probably more me though." When I was younger I had been outgoing and fun. The older I got, and the more families that sent me away, the quieter I became. In high school, it was almost like I completely lost my voice. I was terrified all the time. I didn't want anyone to see me, but at the same time I was silently screaming for help. No one noticed. The problem was that I was good at hiding. Over the years, I had become brilliant at make-believe.

"Look up," Eli said.

I followed his gaze. And I saw a star. One bright star. It wasn't completely dark yet. The sky was still more dark blue than black. But there it was. I just hadn't been looking hard enough before. I looked back at Eli. He was lying on the blanket with his hands behind his head, staring at the sky.

He was breathtakingly handsome. He was better than the star. I inched closer toward him and lay down directly beside him. I wanted to be close to him. For years I had felt like no one was listening to my silent pleas. But I felt like he heard me.

My heart was beating so fast that I was sure he could hear it. I took a deep breath and slid my hand toward his until my pinky brushed against his thumb. And then I held my breath for one second. Eli immediately shifted his hand so that his fingers wrapped around mine. It felt like fire and ice were coursing through my veins at the same time. It wasn't painful. It wasn't forced. It felt comfortable, like I had been holding his hand for years. I slowly exhaled. I didn't even have to wait five seconds. Eli instantly knew that he wanted this to be more. There was no hesitancy at all. It had been years since I had been wanted. It had been years since anyone had truly seen me.

"You're shaking," he said gently. "Are you cold?" He rolled onto his side so that he could look at me.

I shook my head. If anything, I was overheated in my hoodie. I turned my head toward his. "I've been hurt before." That was the truth. I couldn't go into any more details than that. He'd just have to assume whatever he was going to. But maybe that was enough. I needed him to realize that I wanted to take this slow.

"The bruise on your knee..."

"No." He couldn't know. I couldn't tell anyone. "Nothing like that," I lied. I had to force myself to make eye contact with him.

His eyebrows were lowered, like he didn't believe me at all. "Sadie..."

"I don't really want to talk about it." My hand that wasn't holding his was clenched into a fist in my pocket. "I'm trying to move on. I just...I needed you to know. That's why I said I wasn't looking to date anyone. I wasn't sure I was ready. I like you, though. A lot. But that doesn't mean I'm not just a tiny bit scared." *A lot scared.*

"I would never hurt you, Sadie."

And I believed him. When he looked at me like that, how could I not? My hand shook as I lifted it out of my pocket. I lightly touched the side of his face with my fingertips. *Fire and ice.*

His eyes stayed locked on mine as he shifted slightly closer to me.

I kept my hand on the side of his face. "I just...I want to take things slow." But I inched closer to him too.

"How slow?" His breath was warm. It made me lean even closer to him.

Surely he can hear my heart beating. "Pretty slowly."

The tip of his nose brushed against mine. "Sadie." His voice was just a whisper. "Can I kiss you?"

He was asking me if it was okay. I felt a tear slide down my cheek. *He's asking me.*

I tilted my face up toward his until my lips brushed against his. It was gentle. His lips were soft and slightly hesitant, like he was worried he wasn't going slowly enough. He was perfect.

He pulled away far too soon and wiped away my tears with his thumb. "Why are you crying?"

The fact that he asked just made me cry even more. "No one's ever been this nice to me."

He wiped my tears away again. "You've been hanging out with the wrong people then."

Not by choice. "I don't actually just want to be your friend, Eli. I want this."

He laughed. "Good, because I don't want to just be friends either." He ran his hand from my cheek down to my chin and lifted my face back to his. "I want you. And we can go as slowly as you want. I'm patient."

I loved the feeling of his breath against my skin. I pressed my lips against his again. And I loved the feeling of his hand on the side of my face. I never thought I'd be able to enjoy something like this. His tongue parted my lips and I let him in. I had told him I wanted to take things slowly, but my body had a mind of its own. It was practically melting into him. He made me feel so safe and secure, yet alive at the same time. I hadn't felt this excited about anything in years.

His fingers drifted to my neck and I froze. There was the pain. There was the feeling of suffocation. He was barely touching me but I felt the panic in my chest. I put my hand on his chest and lightly pushed him off.

He immediately pulled away and dropped his hand by his side. His eyes searched mine. "I'm sorry."

"You didn't do anything wrong, I just..." my voice trailed off. "I want this. But that doesn't mean I'm any good at it."

"Trust me, you're good at it." His smile seemed to calm me down.

I wanted to tell him everything, yet nothing at all. "I'm worried that I don't know how to love anymore." It slipped out before I even realized what I was saying.

He slipped his hand back into mine. "I'm more than up for the challenge of teaching you how. But I really did just bring you here to look at the stars." He nodded up and I followed his gaze.

There in the sky, if I looked really hard, I could see Sagitta. I could see my constellation.

"I feel like you have a bigger heart than you might re-alize," he whispered into the darkness.

I let myself cry silent tears as I stared up at the stars. I hadn't felt this close to home since I was nine years old at my grandmother's house, staring up at the stars on the roof with Miles. I exhaled slowly, hoping to release the pain in my chest. I wasn't just holding on to fear and grief.

For years I had been holding on to anger. I needed to let it go before there was nothing left of me.

CHAPTER 18
Tuesday

I recognized the inside of the bank from the video footage that Eli had shown me. The teller that had been held hostage wasn't anywhere in sight though. I wouldn't be surprised if she had quit immediately after that.

All the information I needed to give my new employer was in the packet Mr. Crawford had left me. But I was curious to see just how much money I had in my account. I had worked the whole time I was in high school. Most of that money went to food, clothes, and books though.

I put my debit card into the machine and typed in the pin number I already had memorized. A few seconds later my accounts showed up. I clicked on my checking account first. $79. That was right about where I thought it would be. I exited the screen and clicked on the savings icon. *What the hell?* I blinked and rubbed my eyes.

$3,252,101.75 was staring back at me on the screen. I blinked and read the number on the screen again. *Where the fuck did this money come from?* I glanced over my shoulder, but no one seemed to be watching me. I quickly exited out of the screen and pulled my card out of the reader.

Eli had said that the bank robbers had gotten away with a few million dollars. And that it was still missing. I think I may have just found it. I kept my head down as I exited the bank. I wasn't supposed to be attracting attention to myself. And I wasn't going to jail for a crime that I didn't commit. It felt like I was hyperventilating as I pulled my phone out of the pocket of my hoodie. I pressed on Mr. Crawford's name that I had put in my phone the other day.

After two rings he answered the phone. "Sadie. What's wrong?" He sounded concerned.

"I'm in trouble." I tried to steady my voice. God, what was happening? "There was this bank robbery the other day at Union Bank. They got away with a few million dollars and it's still unaccounted for..."

"The bank is insured. You shouldn't be missing any money."

"It's not that!" My voice sounded squeaky. Someone walking by me gave me a strange look. I ducked into an alley. "There's money in my account that isn't mine. They must have...I don't know. It's not mine. What am I supposed to do? They're going to think I was involved. It's over 3 million dollars." I had just gotten out of trouble. Bad luck seemed to follow me around like we were magnetized together.

"Sadie, take a deep breath. I was trying to tell you this the other day, but you didn't want to listen. Your parents both had good life insurance policies. Really good ones, actually. The money was frozen until you turned 18 so it was put in your grandmother's trust until you were of age. Your parents left you everything they owned. Your grandmother also left everything to you. So with both their estates and the life insurance policies, there was quite a bit of money left for you. It was just recently unfrozen."

"My parents weren't millionaires." There hadn't been anything fancy about my house growing up. It was just a normal neighborhood. "And my grandmother certainly wasn't a millionaire. She lived in a ranch house in the middle of nowhere and hoarded old newspaper clippings."

Mr. Crawford laughed. "You'd be surprised by the way some people with a lot of money live."

"There has to be some kind of mistake."

"There is no mistake, Sadie. Your parents and grandmother left you with enough money to be set for a long time. And your college is already paid for. There was a portion of the money that was designated for higher education, so we put that in a separate account and we'll take care of the payments. Everything in your account is yours to do with as you wish."

"I don't want it." I wasn't sure what made me say that. Anyone would be thrilled to suddenly realize they were a millionaire. But I didn't want their money. I wanted them. All I wanted was one more day with them. "I don't need the money."

"Sadie..."

"I can't do this." I leaned my back against the brick wall. It felt like I was breaking. "I can't live like this. I can't..."

"Take a deep breath. The first few weeks are going to be hard. Assuming your new identity is going to be challenging. But it's for your own safety, Sadie."

"That's not my name." I felt like I was spiraling downhill and I didn't know how to stop. I was gulping for air. I hated how stale it was here. Everything smelled like trash.

"Sadie." His voice was stern this time. "We have used every possible resource to make you disappear. We need to make sure it stays that way."

"I didn't ask you to do that. I just asked for your help."

He cleared his throat. "Sadie, I have some news. At first I thought that was why you were calling."

"What news?" But I knew what news. It had been in the back of my mind this whole time. They must have had the bail hearing for Don. I held my breath for one second. *Please. Please let him still be behind bars.*

"The bail hearing was this morning."

For two seconds.

"It didn't go the way we wanted."

For three seconds. I swallowed hard.

"I recommended secured bail given the circumstances. He violated the foster care system's rules. He didn't use the money he was given from the state appropriately. The judge agreed. I thought everything was fine."

For four seconds. It felt like I was choking.

"The bail was set high, but he paid it. All of it. I don't even know where he got the money. I'm so sorry."

For five seconds. I closed my eyes and let the tears stream down my cheeks.

"Sadie? Are you still there?"

"What other evidence did they need? They took pictures of the bruises. Of the scars. They had x-rays."

"It's not about the evidence. The trial date will be set soon. In the meantime he has a no contact order. That's the best we could do. I'm sorry, Sadie."

There was an awkward silence between us. He's sorry? He should be fucking sorry. He promised me he'd put him away. He promised.

"He's free?" My voice came out as a whisper even though I was angry. *This can't be happening.*

"We knew this was a possibility..."

"You promised me. You promised if I told you everything that you'd put him away. He's going to kill me." *God, he's going to kill me.* I could feel his fingers around my neck again.

"I need you to take a deep breath, okay? He has a no contact order and he's out on bail. He can't leave the state. He can't contact you in any way. He won't be bothering you. He doesn't even know where you are. We made sure of that."

"Are you promising he won't be able to find me? Like you promised he'd go to prison and stay in prison?"

"Sadie, we said we'd do everything we could, and..."

"No, you promised you'd put him away. You promised."

"We tried." His voice was softer this time. "We tried everything we could. And we'll do our best at the trial. This isn't over."

Tried and failed. "I don't want to live like this. I can't live like this..."

"Sadie, you need to get a hold of yourself. You are safe. I can assure you..."

"It's not just my safety! I want to be able to tell people the truth. There was nothing in the folder about how to explain the scars away. What am I supposed to say about that? How am I supposed to live a normal life like this?"

"I never said it would be normal."

I leaned back on the brick wall. He hadn't. I just wanted it to be.

"You're allowed to create whatever past you want. Do you know how many people would kill for this opportunity?"

I just want to be me.

"But I am glad to hear you're hitting it off with someone. This process is easier if you have someone to lean on."

"I never said I was hitting it off with someone."

"If you're worried about someone seeing your scars..." his voice trailed off.

I hoped he felt awkward about what he just said. He should have. Was he seriously trying to give me relationship advice? I didn't want to talk to him about Eli. Eli deserved so much more than whatever I could give him. He deserved someone honest. Someone good. Someone pure. I wiped away my angry tears.

"Take another deep breath, Sadie."

I followed his instructions.

"Does anyone suspect anything?"

"No."

"Good. Now, I really need you to only use this number if there is an emergency, okay?"

I was pissed at him. I knew he could tell it too. I doubted I'd ever call him again. "Okay."

"Is there anything else you need to verify while you have me on the line?"

"No."

"Then put the smile back on your face and keep blending in. Be a normal college student. This is a blessing, not a curse. The sooner you can accept that, the better. Understand?"

I nodded, even though I knew he couldn't see me. I was making him an enemy in my head and I didn't even know why. He was the only one who truly knew me anymore. He was the only one on my side. "Thank you for the books."

He paused. "I shouldn't have encouraged you to hold on to the past. I'm sorry about that."

"You didn't. You just reminded me that I should believe that there could be a better tomorrow."

"Good luck, Sadie. And if all goes well, you'll never speak to me again."

Why did he always dismiss me that way whenever we ended a conversation? Even though I was angry, I didn't really want to never speak to him again. I wanted someone to remember me for who I was if I wasn't allowed to anymore. "Thanks for everything, Mr. Crawford."

The line went dead.

CHAPTER 19
Tuesday

I pulled my hair in front of my shoulders to hide the bruises as best I could. For some reason, it hadn't even occurred to me that I wouldn't be allowed to wear my hoodie at work. But as soon as I got there, Joan had handed me a t-shirt that had Corner Diner scrawled across it and told me to change.

I touched the center of my chest. I could feel the Sagitta pendant underneath. There was no reason for me to be here. I had more money than I could possibly imagine. But I wasn't going to use it. I wanted to start over on my own. And this job was going to be good for me. It would help me focus on the present. Besides, the present was a whole lot better than my past. As long as Don Roberts had a no contact order, he couldn't touch me. And as long as I stayed invisible, he wouldn't be able to find me even when he could leave Colorado. Which would hopefully be never after the trial. Not that I had much faith in Mr. Crawford anymore.

No more calling Mr. Crawford. No more imagining people following me. No more getting pulled into my own fears. I was done.

My phone buzzed in my pocket. I pulled it out and looked at the text from Eli.

"See you after work. There's this ice cream place down the street from the diner. Dessert is on me."

"See you then," I quickly typed back. Yes, the present was a whole lot better than my past.

***

My shift was almost over. It had flown by. I liked talking to the customers. I liked getting the tips even better. It would be easy to live off the money I made here. There was no reason why I'd need more money than this.

The diner was still packed even though it was after 9. I started bussing down my last table. I piled all the cups and plates onto my tray and lifted it with one hand.

I glanced out the window. Eli was already standing outside the diner. His eyes met mine and he smiled. I'm pretty sure I blushed. Honestly, I had been looking forward to seeing him all day. I could tell that Tuesdays and Thursdays were going to be my least favorite just because I didn't have any classes with him.

Someone bumped into me while I was staring out the window. I had good balance, but it was just enough to tip the tray slightly to the left. Before I could straighten my hand, the cups and plates slid off the tray and crashed onto the floor.

Shit! I immediately knelt down and started wiping up the mess.

"I'm so sorry," said a deep voice. "I didn't see..." his voice trailed off.

I looked up to tell him it was okay. It wasn't the first time I had dropped a tray. But I lost my voice when I saw his eyes; his perfect brown eyes. I'd recognize those eyes until my dying breath. It felt like my heart dropped into my stomach. *Miles?* I swallowed hard. *Miles fucking Young?* So much for forgetting about the past when the past was literally right in front of me. Part of me wanted to grab his face and kiss him. God, I missed him. I missed his smile and his laugh and the way he made me feel. But a much bigger part of me wanted to slap his perfect face. I hated him. My heart was filled with anger for the way he had left me. He abandoned me when I needed him the most. I felt like I was going to be sick, but I couldn't look away from him. He looked the same, yet so different. His hair was cut close on the sides, but was long on top. It still fell on his forehead in that way that made me gulp. His jaw line was sharp and there was stubble across it. The playfulness was gone from his eyes though. He looked grown up. But really, he looked more tired than anything else. *What happened to you? What happened to us?*

"Summer?"

I immediately shook my head. It took me a second to remember who I was, who I was trying to become. Because when he said my name like that, I just wanted to be what he remembered. I wanted to be that small, happy girl. Even once my parents had died and I started to feel invisible, he had always made me feel seen. But that was a long time ago. "No. That's not my name." It practically came out as a whisper. "I'm Sadie." I didn't put my hand out for him to shake. I didn't want him to touch me. I didn't want to know if I still felt that spark. I couldn't still feel that spark. Some things were better left in the past. I knew that better than anyone.

He lowered his eyebrows slightly. "I'm sorry...you just..." his voice trailed off again. "You remind me so much of someone I used to know. But she had red hair. I don't even know what I was thinking." He laughed awkwardly and shook his head. It looked like he was having trouble processing the fact that I wasn't the girl he had abandoned all those years ago. The one that he cast aside like yesterday's news.

And honestly, I wasn't. The years had changed me. My eyes started to get watery. The years had ruined me. He had hurt me more than years of abuse ever could. That feeling of being unwanted had killed me. I needed him and he had just disappeared. I definitely hated him now more than I had ever loved him all those years ago. "I must just have one of those faces." I immediately looked back down at the broken dishes. I pushed my hair over my shoulder and started to pick up the broken pieces, going as fast as I could while trying not to cut myself.

"Jesus, what happened to your neck?"

I immediately clapped my hand over the side of my neck. *Ow.* He always had the knack for making me feel vulnerable around him. "Nothing. It was just an accident. Clearly I'm clumsy." I pushed my hair back in front of my shoulder and slid the remnants of food back onto the tray with my dishcloth.

"Let me help you with that."

"I don't need your help." And I didn't. I didn't need him. Not anymore.

There was a frown on his face as I stood up. He just blinked at me. He was staring at my hair that was now covering my neck. I needed to get out of there. He could see through my disguise. He could see through my fake smile. He always had been able to.

"Excuse me," I said.

He didn't move, but I stepped around him and practically ran into the kitchen.

"I'm sorry," I immediately said to Joan. "You can take the damages out of my tips." I set the tray down on the counter and started to wash my hands. They were shaking. I tried to take a few deep breaths. Did he believe my lie? Did he believe that I wasn't Summer? I had just ruined everything. I couldn't seem to stop shaking.

Joan laughed. "Don't worry about it. If you hadn't dropped a tray on your first day it would have been a new Corner Diner record. You did a great job today." She gave me a kind smile.

She probably thought I looked upset because of the dishes I had broken. But that wasn't it. I was grateful that she couldn't see through me as well as Miles could. "Thanks, Joan."

"Same time tomorrow?"

I sighed with relief as I hung up my apron. Joan was definitely the nicest boss I ever had. "Absolutely. I'll see you tomorrow." I pulled my hoodie over my head and exited the kitchen before she had a chance to change her mind.

I could feel Miles staring at me, even though I was avoiding looking at him. It was like I could sense his presence. Before I pushed through the doors, I made eye contact with him. He looked truly concerned. It was too late for him to be concerned about me, though. He already had his chance.

"Hey," Eli said with a big smile. "I saw the fall. You okay?"

I laughed. "It was nothing. And my boss is ridiculously nice. She said she didn't even care."

"Good." He slid his fingers down one of the strings of my hoodie.

And just like that, I forgot about the last few minutes. Somehow in the past couple days, Eli had become my anchor. It was easy to forget about my fears when I looked into his eyes. I stepped closer to him and laced my fingers behind his neck. His skin felt so warm against my fingertips.

"So, your first day was okay?" He placed one of his hands on my lower back and pulled me slightly closer.

I ignored the panic rising in my chest. This was good for me. I was safe. "It's a lot better now that I'm with you."

He leaned down and kissed me.

I immediately stood up on my tiptoes so I could kiss him back.

"I missed you today," he whispered against my lips.

We had stayed up way too late last night, staring at the stars and talking. But even though it hadn't been that long since I had seen him, I missed him too. It had been a long time since I had missed someone that I knew I'd be able to see again. I had been protecting myself for years, not getting too close to anyone. "I missed you too."

"Are you still up for ice cream?"

"I'm always up for ice cream."

He kept his hand on my lower back as we walked down the sidewalk. It truly felt like nothing bad would happen to me as long as he was by my side.

I looked through the window as we passed by Miles' table. He was still staring at me. His eyes drifted down to

Eli's arm wrapped around me. And I knew what he was thinking. I immediately snapped my head forward again. Eli would never hurt me. Besides, I never had an issue with physical pain. I could take it. I was stronger than I looked. It was the emotional pain that had a way of hurting me the most. It stuck with me and tried to swallow me whole. Miles was one of the worst offenders.

CHAPTER 20
Wednesday

The first thing I should have done after seeing Miles was call Mr. Crawford. Those were my instructions if I recognized anyone from my past. I couldn't make myself do it though. I was so tired of moving. It finally felt like I was adjusting. I had done what Mr. Crawford had wanted. I even had people I could lean on. I turned my head toward Kins. She was definitely sound asleep. She was even snoring lightly.

It wasn't just Kins I could rely on, though. It was Eli. Thinking about him made my heart race. He was caring and kind and certainly deserved better than me. But I was done beating myself up. Yes, I had to lie every now and then, but it still felt like he was getting to know me. He actually listened. It even seemed like he heard more than what I said. He didn't press me for details because he could sense my restraint. He respected me. He respected my body. I needed that in my life. I couldn't leave now.

Besides, I was still angry with Mr. Crawford. I knew in my heart that he had done everything he could to keep Don in prison. But it still stung that he had failed. He shouldn't have promised me if he hadn't meant it. It almost felt like he had tricked me into telling him everything that had happened over the years I had lived with Don. I felt betrayed. I didn't want to hear Mr. Crawford's voice. I didn't want him to tell me to take a deep breath and plaster a fake smile on my face.

Maybe I was lying to myself, though. Maybe it was more than just my new friends or my new trust issues with Mr. Crawford. Miles played a role despite how much I wanted to deny it. Seeing Miles had been upsetting, yes. But it was also good to know he was okay. He was alive. He looked healthy. He looked good. I shook my head and sat up in my bed.

What did it even matter? I saw him once at the diner. I'd never see him again. He certainly wasn't a threat to my identity. He seemed to believe me when I said I wasn't Summer. If he didn't seek me out when I needed him all those years ago, he certainly wasn't going to seek me out now. I was almost positive he wasn't lying awake thinking about the awkward girl he ran into at the diner. It was over. He could remain in the past.

So why can't I sleep? I thought about the money sitting in my bank account. It didn't seem possible. My parents weren't rich. I wasn't rich. For some reason, I still thought the money from the robbery had ended up in my account. My imagination was running wild.

I climbed out of bed and opened up my laptop. My fingers seemed to have a mind of their own as they typed in Miles Young into Google. A few Facebook profiles came up but nothing else. None of them were my Miles. *My Miles?* I rolled my eyes at myself. He was never mine. I was just too naive and blind to see it back then. It wasn't like this was the first time I had checked. I had tried to find him. But he had made it impossible for me to succeed. It was for the best. Stalking Miles wasn't going to make me feel better about what happened between us. Miles Young was an asshole. I didn't need to know any more than that.

I shook my head and deleted his name from the search bar. Maybe I could make good use of my new insomnia. Because there was actually someone who I needed to stalk. I typed in "New York City vigilante" and pressed search. There were dozens of articles. I clicked on the first one. They made him out to be a hero. The second article made him out to be a criminal. They questioned where the money had gone. During the bank robbers' interrogation, they both swore they didn't know where the money had gone. That was normal, though. Of course they wouldn't tell the cops where they had stashed the money. It didn't mean that the vigilante had taken it. That was a ridiculous assumption.

The best picture of him was of his back facing the camera. He was wearing tight fitting sweatpants and black Converse high-tops. His dark blue hoodie hugged the muscles in his arms. I had seen enough superhero movies to know that he was probably insanely ripped underneath those clothes. But superheroes didn't exist in real life. He didn't even really look like one. He looked like he had just left the gym. Maybe he was just in the right place at the right time.

I zoomed in on the picture. It was like he was actively trying to hide his face. Almost like he knew where the cameras were. I clicked on another image. His face was turned more toward the camera in this one, but it was blacked out. He was definitely wearing a mask too. So how different was he than a criminal, really if he was also hiding behind a mask? Maybe he was at the bank that day to rob it himself and got beat to the punch. But the more I stared, the more I realized that wasn't true. He had saved someone's life. He was good. His clothes were tight and it didn't look like he was carrying any weapons. If he was planning on pulling a bank job, you'd think he'd bring a gun.

I read through dozens more of the articles until I stumbled upon some local blog called The Night Watch. It talked about how over the last few days, hundreds of people who were being evicted from their apartments suddenly had their rent paid for the next few months. "It's a miracle," one lady was quoted saying. "Whoever paid this for us saved us from going to the homeless shelter at the end of the month. Me and my boys had nowhere else to go. No one else to turn to."

And it didn't stop there. Hospital bills had been paid off. Child support had suddenly appeared. The article ended with the quote, "Someone in this city is watching us." It sent a chill down my spine.

***

"Hey," Eli said. He kissed me on the cheek and sat down next to me in class.

I placed the article I had printed out on top of his desk. "He's like Robin Hood. That's his underlying motivation. He's not crazy. He's trying to help people."

"The vigilante?" Eli laughed as he picked up the article. "This doesn't mean he isn't crazy. Putting yourself at risk for strangers is kind of mental." His eyes wandered over the page. "Plus, if that money really was what was used to help those people, that means he stole that money from the robbers."

"Can you technically steal something that's already been stolen? Besides, the bank was insured. It didn't even matter."

"Well, it matters to the insurance companies." He scanned the rest of the article. "And it doesn't mean he's not a criminal."

"It's different if you're trying to do good."

"When did you even have time to do this research? We were out pretty late last night. Don't you ever sleep?" His smile was so charming.

I looked down at my shoes for a second. I was wearing the Converses I had bought for work. For some reason, it almost felt like I could be my own superhero if I wore them. I was living behind a mask too. After reading about the vigilante last night, I felt like I could relate to him. "I've actually been having trouble sleeping."

"Yeah? That's pretty much the exact opposite for me. These late nights are killing me. I could really use a nap."

I laughed and turned my attention to the professor as he walked in.

CHAPTER 21
Wednesday

"Do you want to grab some lunch?" Eli asked as we made our way out of the classroom. He grabbed my hand as we stepped outside.

I immediately intertwined my fingers with his. I loved hanging out with Eli, but I was itching to do more research about the vigilante. "I'm not super hungry..."

"Or we could take that nap instead." He smiled down at me.

"Are you really that tired? I was the one up all night, not you."

"I have 8 a.m. classes, unlike some people."

"Well, how about you take a nap and I do some more research for our project? I'm really excited about what I found. I think we can spin this into a really in-depth study about his psyche."

"Maybe I should have picked a topic that was a little less exciting. I'm starting to think you like him more than you like me."

I couldn't possibly when Eli's smile was so endearing. "Yeah, I don't think that's possible."

"Well, that's good to know. I guess I should let you get back to work then."

I had gotten lost in his eyes. I hadn't even realized that we had stopped in front of my dorm room. "You can come up if you want. You can nap and I can work." I immediately felt awkward and nervous about asking him up to my room again. I wasn't going to sleep with him or anything. He knew that, right?

"Are you sure? I can just head back to my place to get a few hours of sleep. We can meet up later."

"No, it's fine. I have work at the diner again later, so I won't be able to see you until after otherwise. You should take a nap so I can keep you up late again." Why was everything coming out of my mouth laced with sexual undertones?

He smiled. "I'd rather be tired than not get to see you."

"Exactly. So, come on." I pulled him toward the doors of my dorm building. I waved the fob against the reader and the doors clicked open. I had this weird feeling that I was breaking the rules by allowing a stranger into my dorm. But Eli wasn't a stranger.

We stepped onto the elevator.

"Is your bed as uncomfortable as mine?" he asked.

"Are you kidding? It's the most comfortable bed I've slept on in years." That was the truth. I had slept on a couch for the better part of high school. It definitely wasn't the bed here that was causing my insomnia. It was my mind refusing to stop.

He laughed. "Wait, seriously? Didn't you say you had a nanny growing up? I kind of pictured you with a huge king sized bed with pillows everywhere. Did your parents make you sleep on the floor or something?"

I suddenly understood the back story for the new identity Mr. Crawford had given me. He had given me a nanny and said my parents worked all the time because I was rich. My bank account proved that. I bit my lip. "I was just kidding. The beds here are the freaking worst."

"I know. It's like sleeping on concrete." He smiled.

I was starting to think the longer I hung out with someone, the harder it was going to be to maintain my identity. But it was worth the extra effort of being careful. I really liked Eli. I just had to watch what came out of my mouth.

We stepped off the elevator and onto my floor. "My room is right down there." We were still holding hands. The closer we got to my room, the more nervous I got. He was probably reading into this. Was I reading into it? Did I want more? I didn't think I could handle more right now.

I took out my key and unlocked my door. Part of me wished that Kins would be in the room, even though I knew she had class. Another part of me wanted us to be alone.

"Is blue your favorite color?" Eli asked as he stepped into the room.

"How did you know which bed was mine?"

"The fact that you haven't taken off that blue hoodie since we've met was a clue. But I also can't picture you wearing any neon colors." He pointed to the wild neon patterns on Kins' bedspread. He kicked off his shoes. There wasn't anything about the way he was acting that made it seem like he felt uncomfortable. "Plus, I know how much you like the sky."

"You're right. Blue is definitely my favorite color."

He smiled as he sat down on the edge of the bed. "You're sure it's okay if I just take a nap? I feel like I should be helping you do research."

"No, it's fine."

"Okay." He pulled out the iPod from his shirt pocket and his phone from the front pocket of his jeans and set them on the stand by my bed. "Are you sure you don't want to join me?" There was this hopeful hint in his voice. But it wasn't pushy. I had wanted him to ask, even though I knew I wasn't going to say yes.

"I should really focus."

He nodded and lay down on the top of my bed, without crawling under the sheets. "Your bed is just as uncomfortable as mine."

I laughed and opened up my laptop. No matter how hard I tried, though, I couldn't concentrate on the research at all. I was listening to his breathing. It was getting slower and steadier. The sound of it calmed me. I looked up from my computer. He was lying on his side with his eyes closed.

I told my mind to go to hell as I stood up. I wanted to be wrapped in his arms. I kicked off my shoes and slowly climbed onto the bed. He didn't seem to notice until I rested my head on his outstretched arm.

"Mmm."

It was the tiniest noise. I wasn't even sure he consciously made it. But I loved that sound. I moved a little closer to him and closed my eyes. This was the feeling I had been searching for my whole life. He made me feel like I was finally safe.

***

"Sadie." He kissed the top of my head.

I slowly opened my eyes. I had definitely been caught in a compromising situation. My hand had slid underneath the front of his shirt while I was sleeping. I was basically molesting his abs. Geez, who needed a superhero when their boyfriend had abs of steel? I internally rolled my eyes at myself. Eli wasn't my boyfriend. We hadn't had that talk yet. But we spent every second that we could together. And I did love having my hands on his skin. What was I doing?

"Sorry," I said and immediately removed my hand.

"I wasn't complaining." He placed his hand on my lower back and shifted forward so that our bodies were still pressed together. "And I was wrong. Your bed is much better than mine. Or maybe it's just because you're on it with me."

I studied the top two undone buttons of his shirt. I wanted to see him. I wanted to see all of him. My hand shook slightly as I deliberately put it back on his abs.

"You're making it incredibly hard to move slowly with you." His voice sounded strained.

"I don't know if that's really what I want."

His hand slid to my ass.

"I'm trying to be respectful, but you're killing me, Sadie."

I could be whoever I wanted to be. My past meant nothing. The present was all that mattered. And Sadie Davis just so happened to be a little looser than Summer

Brooks was. I grabbed the collar of his shirt and brought his lips down to mine.

He groaned into my mouth as he rolled over on top of me. I wanted his hands all over me. I never thought I'd feel safe enough to be in this position. But Eli was perfect.

"God, Sadie, you're so beautiful." He kissed me again as he pushed my hoodie and t-shirt up the sides of my torso, his palms flush with my skin. "Tell me to stop and I will. Just say the words."

His touch was like fire and ice. I wanted more, but at the same time, I did want him to stop. I wasn't sure I could handle it. I closed my eyes tight. No, I didn't want him to stop. My whole body felt alive. I needed this. I needed to move past my fears. "I don't want you to stop." My voice sounded small, but I meant it. I never wanted him to stop.

"Heyo," Kins said as she walked into the room. "Oh." She coughed awkwardly and Eli's hands fell off my skin.

"Sorry, I'm going to go," she said.

I pushed on Eli's chest, but he was already sitting up.

"Hi, Kins." My voice sounded oddly high-pitched. "No, you're fine, I actually have another class to get to."

"Oh, um..." her hand was still on the doorknob. "I didn't mean to walk in on you guys, my classes just keep letting out early. This college thing is easy."

I laughed. "That's because you haven't started any of the assignments yet."

"I think I've started the same ones that you two have." She winked at me.

Oh my God, Kins.

Eli cleared his throat. "I should probably get going too. See you tonight?"

The look in his eyes made me gulp. There was a promise in his gaze. A promise of what tonight would entail. I nodded and he kissed my cheek. Part of me was glad that Kins had walked in. I wasn't ready for the questions. I awkwardly touched my neck as Eli left the room.

"Hot damn, girl. I really am sorry I interrupted."

"No, it's fine. Nothing happened. We were just taking a nap and..."

"Making out like nobody's business?" She laughed.

Exactly. "I probably should get to class."

"Oh, before you go, here." She handed me a note. "I got all excited because I thought Mr. RA wanted to be alone with me. But there was one for you too. Apparently part of his job is talking to all of us every now and then or something."

I looked down at the note. I was supposed to meet with him at 3:30. "I'm supposed to be at work at 4. Do you think I should see if he'll reschedule?"

"I'm sure it won't take long. Although, I'm hoping my session will take longer, if you know what I mean?" She raised both her eyebrows. "You know...like what you and Eli were just doing."

I laughed. "No, I got it. I just thought it was a rhetorical question."

"There is nothing rhetorical about the things I'm going to do to him. I can't wait for you to meet him so we can drool over him together. Although, your mind already seems preoccupied by Eli."

"It is."

"So, you really like him?"

I smiled. "I do." I slid off the bed and laced my shoes back up. "He makes me feel so...safe."

Kins laughed.

"What's so funny about that?"

"The adjective you used to describe him makes him sound incredibly boring."

"He's not boring at all. We have a lot in common. He's a gentleman and I like that." I really liked that.

"Well sometimes the guys that seem too perfect are actually the weirdest ones. He's probably a freak in the sack."

"Kins!"

"I'm just kidding. Kind of. And who really cares if he is hiding something under that perfect smile? He is seriously gorgeous. Did his abs feel as good as they looked?"

I laughed. There was no such thing as being too perfect. Right? I shook away the thought. I couldn't trust Kins' judgment when it came to men. "Okay, I'm leaving." I pulled my backpack over my shoulder.

"See you later," she said. "I can't wait to hear about how tonight goes."

"I can't wait to hear about how your date with Mr. RA goes. Hopefully a little better than the other night."

"Well it couldn't go any worse. I can't believe those bitches got there before me and monopolized his time all night. We did make eye contact a few times though. And don't you forget it."

"I don't think you'll let me forget it."

"Hardy har har. Well, during my meeting with him tonight I'm going to make him jealous. I have that date with Patrick tonight, so I'm going to rub it in his face."

"Solid plan."

"I thought so. Now I just have to figure out what to wear."

"See you later, Kins." But I wasn't even sure she heard me. She was already rummaging through a drawer of clothes, if you can even call those tiny pieces of fabric clothes.

CHAPTER 22
Wednesday

One thing I was sure about was that finance was my least favorite class. At least I understood why Mr. Crawford had enrolled me in it now, though. I had money that I needed to manage. It was probably irresponsible to have it all sitting in the bank, but thinking about it made my stomach twist into knots. It was hard to believe that it was even real.

It took me a second to realize that everyone was packing up their things. I had been daydreaming during class. I never did that. My eyes gravitated to the notes the person was taking next to me. She hadn't written much more down than I had. Maybe I didn't miss anything important.

I hurried back to my dorm and changed into my Corner Diner t-shirt. Hopefully this meeting with the RA wouldn't take long. I pulled my hoodie back over my head as I walked out into the hallway. There would be no more accidental bruise sightings today. I'd be more careful at work. And I'd tell Eli I wanted to slow things down again. That was fine. I had already told him I wanted to take things slowly. Now I just needed to get my body to agree with my very sound reasoning.

The RA's door was open, but I stopped outside because I heard two people speaking. Well, a girl speaking. I was a little early. I folded my arms across my chest and leaned against the wall.

"I will definitely stop by if I need anything. It was really great talking to you." The girl's voice couldn't have been any more flirtatious. Apparently Kins wasn't the only one competing for his attention.

"Yeah, you too."

I smiled to myself. He didn't sound at all interested in what the girl was saying. Kins definitely had a shot.

"Bye," she said and walked out of the open door.

Maybe I imagined it, but I could have sworn she gave me a dirty look. She shouldn't have been worried about me. My roommate, on the other hand, was a whole different story.

I leaned forward and tapped on the door.

"You can come in," the RA said.

I walked in and froze. *Miles. No.* He was looking down at a notebook on his lap. *Shit. No, no, no.* I took a step backwards and my butt hit his desk. The desk make a squeaking sound as it slid slightly on the linoleum. He raised his head and our eyes seemed to lock. I hated those brown eyes. *Those stupid, beautiful brown eyes.*

"Oh." He immediately stood up. "I'm so sorry about the other night, Sadie."

"That's okay. It wasn't my first time dropping a tray." *This can't be happening.* "I should have been watching where I was going."

He shook his head. "No, it's my fault."

We both just stared at each other for a few seconds. I wanted to turn around and run. Instead, I wrapped my arms around myself as if I was about to fall apart. I needed to hold myself together.

"So you're Sadie," he looked down at his notebook, "Davis?"

"Yes."

He gestured to the chair that was next to his.

I stayed glued to his desk. "I actually have to get to work."

"It'll just take a few minutes."

I glanced at the open door. I could bolt at any second. I could run and call Mr. Crawford. I could never see Miles again. Instead, I slowly walked over to him and sat down in the empty chair.

He stood there for a second and then sat down too.

"I'm Miles." He held out his hand.

"Nice to meet you." I ignored his outstretched hand and kept my arms wrapped around myself. I knew if I let go, I'd fall apart.

He awkwardly put his hand down on his thigh and cleared his throat. "Well, I'm your RA this year. So if you ever have any questions or need someone to talk to..." His eyes landed on my neck.

I tried to shrink into my hoodie as I looked down at my Converses. What happened to my superhero strength? "I'm adjusting pretty well, actually."

"That's good."

I looked back up at him. I wished that the years had changed him more. I wished that it was harder to remember how his hand felt in mine. How his lips felt against mine. *Stop staring at his lips.* I thought about the Sagitta pendant hanging around my neck. I thought about the night he gave it to me and it felt like I couldn't breathe. How could we have turned into strangers? How could he have ignored my pleas for help? My heart was racing, and I didn't know how to make it stop. "Who's Summer?" I shouldn't have asked it. I should have been avoiding the connection.

We locked eyes again and he seemed to be searching my face. I immediately looked away and stared at a poster on the wall. It was of the constellations. *He still looks at the stars.*

"Just someone I used to know."

"An ex or something?" *Stop asking questions about this.* I continued to look anywhere but at him. There was a soccer ball on the floor. *He still plays soccer.*

"Just a friend from when I was younger. I honestly don't know why I even thought you were her. Like I said the other night, she has red hair. I think I just lost my mind for a few minutes or something." He smiled out of the corner of his mouth.

I swallowed hard. God, I missed that smile. I shook away the thought. The important thing was that he be-lieved I wasn't Summer. I was okay. Out of the corner of my eye, I saw him push his hair off his forehead like he had always done when we were kids. I nodded. *A friend.* I knew that. If he loved me, he would have tried to help save me. But I never really needed him. I just had to learn how to save myself.

"How are your classes going?" he asked.

"Pretty good." I wasn't going to sit here and have small talk with him. Maybe this helped other people on my floor, but seeing him only hurt me. "I'm sorry, I really do need to get going. It was great meeting you." It hadn't been great. Now I wished I had never seen him again. He was going to ruin my fresh start. He was going to ruin everything. I stood up and walked toward the door.

"Sadie?"

My feet stopped moving and I closed my eyes. I don't know what I wanted him to say. But all of this was wrong. All of it. I kept my back turned toward him.

"I'm here if you need to talk."

No...you're not. You were never there for me.

"It's not really my business, but I saw the bruises on your neck. If your boyfriend is hurting you..."

I did not need Miles Young to save me. He was five years too late. "You're right, it's not your business. I'm going to be late." I walked away as fast as I could. I thought he was searching my face because a small piece of him didn't believe that I wasn't Summer. But he was just trying to see if I was in pain. From my non-existent abusive boyfriend. Why the hell did he care so much about some random girl he just met more than the real me? Why had he ignored my pain?

CHAPTER 23
Wednesday

I stared at the ceiling. Kins was still out. The silence was starting to drive me crazy. I needed someone to talk to, but no one could know what I was going through. The Sagitta pendant felt heavy on my chest. I should have taken it off and thrown it away. I couldn't make myself do it, though.

My phone buzzed again. I slid my finger across the screen and looked down at the new message from Eli.

"I'm sorry about earlier. I took things too far. I wasn't thinking. I'm really sorry, Sadie. Please pick up your phone."

I had told him I wasn't feeling well, but he didn't seem to believe me. And why should he? I had been lying to him since we met. Ever since I had talked to Miles, I felt on edge. For the rest of the day, the eerie feeling that someone was watching me had returned. It was probably in my head. I didn't feel safe anymore, though.

I found Mr. Crawford's name in my phone. My finger hesitated above the call button. *Call him.* Why couldn't I press the button? I tossed my phone onto my bed and sat up, pulling my knees into my chest. I needed to leave. My identity had been compromised. Those were the instructions I had been given. But I didn't want to leave. I wiped my tears away with the back of my hand. I finally felt like I was fitting in somewhere. It finally felt like I could find a home.

My phone buzzed again. "I'm outside, Sadie. Please just let me up. Please let me in. I just want to talk to you."

I knew he meant he wanted to be let into the building. But my tired mind read it as letting him into my heart. It just made me cry harder. I was leaving. I had to leave. My finger hesitated over the call button again. Why couldn't I do it?

I rested my forehead on top of my knees. The truth was that I wasn't ready to say goodbye. I finally had someone to hold on to, and I couldn't leave. Not yet. I hated goodbyes. I had lost everyone I'd ever loved. I needed Eli. I needed this one glimmer of hope.

A knock on my door made my whole body turn cold. *He found me.* That was the fear gripping at my chest. *He found me.* How did he get in? You weren't supposed to let strangers into the building. *He's found me.* Fear was taking over my mind.

"Sadie, it's me. Eli."

My heartbeats seemed to slow. It wasn't a nightmare. It wasn't my past creeping up to me. It was the boy I didn't want to say goodbye to. *Eli.*

He knocked again. "Sadie, are you in there?"

I slowly climbed off my bed and wiped the rest of my tears away. My eyes were red. I was sure my mascara was smudged. But I didn't care. A part of me knew that Eli wouldn't care either. He was here because he was worried about me. It had been a long time since anyone had cared enough about me to check to see how I was doing. There was no way I was leaving. I had to stay here. I slowly opened the door.

"Sadie, I'm sorry about earlier. I thought..." his voice trailed off as he took in my appearance. There was so much pain in his expression. "Sadie, I'm so, so sorry."

He thought I was crying about him? He was the only reason I had been smiling recently. He was the only person that could make the eerie feeling of being watched go away.

I quickly shook my head. "You didn't do anything wrong. I've just had a really bad day." I could feel the tears biting at my eyes again. Recently all I ever did was cry.

I heard a door close and I glanced to my left. Miles was standing in the hallway with his arms folded across his chest, staring directly at us. He saw my red eyes. He saw my smudged mascara. And he saw Eli. He could jump to whatever conclusions he wanted to. As long as he didn't know I was crying because of him.

I grabbed Eli's arm and pulled him into my room. The door closed with a thud. The past was out there. But the present was in here with me. I looked up into Eli's kind eyes. He exuded everything I had ever wanted. Strength. Kindness. Understanding.

"We should talk about earlier." He set down a bag on my dresser.

I didn't want to talk. Everything was perfectly clear to me. I was staying here because of him and him alone. I remembered Julie telling me that it took at least a few weeks to know if you loved someone. But I had never thought that was true. I had been looking for someone like Eli for my whole life. I refused to let anyone take him away from me. I was done having things stripped from me. Instead of agreeing to talk about earlier, I stepped forward and wrapped my arms around him. "What's in the bag?" I mumbled against his chest.

Instinctively, his arms wrapped protectively around me. "You said you weren't feeling well. I brought you soup."

He brought me soup.

"I'm sorry about earlier. I thought when you didn't tell me to stop that it was okay. But I should have asked you."

"I didn't tell you to stop because I didn't want you to stop." I turned my head and kissed the top of his chest that was showing through the two undone buttons. If I was ever going to get over my past, I needed to do this. I needed to love him and I needed to let him love me.

"I came here to apologize."

I undid another button on his shirt.

"Sadie."

I undid a few more buttons.

"You were just crying. We should talk about what's been upsetting you."

"I don't need to talk." I finished undoing all his buttons. I watched his Adam's apple rise and then fall. "I just need you." I kissed the front of his neck.

I could feel his hands sliding down my back. I tried to focus on how good it felt, instead of the fear pulsing through my veins.

He grabbed my ass and lifted my legs around his waist as his lips crashed against mine.

I'm okay. God, I wanted him. *I'm definitely okay.*

His kisses seemed more passionate as he set me down on the edge of the bed. It was like we were both freefalling into the unknown. There was no stopping me now. I pushed his shirt off his shoulders. He was strong. He'd be able to protect me. He was all that I needed. I wrapped my fingers around his biceps.

"It's okay if you want to wait." He kissed me behind my ear as his hand slipped underneath the back of my hoodie.

I clenched my eyes shut. *It feels good. I'm okay. I'm safe.*

"You know that I'll wait for you."

"I don't want to wait."

"Sadie." He gently touched the side of my face.

Fire and ice. I opened my eyes. He must have seen them shut tightly. "I want this." My fingers slid down his abs. I couldn't wait. I was done waiting. I had been waiting my whole life.

"Is this your first time?"

I swallowed hard. "No." It would be the first time like this. But it definitely wasn't my first time. I didn't want to be talking about this. I wanted his lips back on mine. But he wasn't moving. "I promise that this is what I want. I just need you to go slowly."

He put his hands on either side of me on the bed without touching me. "Going slowly means stopping right now. Let's wait, okay?"

"That's not what I meant. I just...I don't want you to hurt me."

He lowered his eyebrows. "I'm not going to hurt you." He lightly touched the side of my face. "I care about you, Sadie. I'll never hurt you."

"I care about you too."

He stepped forward slightly, spreading my thighs farther apart.

I swallowed down my panic.

"I'll go slowly." He lightly kissed my lips. "As slow as you want." He kissed my cheek.

His words seemed to calm me down. My heartbeats were slow and steady even though my skin felt like it was on fire. *I'm safe.*

"I'll never hurt you." He lightly kissed my jaw.

I let my head fall back, surrendering myself to this moment. I could let go of the past if the present felt this good.

"You can trust me." He kissed the side of my neck and his body seemed to tense.

Damn it. I shifted away from him and put my hand over my neck. *No, no, no.*

He was staring at my hand. "Sadie, what happened to your neck? That's..."

"It's nothing." I pulled my hoodie up higher to hide it. How had I forgotten? How had I let him see? I couldn't let him know.

"They look like choke marks." He wasn't looking at me like he normally did. He was looking at me like I was something damaged. Like he finally saw me for the first time. He looked horrified.

I could feel the air leaving my lungs. I could feel his fingers clamping down around my throat. I closed my eyes. "No, it's nothing."

"It's not nothing. Someone hurt you."

"That's not...it's not what it looks like."

"Sadie." He touched my knee.

It burned. "Stop."

"Tell me what happened." His hand was on my thigh. He was moving closer to me.

"Don't touch me!" I pushed myself away from him on the bed. I felt terror gripping at me.

He put his hands up to show that he wouldn't touch me. "I'm not going to hurt you, Sadie. I would never hurt you. But you need to tell me who did that."

"No one. It was an accident."

"Sadie."

I could tell that my lies hurt him. I could see it all over his face. He wanted to help me. But I didn't need help anymore. I needed to think of something that would explain this away. "I can't talk about it. Please don't make me talk about it."

"Is that why you were upset today?" His voice was getting loud like he was angry.

"No." It felt like I was gasping for air. *He sees me. He knows.*

"You can talk to me."

"I can't." Tears were streaming down my face.

"Please talk to me." He looked angry.

Did he feel my pain? Or was he angry with me? *Don't hurt me.* "Please don't be mad at me. I'm sorry." I hugged my knees to my chest. "I'm sorry."

"Sadie, I'm not mad at you." He ran his hands down his face. "I'm mad that someone did that to you. I'm mad that I didn't protect you from it."

It's not your fault. "It was an accident."

"It doesn't look like an accident to me. We should go to the cops. If someone is hurting you..."

"No. I can't..."

"How am I supposed to protect you if you won't tell me what happened?"

I needed his protection. I needed him and I couldn't tell him why. I couldn't tell him how much. "Can you just hold me?" I wiped the tears away with my fingertips.

"We really need to tell someone about this."

I shook my head and closed my eyes. "Please don't leave me." I couldn't bear to lose anyone else. "Can you please just stay a few more minutes." My voice was laced with desperation.

"I'm not going anywhere."

I felt the bed sag. I opened my eyes. He was sitting on the bed, being careful not to touch me. I shifted forward and collapsed into his waiting arms. He let me cry without asking any more questions. He let my salty tears drip down his chest. He held me until I had no more strength. But his arms around me made me feel like I could keep going. I had messed everything up. They were going to take me away from him.

"No one's going to hurt you anymore, Sadie." He ran his hand up and down my back.

I swallowed hard. I wanted to believe him. But I had never been able to hide for very long.

CHAPTER 24
Thursday

I woke in a tangle of limbs. His fingers on my skin. My cheek on his chest. I took a deep breath. He smelled like sunshine and citrus. It was probably his laundry detergent. But I could smell it on his skin. He smelled like happiness. I clung to him like he was the only thing in this world I needed. I wanted to stay like this forever. No questions. No worried looks. Just this feeling of security. It was more than that though. I lightly trailed my fingers down his six pack. He was a perfect human specimen. I had no idea what someone like him was doing with someone like me. He was whole. I was broken.

"Good morning," he whispered.

I lifted my face off his chest. "Good morning." No one should look as good as he did right after waking up.

He tucked a loose strand of hair behind my ear. "How are you feeling?"

"Better. I'm sorry about last night."

"You didn't do anything wrong." His brown eyes seemed to bore into my soul. "But I wish you would talk to me about what happened."

I propped myself up on my elbow and looked over his shoulder. Kins wasn't in her bed. The alarm clock on my nightstand read 9 am. "You missed your first class."

"I don't care about that. The only thing I care about right now is you. I'm just trying to understand, Sadie. But if you don't want to talk to me about this, maybe you can talk to someone else."

"You mean like a therapist?"

"Or someone else that you trust."

The only person I could talk to was Mr. Crawford. And if I talked to him, he'd take me away. "That's not why I don't want to talk about it. I do trust you." I sat up in my bed.

"Then talk to me."

"I need to keep the past in the past. I'm trying to live in the present. I just don't want to think about it." *I can't think about it.*

"Can I at least ask you one question? That's all I need. Because I don't know how I'm supposed to drop this if I don't know the answer."

"Okay."

"The person that did that to you. Are they here? Are they in New York?"

I shook my head.

"So that's from before you came here?"

I nodded.

He slowly sat up. "So you're safe now?"

Maybe? He had asked me three questions now. Not one. Mr. Crawford thought I was safe here. Eli knowing more would make me unsafe. Miles being here made me unsafe. "I'm safe," I lied. The truth was, I'd never truly be safe. Don would find me. He always found me.

"Can I see it?"

Four questions. "It's not as bad as it looks."

"Please, Sadie."

Would he really let this go? Would we be able to move past this? I slowly pulled my hoodie off and pushed my hair over my shoulders. There was no hiding now. He had already seen it. He already knew.

He pressed his lips together as he shook his head. "Sadie." His voice sounded tight.

Every day it got better. Every day it faded. I needed the memory to disappear with the bruises. I couldn't talk about it anymore. "I'm okay."

"Someone tried to kill you."

"But they didn't."

"I know you don't want to talk to me, but I want to understand. I want to help."

"You are helping. This is helping me." I gestured back and forth between us. "It's been a long time since I've been this happy." I pushed my hair back in front of my neck. "But I get it. If this is too much..."

"Sadie, I meant what I said last night. I'm not going to hurt you."

"I don't want you to feel obligated to stay with me. Trust me, I don't need anyone's pity. I've gotten plenty of that already."

"This doesn't change how I feel about you."

If you knew everything it would.

His phone started buzzing in his pocket. He ignored it and grabbed my hand. "Sadie, I really like you. I felt sick to my stomach all day yesterday because I thought you were mad at me. You know that I care about you. I'm sorry if I'm not reacting the way you want me to react. But of course I'm upset. How could I not be when you tell me something like that?"

"I just want to forget it ever happened. I don't want to talk about it ever again. Please don't tell anyone about this."

His lips parted like he was about to say something, but they immediately closed again. "If that's what you want."

I pulled my hoodie back on. "That's what I want."

We were both silent for a moment. He climbed off my bed and pulled his shirt back on. I watched him slowly button it up.

"Does it hurt?" he asked it without looking at me. He was staring down at the ground.

Yes. But the memory hurts more. "Barely. You're going to be late for your next class."

"I'm sorry. I won't ask about it again."

I followed his gaze. His hands were clenched into fists. He was angry. But it wasn't directed at me. He was angry for me. He did feel my pain. No one had ever felt my pain before.

"Can you walk me home after work again?"

He lifted his head and smiled.

I was worried I'd never see that smile again.

"Of course. Nine o'clock again?"

I nodded.

"I should get going." He stepped forward and placed a gentle kiss on my forehead.

It didn't feel intimate. It felt protective. And I was worried everything had just changed. My past and present were colliding, and I didn't know how to make it stop.

***

Kins walked in and threw her keys down on the dresser. Her hair was askew and her makeup was slightly smudged.

"Hey, Kins."

She jumped. "Geez, you almost gave me a heart attack, Sadie. What the hell are you doing here?"

"My first class isn't until after lunch."

"Oh, right." She yawned.

"How was your date?" I already knew the answer though. I had been here all night. She hadn't come home until right now.

She smiled. "It was good. Much better than my session with the RA. God, I'm starting to think he's gay."

Miles isn't gay. "I didn't really get that vibe."

"Well, he's certainly not giving me the time of day." She sat down at her desk. "So, I noticed that Eli didn't come back to his and Patrick's dorm last night."

"I noticed that you didn't come back here."

"Touché. Did you seal the deal?"

"If you mean seal the deal with a kiss, yes."

Kins laughed. "I sealed the deal with a whole lot more than a kiss."

"I thought you didn't even like him."

"I never said that. I said that I liked him but I could still see how hot our RA is. Just because I like someone doesn't mean I don't have eyes. You agree, right? He's totally dreamy."

"He's not my type." The lie came easily to my lips. I had been trying to convince myself that I was over Miles for five years. The more I thought it, the more real it seemed. But in the pit of my stomach, I still knew it was a lie. Of course he was dreamy. I used to dream about him every night.

"I'm pretty sure he's everyone's type."

"I don't find him attractive at all." I turned my attention back to the most recent blog on The Night Watch. The vigilante had struck again. A woman had gotten mugged last night. The mugger had been dropped off with his hands and feet bound at the police station late this morning. There was a picture on their security feed showing that it was the vigilante who dropped him off. But again, the pearl necklace that the mugger had gotten away with was still missing. I wasn't sure why I was so fascinated by this.

"You must be madly in love with Eli then," Kins said.

"Yeah, I guess." I wasn't really paying attention to her. My eyes continued to scan the article until the last sentence. "Someone in this city is watching us." The same chill ran down my spine as the first time I had read the phrase.

"You love him?"

"What?" I looked up from my computer screen.

"You just told me that you love Eli."

"I didn't say that. I wasn't paying attention. When did I say that?"

"One second ago."

I loved the way Eli made me feel safe. But a part of me knew he wasn't going to drop the issue. I knew he'd bring it up again. I wasn't interested in him pressuring me to go to the cops. They couldn't help me. He didn't understand. And I couldn't explain it to him. "I like him. We're just seeing how things go, you know?"

"Has he asked you to be his girlfriend yet?"

That was weird too. We had almost had sex yesterday. On two different occurrences. But that hadn't come up at all. "No."

"Well, he will. I'm sure of it. Patrick said that you're all he ever talks about."

That made my stomach feel queasy. Could I trust Eli not to tell anyone about my past? Would he tell Patrick who would tell Kins? Kins was great, but she didn't exactly have a great grasp on keeping her mouth shut. "Maybe." I switched off my computer screen. "I should probably get to class. I'll see you tonight."

"Later, lovebird."

CHAPTER 25
Thursday

I stood outside the Corner Diner until 10 o'clock. There was no reason why I should have waited so long. Eli had never been even a minute late to meet me. I pulled out my phone for what seemed like the millionth time. No text. No missed calls. He had stood me up.

The longer I stood there, the less surprised I was. Of course he stood me up. Despite how much I liked him, I had pushed him away by not telling him the truth. It still stung, though. Even more so because he knew someone had hurt me. Why did he want to hurt me too? He had looked me in the eye and promised that he wouldn't.

I turned my head and swallowed hard. The longer I stood here, the more nervous I got. No matter how many times I told myself no one was watching me, I couldn't shake the feeling. I felt paralyzed by the thought of walking through the city alone. My feet seemed frozen, firmly planted, waiting, hoping that Eli would magically appear. He made the eerie feeling go away. How was I supposed to face this city without him? I was terrified all the time when he wasn't by my side.

It made me feel ridiculous, being scared to walk home alone. I stared down the street. It wasn't empty or anything, there were still people walking around. Everything just seemed more ominous at night. I'd be fine, though. I just needed to get safely back to my dorm before it got any later.

After one last hopeful glance at my phone, I started walking down the sidewalk back toward my dorm. I knew that continuously glancing over my shoulder and looking spooked made me an easy target. I should have been walking with my head held high. But I couldn't stop. I picked up my pace. A chill ran down my spine. I glanced over my shoulder again. Someone ducked into an alleyway.

Oh, God. I wasn't wrong. Someone was following me. My heart leapt into my throat. I started running as fast as I could. *He's here.* I ran across the street without waiting for the crosswalk to signal that it was time. A taxi beeped at me and tires screeched. Horns honked. But I kept running. *He found me.* I tripped on an uneven patch of the walkway and fell. My palms slid across the rough cement, biting at my skin.

"Ma'am are you okay?" A man said from behind me. "Let me help you up."

No! Stay away!

He put his hand down in front of my face.

I shrunk away from him. *Don't touch me.* My voice didn't seem to work. I got to my feet and ran from him. I ran as fast as I could without looking back. I threw open the door to my dorm, sprinted up the stairs, and burst through the door to my floor. And I ran straight into someone.

Miles. I didn't even have to look up to know that it was his arms that I had fallen into. Because I didn't even flinch when his hands caught me. His touch didn't burn my skin. It comforted me. It felt like home. I pictured holding his hand for the first time. I pictured falling into the grass with him and laughing. I wanted his arms to stay wrapped protectively around me. I wanted him to be my rock again.

"Whoa, are you okay?" Miles said.

But he didn't remember any of that. He just thought I was some random weird girl on his floor. I quickly stepped away from his hands, no matter how much I didn't want to. It was easier to stay away from him if I held on to the anger. And I needed to stay away. *No. I'm not okay. I haven't been okay since you stopped writing me back.* "I'm fine." I wrapped my arms around myself. My body wanted to betray me. It wanted his hands back on my waist. It wanted to keep feeling that overwhelming sense of home.

He didn't look like he believed me at all. "You're bleeding." He lightly touched my wrist.

I looked down. The heels of my palms were scraped and bloody. "I'm okay." My voice sounded small.

"Come with me." He gently put his hand on my elbow and guided me down the hall.

I couldn't stop myself from following him. The fear that had been engulfing me was fading the longer his hands were on me. He steadied my heartbeat. He made my breath come easier. At the same time, he made my stomach twist into knots. It was the same feeling I used to have before I'd sneak over to his tree house at night.

He opened up the door to his room.

It was like I was being invited into his tree house for the first time. It didn't even feel real. Every part of this felt like I had been transported into the past. I looked around his room again and my eyes landed on the poster of the stars. I was dreaming. That's what this was. I was dreaming about the boy that I dreamed of every night when I was little. And that was a lie. I had never stopped dreaming about him. The pendant felt heavy on my chest. I told myself it was to remember that night, but it was to remember him.

His fingers on my wrist brought me back to reality. "This is going to sting a bit." He sat down on his desk chair and looked up at me.

"Okay."

He poured a little peroxide on my palm. It didn't hurt. Whenever I could tell when pain was coming, I was good at mentally blocking it out. What I did feel was the roughness of his hands. It sent chills down my spine.

He lowered his eyebrows slowly as he dabbed my palm with a tissue. "Do you want to tell me what happened?" He didn't look up at me at all as he grabbed my other hand.

"I tripped." I could have stopped there. His gentle touch made me feel at ease, though, even though he was the last person I should be with right now. I was supposed to be avoiding him. "I'm just not used to the city yet," I said. "I usually have someone to walk me home after work and I was just a little on edge. I tripped on an uneven patch of sidewalk."

He smiled out of the corner of his mouth. "It took me awhile to adjust to the city too. I'm from a really small town out west. But it really is pretty safe here."

I wanted to ask him about his home. Did his family still live in the house next to mine? Were his parents well? Was there a new family in my old house? Did he ever think about me?

"Do you get off at 10 most nights? I can walk you back if you want."

"Oh, no, that's okay." Again, he was trying to help me five years too late. But this time when he offered, it warmed my heart instead of making my blood boil. He hadn't really changed. He was still the same sweet boy. I just wanted to know why he had stopped caring about me.

He smoothed Neosporin on the scratches and placed a Band-Aid on top of them. "Well, if this is when you get off, it's about the time I head for the observatory anyway. I don't mind walking you home while I'm already out."

For the first time, I noticed that there was a telescope sticking out of his backpack on the floor. "I didn't realize there was an observatory near here."

"Yeah. It's above Grenada Hall."

"Are you an astronomy major?"

He laughed.

It made my heart race.

"No, I wish," he said. "My dad didn't exactly approve of that idea. But I do try to take one astronomy class every semester." He lifted up my other hand and slowly placed a matching Band-Aid on the heel of my palm. He didn't drop my hand when he was done. He just let it rest in his.

"Is your class right now?" I didn't want him to let go of my hand. I wanted him to fix me like he had fixed my cuts. It wasn't a secret that I was broken. I could tell that he saw it. Why else would he be taking care of me right now?

"No, it only meets once a week, but I still like to go to the observatory most nights. Honestly, I prefer to look at the stars alone anyway."

That's not true. You liked to look at the stars with me. I nodded my head.

He slowly let go of my hand. "Actually, I was hoping
to run into you. I got something for you." He stood up
and grabbed his backpack.

He got something for me. For just a moment, it was like we
were back in his tree house again. That night that he had
given me the Sagitta keychain, I could have sworn it was
the best night of my life. That moment was short lived,
though.

He handed me a brochure. I looked down at the picture of the support group. I didn't need to open it up to
know that it was for abuse victims. The quotes on the
front made that perfectly clear. "*I learned that I wasn't to
blame.*" "*I learned to open up.*" "*I learned to fight back.*"

It definitely wasn't a Sagitta keychain kind of present. I
looked up at him.

"If you don't want to talk to me about it, you probably
should talk to someone." There was sympathy in his eyes.

I hated that look. I wanted to snap at him again and
tell him it wasn't his business. But there was something
else in his eyes that made me bite my tongue. It wasn't just
sympathy. It looked like he honestly cared. I didn't know
what to say. So I didn't say anything at all. I just stared at
him and silently willed him to tell me why he had stopped
writing. I silently begged him to tell me why he had broken
my heart.

"And the offer stands if you change your mind," he
said, not seeing my silent pleas. "To talk or to walk you
home. Or both." He smiled out of the corner of his
mouth.

For some reason, I wanted to take him up on his offer. I wanted to go back in time to when we were best friends. But I had to keep my distance. I needed to be avoiding him, not asking him to walk me home. I swallowed down the lump in my throat. "Thank you for offering, but I'm really okay."

He nodded. "I should probably get going."

It took me a second to realize I was blocking his path to the door. "Right." I turned around and walked back into the hall.

"You're sure you're okay?" He lightly touched the back of my hand.

I swallowed hard and nodded.

"Have a good night, Sadie."

I just stood awkwardly in the hallway until he disappeared down the stairs. I was terrified to face this city on my own. But that didn't mean Miles was the one I should be facing it with. I could still try to fix things with Eli. And I had Kins. Neither one of them knew the real me, though. No one knew me as well as Miles. I shook my head. He didn't know me anymore. I wasn't even sure I knew myself.

CHAPTER 26
Friday

"I can't wait until the game tonight," Kins said as we sat down in the front of the room. She had stopped protesting about our seating arrangement after our second sociology class. I was pretty sure she actually loved it. The class was interesting and there were no distractions in the front row.

"You said you were going with Patrick, right?" Apparently the soccer team here was amazing. I thought that I'd be going to the first game of the season with Eli. We had even talked about making it a double date with Kins and Patrick. But I hadn't heard from Eli since yesterday morning. I hadn't mentioned Eli's sudden lack of interest in me to Kins yet. I didn't feel up to talking about it.

"Yeah. But, I almost forgot to show you." She pulled out a flier from her backpack. "Our whole floor is going together."

I didn't want to face Miles again. I didn't want him to ask if I was going to go to the support group. Part of me wanted to go. But I couldn't talk about my problems. My problems weren't supposed to exist anymore. "So are you going with Patrick or the floor?"

"Both. Patrick already agreed to sit with our floor."

I pressed my lips together. She didn't say it, but I knew what she was doing. Clearly she wanted to use Patrick to make Miles jealous. Even though I couldn't hang out with

Miles, for some reason I didn't want Kins to either. Not that I was jealous. I sighed. *Am I jealous?* Either way, I didn't think I could stand to watch her flirt with him or later hear her casually talk about hooking up with him. No matter how small, a tiny piece of my heart would always belong to the first boy I had ever loved. I almost felt protective of him. Maybe I did want to see him again. I liked how my hand felt in his. I liked the way he offered to walk me home. I liked that he was trying to look out for me. But that was his job. It didn't mean he really cared. So why was my heart telling me that he did? Our past meant nothing because I wasn't Summer Brooks anymore.

I ran my fingers across my Band-Aid, imagining it was Miles' touch. I had dreamed of him last night. I wanted to push it aside and blame it on the fact that I missed Eli. But that wasn't it. When Miles looked at me, when he touched me, it felt different than it did with Eli. It made me feel like Summer again. And that's what was so scary. It was almost like I wanted him to know it was me. That's why I needed to avoid him. I needed to ignore my feelings.

"So you're coming, right?" Kins said.

"I'm not sure. Soccer isn't really my thing."

"Oh, come on. It's not mine either. But all those sexy players..."

I laughed. "Well, now that's tempting." I was being sarcastic, but her eyes seemed to light up. "I'm sure you're just going to be flirting with our RA the whole time anyway." I was certainly acting jealous. Just thinking about Kins flirting with Miles made me frown. I didn't want that. How could I deal with that?

Kins laughed. "No, but I will be staring at him."

"What do you mean?"

"He's the team's striker. God, I can't wait to see him in action."

I looked down at my notebook. I remembered when Miles first found out he'd be the striker for his youth league team. It felt like a lifetime ago. He had been so excited. Good for him for sticking with it. I knew it was a huge deal for someone to make the team here.

"Sadie, it's going to be so much fun. And I know you have off tonight. We can go tailgating beforehand."

"You want to sneak away and get drunk? Are you trying to get thrown out of school?"

"No, I'm trying to get the full college experience." She lightly nudged my shoulder with hers.

I tried to hide my cringe.

"So, you in?"

What else was I going to do on a Friday night? I was supposed to be blending in and everyone was going to the game tonight. Besides, I had never gotten to go to one of Miles' games. I always wished I had. "Okay, yeah, I'm in."

She beamed at me.

***

I walked slowly to my Psych class. It had been a long time since I could rely on someone. I wasn't sure why I had trusted Eli so easily. We had only known each other a few days, but for some reason he made my demons seem far away. Kins was right, though. He was too perfect. At least, too perfect for me.

When I walked into the room, I made my way to the back. If Eli was going to ignore me, I could ignore him too. Although, I knew I couldn't avoid him forever. We had a project we needed to do. Honestly, though, I could do it myself. He had come up with the idea for our project, but I seemed way more interested in it than he did. Last night I had even emailed The Night Watch blog to see if I could interview them. I wanted to know how they knew so much about the vigilante. Who knows, maybe the vigilante was writing the blog himself. Now I just had to wait and see if they'd write me back.

I sat down and stared at my Converses. I wondered what it would be like to hide behind an actual mask instead of a figurative one. I wondered what it would be like to be strong enough to beat the bad guys. I wondered what it would be like to be fearless.

"Hey, Sadie," Eli said as he sat down next to me. "I'm so sorry about last night. I had something that took longer than I thought it would."

Vague. I looked up at him. There were dark circles under his eyes.

"I should have texted you, but by the time I realized I was late, I figured you were already in bed. And an apology is always better in person." He placed a daisy down on my desk.

He bought me a flower. I couldn't not smile at that. "Where were you?" I didn't want him to know how I had waited an hour for him. It was pathetic. I didn't want him to think I was weaker than he already thought. The bruises were taking longer to heal than I hoped. I was still bound to my hoodie.

"I...um...started a new class."

"One that meets at night?"

"Not a class for school. A boxing class."

"Why the sudden interest in boxing?"

"I want to be able to protect you, Sadie."

I didn't want him to bring it up. But if he had to, this was probably the sweetest way possible. "That's incredibly sweet. I'm safe here though. Especially if you're hanging out with me instead of standing me up."

"I really am sorry, Sadie. It ended late. Trust me, I'd rather have been with you too. I got my butt whooped."

I laughed and picked up the daisy. "Thank you for this."

He leaned forward and kissed my cheek. "Does that mean you forgive me?"

I turned toward him until the tip of my nose brushed against his. "I thought you were avoiding me."

"I like you too much to avoid you." He leaned in closer until his lips pressed against mine.

I didn't hesitate to kiss him back. I thought he didn't want to see me anymore. But really he had just been doing the sweetest thing ever. The truth was, I needed Eli. I didn't want to walk home alone at night. I didn't want to adjust to this city without him. And I needed to forget about Miles. He needed to stay in the past, no matter how tempting it was to allow the past to combine with my present.

Eli put his hand on my knee when he pulled away.

Fire and ice. Unlike the bruise on my neck, the one on my knee had faded, so I was finally wearing shorts again. I gulped as the professor walked into the classroom. But it wasn't because of him. Eli's hand was slowly drifting up my thigh.

"By the way, I really like these shorts," he whispered. His fingers traced the hem of them on my thigh. Really, he was just mainly touching my thigh. His fingers on my skin made my heart race. In a good way.

I smiled at him. God, I was so lucky that he still wanted me. He kept his hand on my thigh even though class had started. It was protective. Possessive. Exciting. He was taking action to make sure I stayed safe. Maybe I should be too. I could take a class. That seemed like a better idea than going to some support group. I was going to be stronger. I needed to be.

The professor was writing down everyone's topic ideas on the blackboard. Only a few names had been called so far and already James Hunter was on the board twice. For a second I thought that maybe he was the vigilante. He was an extremely wealthy tech mogul who always seemed to be in the news. Sometimes superheroes were rich men, like Batman and The Arrow. But those superheroes were also bachelors. James was happily married. It probably wasn't him. Also, the motivation didn't fit. If James wanted to give people money, he could just do that. He was a billionaire. He didn't have to steal from criminals. At the same time, though, he did have the necessary technology. Batman and The Arrow only had their strength, wits, and tech. No superpowers or anything.

"Maybe James Hunter is the vigilante," I whispered to Eli.

Eli laughed. "Yeah, I don't think so."

"Why do you say that?"

Eli shrugged. "I just don't get that vibe from him."

A vibe? I almost laughed, but I got caught up in studying the dark circles under Eli's eyes. It had been his idea to choose the vigilante in the first place. He said he had seen it on the news, but maybe it was more than that. Maybe he wasn't taking boxing classes late at night. Maybe he was fighting bad guys. "Why, is it you?"

He laughed. "I'm pretty sure if it was me, I wouldn't need to take boxing classes to protect you."

"That's not a no."

He winked at me.

"Sadie Davis and Eli Hayes?" Professor Bryant said.

"We'll be doing our project on the New York City vigilante," Eli said.

"Interesting choice," the professor said and wrote it down on the board.

"Notice how I didn't say Eli Hayes?" Eli whispered at me.

I shook my head. What if it was him? He had abs of steel. And his biceps were mouthwatering. He claimed he was tired from late nights with me. But it could have been more than that.

"It's not me, Sadie," he said, like he could read my mind.

Maybe mind reading was his superpower. I internally rolled my eyes at myself. There was no way it was him. If it was, he wouldn't want to know my secrets so badly. He'd be happy that we both had them. Besides, I was pretty sure I could recognize him in sweatpants and a hoodie. Right?

"This is definitely going to be a problem," Professor Bryant said as he wrote down James Hunter on the board yet again.

I shook my head. Professor Bryant would have had more interesting topics if he hadn't grouped so many girls together for the project. By the time all the names were called, James Hunter was written down six times.

Professor Bryant placed the chalk down and brushed the dust off his hands. "We can't have any repeats. So the groups that chose Hunter need to talk and decide on some new ideas. Everyone else is dismissed."

"Want to get some lunch?" Eli's hand fell off my thigh as he stood up.

"That would be great. I'm starving. We can finally check out the dining hall together."

As soon as I stood up, he slid his hand into mine.

"What happened to your hand?" Eli turned over my palm.

"I tripped. It was nothing."

Something flashed across his eyes. I could have been wrong, but it seemed like anger. Again, it felt like he truly felt my pain. It was comforting. I knew without a doubt that Eli wouldn't stand me up again. He did care.

He lightly kissed my palm.

Maybe Eli wasn't the vigilante. But that didn't mean he wasn't my superhero.

CHAPTER 27
Friday

I took another sip of beer. The more I drank, the less I seemed to look over my shoulder. It calmed my nerves. It made me blend in. It made me feel like a normal college student.

"I told you this would be fun," Kins said. She tapped her red solo cup against mine. Some beer sloshed over the rim and she laughed. She was definitely drunk.

I giggled and looked down at my half empty cup. Was this my third? *Crap.* I was definitely drunk too.

"Oh, there he is!" Kins shouted. She ran over to Patrick and jumped into his arms.

He laughed, despite the fact that she just spilled some beer onto his shirt. I wasn't sure why she couldn't see how great he was. No, he wasn't a bad boy like she wanted. He was cute though. He had shaggy blonde hair and green eyes. Every time I had seen him he was wearing some grunge band t-shirt. Was he in a band? How was a rock star not what she was looking for? Especially one that looked like Patrick.

I looked away as they started making out. I thought Eli was coming with him. My eyes wandered to the entrance of the stadium. Students were starting to head that way. The game would be starting soon. Without Eli here, I felt weird about going in. It made it seem like I had just come to see Miles. And that definitely wasn't the case. I bit my lip. So why wasn't I walking away? It felt like something was drawing me to the stadium.

"Hey, Sadie."

I jumped when Patrick touched my shoulder. "Hey, Patrick." His arm was slung around Kins' back and she was clinging to him. It didn't look like she had Miles on her mind at all. I was surprised by how much that relieved me.

"Eli wanted me to tell you that something came up and he couldn't come."

Not again. I had a sinking feeling in my stomach. "Did he say why?"

Patrick shrugged. "Something about a new class."

"Oh, yeah. He did mention that." He just hadn't mentioned that he'd be standing me up again. I took another sip of my beer as I pulled my phone out of my pocket. There was a missed text from him that I must have not heard come through because of all the rowdy soccer fans. I clicked on it.

"Sorry, I can't make the game tonight. I'll make it up to you tomorrow, I promise."

"No problem," I typed out and pressed send. But it was a problem. He said he was taking the boxing classes for me, so why did it feel like he was avoiding me? I tossed my now empty cup into the trash and followed Kins and Patrick into the stadium. It was packed with screaming fans.

"It's already started," Kins said and grabbed my arm. "Let's find a seat."

We had lost our floor a long time ago in the sea of tailgaters. But it didn't really matter. I preferred to hang out with Kins anyway. Now that Patrick was here though, I kind of wished I wasn't the third wheel. We squeezed our way into the front row. I was all for sitting in the front row of class. But standing in the front row of a game I barely understood wasn't exactly something I normally did. The crowd was electrifying though. I wasn't sure if it was the booze or the fact that my eyes had just landed on Miles, but I started cheering along with them.

Miles was easy to spot. He was without a doubt the most handsome man on the field. It was almost like he could sense my presence. He looked over his shoulder and our eyes locked. And there was that smile. The one that made my heart race when we were younger. Except, it was racing now too. I could have dismissed it as the alcohol coursing through my veins, but that wasn't it.

I watched him push his hair off his forehead and turn his attention back to the game. I was completely en-thralled. I couldn't seem to turn my mind off. His touch. His smell. His laugh. God, I still had feelings for him. And I couldn't look away.

He scored a goal and slid, knees first, onto the grass. I had never seen him with such a big smile on his face. I chanted "Young" with the rest of the crowd while his teammates slid onto the grass beside him, cheering. He glanced toward me again. I could have sworn that he winked at me. *He's winking at me.* I felt like my eight year old self again. My heart was racing.

I couldn't seem to tear my eyes away from the field. He was perfection. He assisted another goal and the crowd chanted his name instead of the guy that actually made the goal. It didn't take me long to realize that Miles had become a soccer God. And he looked good doing it. Really, really good.

"We're going to go to the bathroom," Kins said as soon as the team exited the field for halftime. At first I thought she meant she wanted me to go with her, but then I saw her dragging Patrick with her. I didn't have a doubt in my mind that they were about to bang in the public restroom. Normally something like that would completely appall me, but when I had been staring at Miles Young, I totally got it. I wished I was in the locker room with him right now.

I shook away the thought. What was I doing here? I had a boyfriend. *Sort of.* I bit my lip. I didn't have a boyfriend. What I had was a guy that I liked who kept ditching me. I wanted a constant. I wanted my rock back. My appearance may have changed, but the longer I stood here, the more I realized that my feelings definitely hadn't.

When Miles appeared back on the field, I cheered along with everyone else. I watched him score another goal. They were completely shutting out the other team. The chanting was growing even louder. I jumped up and down with everyone else, screaming at the top of my lungs.

Summer Brooks had lost the love of her life. But Sadie Davis didn't have to. This was a fresh start. I hated Miles Young for forgetting about me, but I had never stopped loving him. I wasn't sure I ever would. And that's why the dismissal from his life had hurt so damn much. That's why it still hurt. I was tired of hurting though. Miles Young was home to me. He was my past, present, and future. God, he always had been. I wiped away a tear that had escaped from my eyes. I needed to tell him. There were only 5 minutes left of the game.

I wanted to call his name until he came back home to me. I had been waiting five years to have him back. Five terrifyingly horrible years. Nothing seemed so dark when I looked at his smile though. Nothing would be bad again if he was beside me.

He looked up at me in the crowd again and lifted up his hand. *He's waving at me.* Maybe I wasn't Summer Brooks anymore, but our chemistry was undoubtedly still there. I was about to lift my hand up to wave back when a few girls behind me started screaming his name.

I turned around. They were wearing bikini tops with his name written across their perfectly tanned stomachs in bright, bold colors. As they jumped up and down, their huge fake looking tits bounced with them. My face turned red. He hadn't locked eyes with me. He hadn't winked at me. He hadn't waved at me. He had been staring at them the whole time.

What was I doing here? I was dating a nice guy. A good guy. I shouldn't have come here. It was the alcohol manipulating my mind about Miles. That's what alcohol did. It made me think stupid thoughts. It was all a lie. I still hated him. I hated Miles Young. He left me. He left me alone. I couldn't seem to swallow down the lump in my throat.

Where were Kins and Patrick? Had they not come back from the bathroom? *I'm alone.* I pushed through the people in the front row. *I'm all alone.*

"Watch it," someone slurred at me.

I didn't see anyone I knew. It was a blur of drunken faces. I ran down the steps of the bleachers. *Kins? Where are you?* There was a huge line to the women's bathroom. I thought about texting Eli. But if he had wanted to spend time with me, he'd be here. He'd been avoiding me ever since he saw my neck. Ever since he found out I was damaged. *I'm all alone.*

I turned in the opposite direction and ran out of the stadium. I needed to get as far away from Miles Young as possible. The long pathway back to the dorms was deserted. I ran for as long as I could and then slowed my pace. I was out of shape. My body was weak. I had always been weak. Tears blurred my vision as I continued walking down the path. My heart seemed to ache. It was like it had repressed all these feeling for Miles and as soon as I released them, they needed to be beaten away again. I put my hand in the center of my chest. People like me didn't get happy endings. People like me belonged in the shadows where no one could see them. Damaged. Alone.

I glanced over my shoulder. It seemed impossible for me to shake the nagging feeling that someone was watching me. *It's just in my head.* I was going crazy. My mind was playing awful tricks on me. *How far away from my dorm am I? Did I make a wrong turn?*

"Suuuummer." The voice sounded like a hiss.

It felt like there was ice in my veins as I turned around. "Suuuummer."

I turned the other way.

"Who's there?" I tried to stay calm. *He's here. He's here.* "Suuuummer."

I was imagining it. No one was here. *I'm going crazy.* I spun around again and came face to face with a beast. That was the only way to describe him. He was hideous. And huge. He towered over me. His face was greasy and there was a scar under his eye. But he wasn't Don. He stepped toward me.

I tried to scream but nothing came out of my mouth. I had always become silent when I was in danger.

"You are pretty, aren't you?" He slid his thumb down the side of my face.

Don't touch me! I was completely frozen. No, he wasn't Don. He was here for Don, though. There wasn't a doubt in my mind. He didn't need to say it. I could see it in his eyes. That dead stare. He had killed before. It was his job.

Scream. Do something. My whole body was defying me. I wanted to scream. I wanted to punch and kick and fight him. *Damn it!*

He clamped his hand over my mouth, even though I hadn't said a word, and pulled me into the alley. He shoved my back against the brick wall. The smell of trash filled my lungs. I was going to die in this disgusting city in this dark alleyway. *Scream. Do something.* But my body hung limp against the wall, still defying me. I saw a glint and noticed the pocket knife he was raising to my face.

"This is going to hurt, darling."

Tears bit at my eyes as the knife came in contact with my skin. It didn't slice my neck, though. My eyes flashed down to the blade against the side of my jaw. He wasn't trying to kill me. What the hell was he doing? The knife slid under my skin. The pain was blinding.

He coughed and the knife clattered to the ground. He released his hand that was clamped down over my mouth and my body slid down the brick wall. When my feet hit the pavement, I should have run. But I couldn't seem to look away. He slapped his hand to his neck as he stumbled sideways. He coughed again and teetered slightly.

I heard a noise behind me and spun around.

The Converses. The sweatpants. The dark blue hoodie. The New York City vigilante was crouched down on the other side of the alley, with one hand splayed against the pavement like he had just jumped down from something. He lifted his face slightly, but not enough for me to see in the shadows.

"Run." His voice was low and rumbled slightly. It sounded like it was being altered somehow.

I just stared at him. I didn't want to run. I wanted to thank him. He had just saved my life. But my body was still defying me. No words came to my lips.

"You need to go home. Now. It's not safe for you here."

I didn't have a home. Where was I supposed to go? Sirens started to wail in the distance.

"Run, Sadie."

His words gave me chills. *He knows my name.* I took a step back. That had seemed to be enough to get my feet moving. How did he know who I was?

There was a crashing noise and my head snapped toward the man who had tried to kill me. He had just fallen into a pile of garbage. When I turned back to the vigilante he was gone. I looked up. There was nothing. Where had he gone?

The sirens were getting closer. He told me to run. He told me I wasn't safe. I willed my feet to keep moving as I ran as fast as I could out of the alley. And I kept running until the door to my dorm room was safely locked behind me.

Had I just imagined that whole thing? The blood dripping down my jaw was evidence enough that at least that part was real. But the vigilante? I touched my forehead. I was drunk. I was scared. Had I imagined that I saw him?

I thought about the way his voice rumbled. The way his muscles seemed to bulge underneath the fabric of his hoodie. The way he knew my name. I felt safe when I was with Eli. I felt like I was home when I was with Miles. But no one made me feel as protected as the vigilante did. He had saved my life.

CHAPTER 28
Saturday

I woke up panting. I dreamed it was the vigilante pushing me up against the wall in the alley. I imagined it was his thumb tracing my cheek. What's wrong with me? My stomach seemed to churn. I threw my hand over my mouth and ran out of my room toward the bathroom. I was just able to open the stall door when I started to throw up all the alcohol I had consumed last night.

Shit. I melted down onto the floor in front of the toilet and wiped my mouth off with a wad of toilet paper. Last night was a blur. When I closed my eyes, all I could picture was the vigilante. My mind wasn't focused on the person who had attacked me at all. I was consumed by images of the vigilante. I had been paralyzed by fear. But not fear of him. The more I thought about it, the more I realized that I wasn't scared of him at all. I was intrigued by him. And apparently I enjoyed fantasizing about him while I slept. I placed my hand on my forehead. This was probably the worst headache I had ever had. *I'm never going to drink again.*

I should have been terrified. I should have been calling Mr. Crawford, telling him I had been attacked. But I didn't feel like I needed to. I wasn't in danger if the vigilante was looking out for me, if he was watching me. A chill ran down my spine. Was that why it felt like I was being watched? Had it been the vigilante watching me the whole time? And the attacker could have just been a coincidence. There was crime in New York City. He didn't say that Don had sent him. It could have been a random attack.

The only thing I was sure about was the fact that I needed to see the vigilante again. I needed to thank him. I needed to figure out how he knew my name. There were a million questions I wanted answered. And it wasn't just for the project, it was because I honestly wanted to know who was hiding behind that mask.

I flushed the toilet and walked over to the sink. I had covered the cut on my jaw with a huge Band-Aid. For the life of me, I didn't understand why he had cut me there. He could have ended my life with one swipe across my throat. It was as if he wanted something from me. The thought made me shiver.

It was a random attack. I took a deep breath. I refused to leave this city. This was going to be my new home, and I was determined to keep it that way. That meant getting into better shape. I nodded at my reflection in the mirror. It was time to fully become Sadie Davis. And Sadie Davis was independent and strong. *I can do this.*

***

I leaned over and placed both my hands on my knees. *Jesus.* I could barely catch my breath. Apparently wanting to be in shape and actually getting in shape were two entirely different things. But I had run the two mile course I had mapped out for myself. It had taken me way longer than it should have, but I had done it. That was all that counted.

I slowly stood up and walked back into my dorm building. The stairs seemed daunting, but I forced myself to take them. When I finally got to my room, I was ready to collapse. My thighs were screaming in protest as I put my key into the lock. I wasn't surprised to see that it was already unlocked. Kins usually found her way back to our dorm around noon. I pushed the door open. Even my arms hurt. I wasn't even sure why.

"I texted you like ten times," Kins said.

I just blinked at her. She had way too much energy for having drunk as much as me last night. "I went for a run. What's up?" I didn't mean to sound pissy, but I was a little mad at her. She had completely ditched me last night. I shook away the thought. If she hadn't, though, I may never have met the vigilante. Really I should have been thanking her.

"We're having a double date. Geez, what happened to your face?"

My hand instinctively touched the bandage. "I drank way too much last night and tripped on the way home. It was stupid."

She laughed. "Wasn't last night fun?"

"Yeah, it was." Just thinking about the vigilante made my heart race.

"We really have to get going. I told Patrick and Eli we'd meet them at the dining hall in an hour..." she glanced at her cell phone, "...half an hour ago. So you need to get ready." She handed me my shower caddy.

I really wasn't up for a double date. My head was still pounding and my muscles ached. Besides, I was working a double shift at the diner. I had to be there at 2. Not to mention the fact that I was annoyed with Eli. Things made sense when we were together, but when we were apart, it really didn't seem like he liked me at all. "I don't know..."

"Please, Sadie. Patrick is getting way too clingy. I need you there."

I thought about the way she jumped into his arms last night. I wasn't exactly sure Patrick was the one being clingy. "Didn't you just spend the night with him?"

"No, obviously I spent the night with Mr. RA."

"What?" The pain in my chest from last night seemed to return. She slept with Miles? I was trying to repress my feelings for him, but I couldn't seem to ignore that pain in my chest. Miles was such an asshole. He had probably slept with one of those bikini-clad girls from the soccer game too. Of course he had moved on. It wasn't like I thought he had been pining over me for five years. *The way I have been pining for him.* I bit the inside of my lip.

Kins laughed. "Just kidding. Obviously. Geez, I heard that he was a player, but he doesn't seem to be playing the field at all. I literally haven't seen him with a single girl this semester. His reputation is such a lie. I actually heard a rumor that he only has one night stands. Why oh why can't one of them be with me?"

So he had definitely moved on. Probably with dozens of women. If the rumors were true, though, he probably would have already slept with Kins. She was gorgeous with her perfectly smooth blonde hair and perfectly tanned skin. Anyone with eyes could see that. So maybe Kins was right. Maybe all the rumors were a lie. *Maybe he is pining after me.* I sighed. No, not me. I wasn't Summer anymore. "You slept at Patrick and Eli's place then?"

"Indeed. See. He's clingy. I just spent all night with him and now he wants to have lunch."

I laughed. "At least he likes hanging out with you."

She pressed her lips together. "Is that supposed to be a stab at Eli? Trust me, when he's not with you, he's thinking about you. God, I've never heard someone go on and on as much as him. We're going to have to set both of them straight and tell them we don't want anything serious."

"I never said I didn't want something serious." I pictured the vigilante.

"Ugh. College is about having fun. Not being tied down. You're supposed to be sowing your wild oats."

"I'm pretty sure that's a guy thing."

She shrugged. "Whatever. Just go get your ass in the shower. It's fine if we're fashionably late, though. We don't want them to expect too much from us."

I laughed as she tossed my towel at me. I was pretty sure Kins was all talk. She seemed so smitten with Patrick. And despite the fact that I was avoiding Miles, I didn't want her to be with him. I wouldn't be able to handle that rejection.

***

"Hey, babe," Patrick said as Kins sat down next to him. She smiled as he kissed her cheek.

Definitely smitten. Maybe I could convince her that they were a perfect match.

Eli smiled at me as I sat down. Just a smile. No apology for last night. No kiss. Our relationship had changed ever since I had revealed too much information about my past. I wished we could go back to that night we went stargazing. There had been so much potential. I really liked him. But he wasn't looking at me the way that Patrick was looking at Kins. He was looking at me like he wanted to take care of me. That's why he made me feel safe. That's why Kins said he was boring and too perfect. There wasn't any sizzle.

I shook my head. Safe didn't have to mean boring. I just needed him to realize that I could take care of myself. I didn't want a bodyguard. I wanted a relationship. A real one. One where each person gave as much as they got. I had never had that before.

"What happened?" Eli said as he lightly touched my chin.

Fire and ice. His touch still excited me. Just like Miles' eyes on me did. Or the vigilante knowing my name. Now I wasn't even sure that any of that was a good thing. I was confused. I wanted more, but none of them could give me that. I could never have a real relationship again, despite what Mr. Crawford said. A foundation built on lies would always crumble. I swallowed hard. "I tripped on the way back from the game. It's nothing."

"You've been tripping a lot lately." He looked down at my hands. I had taken off the Band-Aids, but the cuts were still visible.

You've been ditching me a lot lately. I wasn't sure why I couldn't voice my concerns too. But something always held me back. I bit my tongue. I was used to people treating me badly. Maybe Eli wasn't doing it on purpose, but he was doing it. "I'm clumsy. How was boxing practice?" I took a big bite of the salad on my plate.

"Good."

Patrick laughed. "Is that what you call getting your ass handed to you? You should see all the bruises he's sporting."

"Seriously," Kins said. "He's like a punching bag."

"Were you perves watching me change last night?" Eli said with a laugh.

"Absolutely not," Kins said and winked at me.

I laughed. I had no doubt that Kins was watching him change. "You really don't have to take that class, Eli. I don't want you to get hurt."

He shifted slightly so that his lips were by my ear. "You're worth taking a few punches for, Sadie."

And just like that, I felt like an asshole. I needed to stop thinking about Miles and the vigilante. Eli was good and sweet. I was making him a villain in my head and I didn't even know why. His reasons for ditching me were sound. Why was I questioning a good thing?

"They're seriously embarrassing to hang out with." Eli nodded toward Kins and Patrick.

They had abandoned any idea of eating and were just making out hardcore.

Eli and I both stifled our laughter. I smiled up at him. Safe was what I needed.

CHAPTER 29
Saturday

I set down a tray of dirty dishes in the kitchen. My shift ended in 30 minutes and all my tables were already eating. I'd probably get out early.

"You were just requested at table seven by a very handsome gentleman," Joan said.

I smiled. Eli promised he'd be here to walk me home tonight. It was sweet of him to come early to hang out for a bit. "Thanks, Joan."

"Is he your boyfriend?" she said as she raised both eyebrows.

"We'll see. Nothing's official yet."

She laughed. "Atta girl. Make him work for it."

I walked out of the kitchen with a huge smile on my face. But it disappeared when I saw who was sitting at table seven. *Miles.* Now Joan was going to think that I wanted Miles to be my boyfriend. And I didn't. I didn't want a one night stand. I wanted to be loved the way I loved him.

I shook away the thought. This didn't have to be weird. He didn't know that I thought he was flirting with me at his game. He knew I worked here and that's why he requested me to serve him. He was just being a sociable RA. I walked over to his table. "Hi, Miles." My voice sounded oddly high pitched. *Stop being weird.*

He smiled out of the corner of his mouth. "Hey, Sadie. I was hoping you'd be working tonight."

I tried to tell my quickening heartbeat to take a chill pill. He meant it in a friendly way. So why did the center of my chest ache? Why couldn't I stop looking into his eyes? I felt like my feet were melting into the ground.

"Sadie?"

"What?" I shook my head, hoping it would dismiss my wandering thoughts.

He smiled again but then he lowered his eyebrows slightly. "What happened?" He lightly touched the side of his jaw.

My fingers found the Band-Aid on my cheek. "I tripped."

He pressed his lips together. "You should have stopped by my dorm. I wouldn't have minded bandaging you up again."

Is he flirting with me? No. He's just being a good RA. "I'm okay, really."

"When do you get off?"

"10." I swallowed hard. Did he really come to walk me home? I told him he didn't need to.

He glanced at the clock on the wall. "Maybe I'll just take a chocolate chip cookie and a glass of milk then?"

I nodded and wrote it down in my notepad even though I knew I wouldn't forget it. Some nights he'd sneak cookies and milk into his tree house. It was his favorite snack. I saw the telescope sticking out of his backpack. He was on his way to the observatory. Did he remember pairing those things together? I had always been a part of that equation. "I'll be right back." I didn't make eye contact with him before I walked away.

Some weeknights it had been harder to slip away. But we were always together watching the stars every Saturday night. He was still looking. Maybe he was still waiting. He couldn't wait for me, though. I wasn't Summer Brooks anymore. She had died five years ago. There was nothing left of her. Except him. *Stop.*

I was torturing myself for no reason. Kins said he was a player. He had moved on. I needed to too. I put my hand on the center of my chest. This wasn't living. I grabbed one of the cookies off the cooling rack and poured a glass of milk. I walked back to his table and put the plate and glass down in front of him. "Here you go. Just let me know if you need anything else." I was staring at my Converses instead of him.

"Hey." His fingers grazed my forearm, sending a chill down my spine. "You came to my game last night."

"I'm pretty sure the whole school was at your game."

"Yeah, maybe. But I wasn't paying attention to them."

My eyes met his. He knew I was staring at him the whole time yesterday. He always could tell what I was thinking. I tucked a loose strand of hair behind my ear. "I'm pretty sure you noticed the two girls behind me in bikinis too."

He laughed. "I was a little too preoccupied to notice."

"Right. With the game."

"No, not with the game." His gaze was suddenly so intense.

The heat behind it made my whole body feel warm. There was no doubt that he was flirting with me. What I didn't understand was why. "I should probably go check on my other tables."

He pushed his hair off his forehead. "Okay, Sadie."

I walked around the diner for several minutes, mainly to ignore him. I stole a glance as I refilled someone's water glass. He was staring directly at me. I immediately looked back down at the pitcher in my hand.

This was ridiculous. Getting involved with him would put us both in danger. Plus, I was pretty sure that dating your RA was against the rules. And the whole thing was ridiculous anyway. He was the star soccer player here. Girls practically threw themselves at him. He was just being nice. I was imagining the heat. I was pretending I was that little girl that used to spy on him from my bedroom window. I was being completely insane.

My shift was almost over. Eli wasn't outside yet. I bit the inside of my lip. I needed to squash this thing. I needed to get the ache out of my chest. I needed to forget. The sooner I got out of here, the better. I grabbed his check and placed it down on his table. "Here's your check. Thanks for stopping by the Corner Diner." It was what I had been trained to say, but I left off the "We hope to see you again soon."

There seemed to be a twinkle in his eye.

I hadn't said anything funny.

"I'm walking you home."

"It's okay, my...friend is coming to walk me home." It would have been better if I had been able to call Eli my boyfriend. Then Miles would get the hint. But Eli hadn't asked me out.

Miles glanced out the window. Eli still wasn't outside. "I want to."

He wants to. I needed to push him away. "There are a million girls at this school that would love your help. And I'm sorry, but I'm not one of them." There was still some anger underneath the ache in my chest. It was easier than I thought to snap at him.

The twinkle remained in his eye.

"Someone is coming to walk me home." Saying it a second time made it sound like a lie. "Really," I added.

"Okay." He pulled out his wallet and placed some money down on the table. It was only a few cents over the bill.

Did he seriously not leave me a tip? "I'll be right back with that." I angrily grabbed his three pennies of change and brought it back to his table. "Here you go."

He picked up the pennies and slid them into his pocket.

Asshole.

"If you want your tip, you'll have to let me walk you home." Again, it was like he could still read my thoughts.

I laughed. "I don't know why you don't believe me. I'm not walking home alone tonight." The clock on the wall said 10:02. *He'll be here.*

"If you say so."

"I do."

He shrugged his shoulders innocently.

I shook my head as I walked away from him.

"He's really cute," Joan said as I entered the kitchen.

I took off my apron and pulled my hoodie on over my head. "He's okay."

She laughed. "If you say so."

Why was everyone questioning me tonight? "Good-night, Joan."

"See you tomorrow, Sadie. Have fun." She winked at me.

I walked out of the kitchen and saw that Miles' table was empty. I exhaled slowly. It should have made me feel relieved, but I felt slightly disappointed. He was probably antagonizing me because he was popular and gorgeous and I was invisible.

When I stepped outside, I froze. He was waiting for me. I had hoped and prayed that he had been waiting for me this whole time. "You waited."

He smiled out of the corner of his mouth. "You ready to go?"

"No...I'm...someone's coming to walk me home already."

Miles glanced around at the empty sidewalk, emphasizing his point. "Then I'll just wait with you."

"You don't have to."

"I want to."

Why did he keep saying that? I folded my arms across my chest. I didn't want to stand here with him and pretend like he hadn't hurt me. And honestly, I didn't need him or Eli to walk me home. I was going to learn how to defend myself. In the meantime, there wasn't a doubt in my mind that the vigilante was out there watching me. I looked over my shoulder. It felt like he was watching me right now.

I turned back to Miles. "Are you going to the observatory tonight?" It was a stupid question. The telescope was sticking out of his backpack again. Obviously he was going.

"Yeah. Do you want to check it out?"

Did he just ask me out? I swallowed hard. I wanted to see it, but it would be better if I went alone. "Maybe a different time."

"Right. When you're not waiting for someone." He smiled.

I am waiting for someone. "Why are you so obsessed with the stars anyway?"

His smile seemed to fade as he thought over the question. "They remind me of being a kid. When I look at them, I feel closer to the people I left back home."

They didn't remind him of me? Every time I looked at the stars I pictured him beside me. I don't think I'd ever stop picturing him with me. "What about that girl? I think you said her name was Summer? Do they remind you of her?" I was acting desperate. But he didn't know that. He didn't know that I was her.

He lowered his eyebrows slowly. "Yeah, actually. When we were little we used to stare at the sky for hours together in my tree house."

"I guess you haven't seen her recently?"

"No. Not in years." He looked like his mind was far away. Remembering a time when we made sense.

Nine years. Had it really been that long? We had written to each other all the time, but I hadn't seen him since I went into the foster care system. I was holding a torch for someone who couldn't possibly be the same as I remembered him. For some reason I found myself stepping closer to him. "What happened with you and her? If you don't mind me asking."

He shrugged his shoulders. "She moved away. And eventually she stopped writing me back."

Liar. I put my hands into the front pocket of my hoodie and dug my fingernails into my palms. I stopped writing him when he hadn't written me back in years. I stopped because he had already forgotten about me. "Are you sure you didn't stop writing her back?"

He laughed. "Yeah, I'm positive about that. Sometimes I still write to her even though she hasn't written me back in five years. It's stupid, but I can't seem to stop. I don't even know if I have her right address anymore."

You're lying. He had stopped writing back to *me* five years ago. He had forgotten about *me.* But if he had, why would he have thought I was Summer when he first bumped into me in the Corner Diner? A forgotten person's name wouldn't come to his lips so easily. My eyes wandered to his lips. His perfectly kissable lips.

"Hey, Sadie," Eli said.

I jumped when his arm wrapped around my waist. And I cringed when he kissed the side of my forehead. I wasn't sure why his touch burned my skin tonight. There was no ice. Just fire. It was probably because I was mad that he was half an hour late to pick me up. But maybe it was because I'd rather have Miles' arm wrapped protectively around me. Maybe I had never stopped wanting that.

Miles was searching my face.

It took me a second to realize I was being incredibly rude. I cleared my throat. "Eli this is Miles. Miles, Eli," I said and gestured back and forth between them.

Eli let his arm fall away from me as he grabbed Miles' outstretched hand.

I watched the knuckles on both their hands turn white as they shook hands. *What the hell are they doing?*

Eli clapped another hand on the other side of Miles' before pulling away. "How do you two know each other?" he asked as he slid his hand back around my waist.

Fire. The way he was being possessive should have comforted me. But it didn't. I felt trapped.

"I'm her RA," Miles said.

"Oh, okay." Eli seemed relieved as he shifted even closer to me.

I felt like I was suffocating.

"And you are?" Miles asked.

"Her boyfriend."

I stood there dumbfounded. Eli wasn't my boyfriend. We had never talked about that. And I didn't like him making that assumption without asking me. For some reason, I didn't say a word though. It was easier this way. I needed to stay away from Miles. I had to. But I hated the way he was searching my face, as if he could still hear my thoughts. *You can't save me. You have to stay away.*

"We should probably get going, babe," Eli said.

Babe? He had never called me babe. That's what Patrick called Kins. This whole thing seemed unnatural and forced. What was Eli doing?

"We'll see you around, man," Eli said and pulled me away from Miles.

I glanced over my shoulder.

Miles' hands were stuffed in his pockets and he was scowling. Not at me though. He was staring daggers at Eli.

The look made my heart race. He saw the way I flinched at Eli's touch. He saw the shocked look on my face when Eli said he was my boyfriend. He saw the way I cringed at Eli calling me babe. He saw me. He had always been able to see me.

I turned my head and swallowed hard. The only problem with that was that Miles was wrong. Eli was sweet. And kind. And good. So why did it feel like his fingers were digging into my hip, biting at my skin? Why did it feel like he was forcing me to walk forward. Why did all of this suddenly feel so wrong? This didn't feel sweet. Or kind. Or good.

"What was that?" I asked.

"I could ask you the same thing."

"He was just keeping me company while I waited for you."

"I was just a few minutes late. I told you I was coming."

"It wasn't a few minutes. It was half an hour. And it wouldn't have been the first time you stood me up."

"For a guy that was just keeping you company while you waited for me, he seemed pretty surprised when I walked up to you. Didn't you tell him about me?"

"I told him that my friend was coming to walk me home."

Eli laughed. It sounded strange. "A friend? I could have sworn we already talked about this. We both agreed that we wanted to be more than friends." His fingers seemed to grip harder at my waist.

You're hurting me. But my voice was gone. I blinked away the tears forming in my eyes.

"I don't want you to see anyone else, okay?"

I didn't say anything.

"Okay?" His voice was sharper as we came to a stop outside my dorm building.

I looked down at my Converses. I needed to find my voice. I needed to be stronger than this. "Please don't yell at me." I was surprised at the words that seemed to fall out of my mouth.

His hand fell from my waist. "I'm not yelling. I'm trying to have a conversation with you."

I forced myself to look into his eyes. The kindness was back. He looked concerned. Had I imagined his fingers digging into my waist? Had I imagined his tone? He was just upset because he thought I had been flirting with Miles. And hadn't I been? He deserved to feel betrayed. We hadn't talked about being exclusive, but I didn't want him to be flirting with other girls. I would have been hurt if I had caught him doing that.

"I'm sorry." My voice sounded small, but I meant it. I felt like my life was a mess. I was daydreaming about the vigilante and Miles, but I had a great guy right in front of me. It was like I didn't know how to be happy. I was sabotaging a good thing.

"It's okay. I'm sorry that I got upset. Can I come up and hang out for a bit?" He touched the side of my face.

Fire. I quickly shook my head. "I'm exhausted. I really just need to get some sleep."

"You sure?"

"Yeah." *I am sabotaging myself.* "No. I mean...I just meant I haven't seen your dorm yet. Can we hang out there instead?"

He smiled. "You sure you don't want to spend the night in your own bed? I'm pretty tired too. We could just call it a night."

I wasn't sure why, but him not jumping on that idea made me feel even more panicked than his touch. Why didn't he want me to see his room? He was hiding something from me. I needed some space. It felt like I couldn't breathe. "If you're sure that's okay. Rain check though?"

"Absolutely." He pulled me against his chest and kissed me.

It was hard and angry and wrong. I tried to ignore the panic rising in my chest, but I couldn't seem to stifle the feeling. It was like I was being engulfed in flames.

CHAPTER 30
Saturday

I bit the inside of my lip as I stared down at my phone. It shouldn't have been a hard decision. Someone had tried to kill me. Eli didn't seem as trustworthy as I had first made him out to be. I knew someone here from my past. And the vigilante had told me I wasn't safe here. I had to call Mr. Crawford.

Even though it felt like giving up, I pressed on his name in my phone. I held my breath for five seconds before his voicemail clicked on. Maybe he really was just busy and couldn't come to the phone. But to me, it felt like fate. Mr. Crawford hadn't picked up for a reason. I didn't need him to whisk me away and change my identity again. I could take care of myself.

Besides, all the bad things here could be easily explained away. The man with a knife was just a normal psycho from the city. Miles believed that I was Sadie, not Summer. The vigilante just meant to go home to my dorm and that it wasn't safe in that dark alleyway. And I felt differently about Eli because I was harboring feelings for Miles. *Ugh.* I lay back on my bed. Hopefully Mr. Crawford wouldn't call me back. I could fix this by myself.

My mind seemed to stay fixated on Miles. He had flirted with me. That should have made me feel good, and it did, partially. But it stung too. It meant he had moved on from Summer. Why had I never moved on? I shook my head. The answer was obvious. Miles was the last person who truly knew who I was. I wanted to be that little girl again, full of life and smiles. Don had stolen my identity before I even had to change my name. He had made me a ghost of who I used to be.

But Miles remembered. He still wrote letters to me. At least, he said he did. Could it have been some kind of miscommunication? Had Don been stealing my letters? I had never told Don about them, but he could have found out. Or maybe Miles had been sending them to the wrong address. Don made a habit of moving a lot. What if Miles was telling the truth? What if he was having one night stands because he couldn't commit to loving anyone else because he was still in love with me?

I laughed out loud. It sounded like a sad noise in my empty dorm. I sat up. None of that mattered. I couldn't pursue my feelings for Miles. It was too dangerous. Besides, there was one other person who did seem to know me. A chill ran down my spine just thinking about the vigilante. He had called me Sadie. He didn't actually know me. But I knew he was watching me.

A few days ago I had filled out a contact form on The Night Watch blog. I hadn't heard back. Maybe they'd respond if they knew I had met the vigilante. I leaned over and grabbed my computer off my bed. I pulled up the blog and read the most recent article.

My heart started to race. It was about me. Well, not really about me, it didn't say my name or anything, but it was about last night. The article talked about how the vigilante had broken his normal routine. He hadn't robbed any robbers. Instead, he had taken down a convicted felon with a lengthy rap sheet. There was a mugshot of the man who had attacked me. The scar under his cold gaze reminded me of the fear in my chest. It reminded me of the death in his eyes. I swallowed hard.

The question was, how did the author of the article know it was the vigilante who had subdued him? There were no photos this time. No proof that it was the vigilante. *It's him.* The vigilante was writing the articles. It had to be him. So, why had he broken his usual MO for me? Why was he watching me?

I read the last line of the article. They always ended the same way. "Someone in this city is watching us." The now familiar chill ran down my spine. It was the same reaction I had to seeing the vigilante in person.

I clicked on the contact form again. This time I told the author of the blog that I knew why the vigilante had broken his usual MO. And I told them that I had met him. If that didn't get me a response, then nothing would. I pressed the send button and drummed my fingers against my thigh.

My mind seemed to flood with possibilities. Maybe the vigilante really was Eli. Patrick and Kins had mentioned that he had tons of bruises from his boxing classes. What if it wasn't from boxing? What if it was from fighting bad guys? I typed Eli's name into Google and scrolled through the results. None of them were him. I typed in his name with Facebook after it. The second result was him. He was smiling at the camera with a couple guys next to him. They were clearly laughing about something. Why would someone so carefree suddenly decide to move to the city and rob from the rich? The motivation wasn't there.

No matter what I did, my mind always seemed to wander back to Miles. Maybe he wasn't stargazing at all. Maybe he was searching the city with his telescope for criminals. It couldn't be him, though. The soccer game was almost over when I left the stadium. It would have been nearly impossible for him to change and find me. And what would be his motivation?

"Hey," Kins said as she walked into the dorm.

I looked up from my computer. "Hey. I'm a little surprised to see you. You've been spending most nights at Patrick's."

She laughed and jumped onto my bed beside me, invading my personal bubble as usual. "I needed some girl time. It's weird, right?"

"What is? Hanging out with me?

Kins laughed. "No, I love hanging out with you. That's weird," she said and pointed to my computer screen where Eli's Facebook picture was still on my browser. "He only has like 10 pictures on his Facebook. There's quite a few friends in them, so you'd think he'd be tagged in more."

"Maybe it's set to private."

Kins shrugged. "Maybe. Did you know he didn't even accept my friend request? And I'm in his dorm all the time. It's not like we aren't friends. I feel like we're pretty close. Why do you never come over, anyway?"

"He's never invited me over actually."

"Huh."

I bit the inside of my lip. "What does he do while you and Patrick hang out?"

"Honestly, he's not there very much. But when he is, he watches TV with us or is on his computer. I would have assumed he was on Facebook, but that doesn't seem to be the case."

Interesting. I wanted to tell Kins about the vigilante. But having a criminal looking out for you didn't exactly seem normal. I was supposed to be blending in. So despite me wanting to confide in her, I bit my tongue.

"Here, let me show you something." She pulled my computer onto her lap. She logged into her Facebook and pulled up Patrick's page. His profile picture was of the two of them. She was smiling at the camera and he was kissing her on the cheek.

"That's adorable."

"It's not adorable. It's all moving too fast. Who makes their profile picture of a girl they just met anyway?"

"You two seem so happy when you're together."

"I do like him, don't get me wrong. But I don't want to settle down yet. I'm not an old lady. I want sexy, spicy, raunchy, smoldering hot sex three times a day so that I physically can't move."

I laughed. "And Patrick can't give that to you?"

She kicked her feet out in front of her. "I'm still moving and there's only an hour left of Saturday. So no, I guess not."

I laughed again. "Kins you're being ridiculous."

"Am I? I don't think so. Because I know who can give me what I want." She typed in Miles Young into the Facebook search bar.

My heart seemed to drop into my stomach. I didn't want to hear Kins talk about her growing crush on Miles.

And I certainly didn't want to hear about her having raunchy sex with him. I didn't want to think about anyone having sex with him.

"Weird."

I looked at the Miles Young profile options that had come up. None of them were his, which I already knew. "Miles doesn't have a Facebook profile."

"No, he does. Something is just wrong with your computer." She handed it back to me and typed in Miles' name on her phone. "See."

What the hell? I grabbed her phone from her. Miles did have a Facebook account. And there were tons of pictures of him. I scrolled through them slowly. His arm slung around some girl at a party. Him with his soccer jersey on. Him with another girl. And another. And another. He was a player. He probably played girls as well as he played soccer.

"Sex with him would be mind-blowing, don't you think?"

I blinked away the tears in my eyes as I started scrolling faster. Him at prom with some girl I didn't recognize. Him with his parents at graduation. I felt like I had missed out on his whole life. All those years that I had held out hope, he truly had forgotten about me. *I'm invisible.* "He's a pig. There's a different girl in every single one of his pictures."

"Exactly. Which means he has a lot of experience in bed."

I shook my head. I loved Miles Young when we were both little. When we shared our first kiss. When we held hands for the first time. When he wrote to me every week after my parents died. I wasn't in love with this version of him. My love had turned into hate over the past few years. And that's where it needed to stay. I hated him. Tears continued to prick at my eyes. Why couldn't my words convince me? Why couldn't these pictures convince me? Why was my heart so fucking stupid?

"You deserve better than him, Kins."

She smiled. "Thank you. But there is no one better than him. Every girl on campus loves him as much as me. Except you apparently. Oh my God, let me show you my favorite picture." She grabbed her phone back. A few seconds later she was holding it out for me again.

Miles had his jersey tossed over one shoulder, baring his perfect six pack. He was tan and muscular and everything you could possible want in a man. His chest glistened with sweat like he had just finished a game and he was pushing his hair off his forehead. If I wasn't trying to hold back tears I'd probably be drooling.

"Right there," Kins said, pointing to a line sticking out beneath his jersey. "I am dying to know what he has a tattoo of. I can't find a picture of it anywhere."

I stared at the line that disappeared beneath his jersey onto the left side of his chest. The whole tattoo must be over his heart.

"One day, I'm going to see that tattoo, I swear." She collapsed backward onto my bed. "I just need one night with him, that's all I'm asking. One night and I can move on. God, it's like an itch that I just can't seem to scratch."

One night and I can move on. Kins was getting in my head. But I couldn't help but wonder. Would I be able to move on if I had Miles for one night? I had a feeling it would just make me want him even more. I stared at the picture. Maybe I imagined it, but there was one thing every picture seemed to have in common. His smile didn't quite reach his eyes.

CHAPTER 31
Sunday

With each step, I felt like I was walking farther and farther into a bad part of town. I glanced over my shoulder. The hairs on the back of my neck seemed to prickle and I picked up my pace. My legs were sore from another run this morning, and they seemed to protest with each movement.

A cat scampering across a path made me jump. Why did the author of the blog have to live in the sketchiest place ever? I had been happy when they had written me back. But the message was blunt. It was just an address and a time. Now I was regretting my decision. This was something a stupid girl in a horror flick would do. My feet kept moving though.

I had convinced myself that the vigilante was writing the blog himself. Which meant I was about to come face to face with him. A few sirens and beggars on the streets weren't going to scare me away. I stopped in front of a rundown building. Some of the windows were boarded up. *This can't possibly be right.* I pulled out the piece of paper I had written the address down on to double check. 255 S. Broad Street, apartment 1057. The number above the front door verified that I was indeed in the right place.

I glanced over my shoulder again. I was starting to get used to the feeling of being watched. The vigilante was out there. I could feel it. It was more comforting than alarming now. I turned my attention back to the front of the building and pressed on the button for apartment 1057.

The door immediately buzzed. I grabbed the handle and walked inside. I jumped as a rat scurried across the floor. Why would the vigilante live here? He should have kept some of that money he had given away for himself. I pictured a poor boy, wanting to fight for people like him. I wasn't at all surprised when the button for the elevator didn't do a thing.

I found the stairs and slowly started walking up. My muscles were screaming at me. Each step up, I'd look down at my Converses. I was going to meet the vigilante. I wanted to prove to him that I was strong. Hell, I wanted to prove to myself that I was strong.

I opened the door to floor 10. It made a terrible squeaking noise. One of the lights in the ceiling was flickering. It seemed more like I was walking into a villain's den than a superhero's. I stopped in front of the door marked 1057. This was it. My heart seemed to be beating out of my chest as I lifted my hand. My knock seemed to echo in the empty hallway.

There was a scuffling noise inside. And then it sounded like someone was undoing a dozen locks. A moment later the door opened. A girl with frizzy dark hair and big glasses was standing in front of me. "You're Sadie Davis?" She pushed her glasses up her nose.

It took me a moment to find my voice. She wasn't what I was expecting at all. "Yes. And you're the author of The Night Watch?" I tried to hide my disappointment. I had been expecting the vigilante.

"Shhh." She stepped out into the hall and looked both ways. "You'll ruin everything. Come in, hurry."

I flinched as she grabbed my arm and pulled me into her apartment. I stood awkwardly in the center of a barely furnished studio apartment as she bolted the door. There were newspaper clippings strewn all over the place. A single couch was the only furniture in the living room. But the whole right wall of her apartment was filled with computer monitors, showing different angles of the city.

"Everyone thinks I'm crazy."

I turned around to look at her standing by the door. She looked crazy. Her apartment was insane. But I knew that wasn't what she was talking about. She meant that no one believed in her articles. "I don't think you're crazy."

"No one sees the connection." She started pacing back and forth. "The missing money. The apartment payments. The charity donations. Why does no one see it? It's not just a correlation."

"I see it."

She stopped pacing as she stared at me. "I was at the bank that day. He's a hero. So many people are making him out to be a villain."

"He saved my life. I know he's a hero."

"But why? Why did he save you? There was no money involved. It doesn't fit. Why you?"

"I don't know. But he knew my name. I feel like he's been watching me."

She pushed her glasses up the bridge of her nose. "He has been. I'm trying to figure out why."

"What do you mean he has been?"

"He hacks my computers." She walked over to her monitors. "Well, I should say that I let him hack them. If I didn't want him to be able to, I could block him. His hacking skills aren't exactly great."

I didn't know anything about hacking. My mind was still fixated on the fact that she said he'd been watching me. "But how do you know what he sees?"

She stared at me blankly. "I'm good at what I do. For example, you just started school at Eastern University. Which just so happened to be one day before the vigilante's first appearance. And he was at the bank where all your money is. Which is a lot for someone your age. It's all connected somehow, I just don't know how. Your appearance set off this timeline of events. It jumpstarted something. He was waiting for you."

I shook my head. "None of this makes sense."

"It's basic cause and effect."

"No, I mean...I'm not involved in this. I don't even know who he is."

"That doesn't mean you didn't cause it. Look." She pointed to one of the monitors. The imaging was rotating, giving another view of the street. "He's looking for you."

A chill ran down my spine. "He's looking for what to do next. It has nothing to do with me."

"It has everything to do with you."

I stared at the monitor. This crazy girl wasn't touching anything. It was almost like a ghost was controlling it. Was he really looking for me? It should have scared me. But I wasn't scared of him. I knew he wouldn't hurt me.

"You have virtually no cyber footprint except for the information about your school enrollment and your bank account," the girl continued. "Which means you're not really who you say you are."

"I don't know what you're talking about. I'm Sadie Davis."

"And I'm the Queen of England."

I laughed.

She didn't look like she thought it was funny.

"I just don't like computers. That's why you couldn't find much on me."

"Who doesn't like computers?"

"I didn't grow up with one. I..."

"What kind of person who has 3 million dollars sitting in their bank account doesn't have a computer growing up?"

It was strange. But not as strange as the fact that she had hacked into my bank account. "I..."

"Why are you here, Sadie?" She put Sadie in air quotes. "In your email, you said you knew why the vigilante had broken his usual MO. So tell me why."

I shook my head. "Honestly, I thought maybe you were the vigilante. I just wanted to meet you. I didn't understand how you knew that it was him that had turned in that convict. It didn't fit his MO. So I thought maybe you were him. Because you had to be watching me."

She shook her head. "I wasn't watching you. It was the sedative the vigilante used. It's an odd mixture of ingredients. It's easy to trace the connection after you hack into the files from the NYPD."

"You hacked into the NYPD computers?"

"Yeah. It was easy." She sat down in the chair and swiveled to face her computers. "You just..."

"You don't have to show me."

She shrugged her shoulders and turned back around. She just stared at me, like she was waiting for me to answer a question she hadn't asked.

"What's your name?" I finally said, breaking the awkward silence.

"Liza. Or maybe I'm making it up. I guess you'll never know."

I laughed.

This time she responded with a small smile.

Now seemed like as good a time as ever to ask for a favor. "Actually, since you're so good with computers, I was hoping you could help me."

"You're right. I am good with computers. What do you need?"

I slid my backpack off my shoulder and pulled out my laptop. "I was trying to check someone's Facebook profile the other day. And for some reason I couldn't see it on here. But my roommate easily pulled it up on her phone."

"Whoever it was probably blocked you."

"But we only just met."

She shrugged her shoulders. "I don't know what to tell you."

"Could you maybe just look at it?" I held out my computer toward her.

She sighed and grabbed my computer. "What's the password?"

"Password."

"Seriously? No wonder someone messed with your computer." She pushed her glasses up her nose and then started typing furiously. "Overprotective parents?" she finally said.

"Something like that, I guess. Why?"

"You have parental controls set. It's weird that they'd involve phrases including names. That's not usually what they're used for. I can override them if you want or..." she stopped talking as the computer screen turned blue. Numbers and letters started scrolling across the screen. "What the hell?" She started typing furiously again. "This isn't like any normal settings I've ever seen before. It's extremely high tech." A red light started beeping on the keypad. Liza's fingers stopped as her eyes scanned the screen. "Fuck. Why would you bring this here?" She slammed the lid shut and ran over to the window.

Before I could stop her, she had opened up the window and thrown my laptop out of it.

"What did you just do?! What is wrong with you?!" I ran over to window and stared out. I couldn't even see it, we were so high up.

Liza hadn't answered me. I turned around and she was pacing again. It looked like she was mumbling something under her breath.

"Why did you do that?" I tried to ask a little more calmly.

She stopped mid-pace. "It had a tracking device in it. The vigilante isn't the only one watching you. You need to go. When they realize the transmitter isn't working, they might try to come for you. You have to go."

It was just Mr. Crawford. It made sense that he wanted to know where I was. To make sure I was safe. "It was just my parents," I lied.

"That was some next level government shit, Sadie. Someone is after you. And the vigilante isn't high tech enough to pull that off. It's someone dangerous, with deep pockets. You have to go."

"But I..."

"You coming here started something, something bigger than the vigilante." She hit something and all her monitors went black.

"Let me help you figure out who he is. I need to know."

"I don't want your help with this. You're not who you say you are. You're involved somehow and I don't want..."

"Please. Please help me."

She stared at me for a moment before handing me a card. "Don't use whatever phone you currently have. It probably has a tracker on it too. You need to dump it. Give me a few days. I'll have a new headquarters by then." She unplugged a fistful of wires.

"Isn't this where you live?"

"In this dump? No way. Now go before they find you."

I knew it was Mr. Crawford, so why did her words send a chill down my spine? Who else had access to my computer? Just a few other members of the witness protection program. And Kins. And I guess anyone else who had come into our dorm. Patrick. Eli. Maybe a few people from our floor. *It was just Mr. Crawford.*

I unbolted all the locks on the door and left Liza to her computers. She said people thought she was crazy. And maybe she was. She was intelligent too, though. It was hard not to take her warning seriously. The flickering light in the hall seemed more ominous now. I quickly made my way down the stairs and out onto the city street.

It was virtually deserted. I looked up at the sky. Not a single star was visible tonight. I looked down at my Converses instead. They had given me the strength I needed recently. I was letting go of my obsession with the stars and holding on to something new for once in my life. I needed the vigilante. He helped me forget about my pain. He helped me want to be Sadie Davis.

A clanging noise made me jump. I looked up at a fire escape just in time to see the vigilante leap off of it and land several feet away from me. He was at the entrance of an alleyway, and he was bathed in darkness. The moonlight cast shadows across his masked face and his hood was pulled low over his eyes.

"I told you to go home." The rumble in his voice didn't scare me.

"And I did. I went back to my dorm." I took a step toward him.

He held his ground. "You know that's not what I meant. This city isn't safe for you."

"I don't have a home."

He shook his head. "You can't stay here, Sadie."

"How do you know my name?" A few more steps and we were less than two feet apart.

He didn't answer my question.

"You've been following me. Why?"

"You're reckless. You shouldn't walk the streets alone at night."

"Neither should you."

His laugh rumbled low and deep. I wanted to know what it sounded like without whatever mechanism was changing it. I took another step toward him. I thought he might step back, but again he held his ground. I could feel his body heat. I could smell his sweet cologne. He smelled like a million bucks.

"Home. Now, Sadie."

"Do you know who else is following me?" I asked, ignoring him.

"You've brought darkness to this city. Trust no one."

He was talking in riddles. But it was similar to what Liza had said. That somehow I had caused all of this. "And what about you?" It was like my hand had a mind of its own. I reached out and lightly touched the side of his masked face.

A low hiss escaped his lips. It was like my touch pained him. I knew how that felt. I immediately pulled my hand away, but I stayed right in front of him. It was like the whole world was silent when we were together. I was drawn to him. I could tell that he was drawn to me too.

"There's darkness in everyone."

His words made me gulp. "How do you know my name?" I asked again.

"You're the only reason that I'm here, Sadie."

The rumble in his voice made my insides flip over.

"There's darkness in me too," I whispered. I was certainly thinking dark thoughts about him. I wanted his lips on mine. I wanted to feel the hard lines of his muscles. I wanted all of him.

He shifted closer to me so that I could feel his hot breath on my ear. "All I see is light."

It felt like my heart was beating out of my chest. "I want to help you. I want to be a part of this."

"You already are a part of it. You're everything."

I closed my eyes as I relished his breath on my skin. *Everything?* What did that mean? Everything to him? Everything that was causing problems? I didn't really even care. He was here because of me. That was all that mattered.

A clanging noise made my eyelids open. I hadn't even heard him walk away from me. But he was gone. I had felt invisible for five years. Now that someone saw the light in me, I didn't feel so invisible anymore. I couldn't leave the city. The ironic part was that the main thing keeping me here was the person telling me to leave.

CHAPTER 32
Monday

"Don't you already have a computer?" Eli said.

I shrugged my shoulders as I stared at the price differ-ence between the Dell and HP. I hadn't asked Eli to come with me. I told him I needed to do some shopping and he had insisted on coming with me. It made my stomach feel uneasy. At first, I wanted to tell him about meeting Liza from The Night Watch blog. But I hadn't actually learned much from her besides for the fact that the vigilante and someone else were watching me. I wasn't sure why, but my gut was telling me that the other person was Eli. He had been one of the only people that had access to my com-puter.

It was Mr. Crawford. It didn't make me feel any better though. There was someone in this city that the vigilante wanted me to get away from. The vigilante had probably seen me with Eli. But he had also probably seen me with Miles. And Kins. I shook away the thought as I glanced over at Eli.

He smiled. "Seriously, what happened to it? It looked brand new."

He had studied my computer. I pressed my lips to-gether, trying to think of a good lie. "I dropped it." Technically, it had been dropped. That much was true.

"And that broke it? It must have been a pretty crappy computer. Do you want me to take a look at it? I might be able to fix it."

"I already threw it out."

"You should've at least recycled it," he said with a laugh.

I shrugged my shoulders. "Either way, which do you think is better?" I gestured at the two computers on display.

"The processor is a lot faster on that one," Eli said and pointed to the more expensive one. "But if you're just going to be using it for writing research papers and stuff, the basic one is fine."

"So you know a lot about computers?"

"A fair amount."

Hmm. Liza had said that the vigilante wasn't the best hacker. Could it possibly be Eli?

"What are you looking at?" he said with a smile.

"Nothing." I realized I had been awkwardly staring at him. I was bordering on the edge of paranoia. Just because the vigilante knew me, it didn't mean I knew him. I stared at the computers again. The more expensive one was a different brand than the one Mr. Crawford had given me. And I did want it for more than just school papers. I wanted to help Liza. I wanted to write for her blog and spread the truth about the vigilante. I wanted to be as close to him as possible.

"Can I help you two with something?" a sales girl asked.

"Yes," I said and turned toward her. "I'll take this computer." I gestured to the more expensive one. "And I was hoping you could show me some cell phones too?"

"Something happened to your cell phone too?" Eli asked.

"Um, no, but I think it's time for an upgrade."

"You have the iPhone they released less than a month ago. There is nothing better than that."

He had definitely been paying attention to my devices. "Yeah, maybe. I think I'm just more of an Android girl."

"Me too," the sales clerk said. "I have the Samsung Galaxy and I love it. It's really easy to use and..."

"Okay, I'll take that one."

"Do you have a plan that you want to switch over?"

There was probably a plan on my current phone. But I didn't want anyone to automatically have access to my new account too. "Nope."

"Did you want to keep the same number?"

Liza hadn't said anything about that. I wanted Mr. Crawford to have my number in case he needed to contact me. "Yeah, that would be great."

"Awesome. I'll ring you up and one of our tech guys will get your phone all set up." She pulled out a key, unlocked the case below the display, and pulled out a box with a picture of the computer on it. We followed her to the check-out and waited while she went to go fetch the phone.

"Are you sure you want that computer, Sadie? It's awfully expensive. Especially if you're getting a new phone too."

"Mhm." I hadn't dipped into the account my parents had left me at all. If there was ever a reason to do it, this was it. They would have wanted me to be safe. I just hoped Eli wouldn't keep questioning me about the money. "You know what, you should look into getting a new iPod while we're here."

Eli looked down at the earbuds sticking out of his pocket. "Oh, no, that's okay. I got it working again actually."

"That's great. Maybe I should have let you look at my computer." I gave him what I hoped was an innocent smile.

"We can transfer all your contacts to your new phone, if you don't mind waiting a few minutes," a tech guy said as he opened up the Samsung box.

"No, that's okay."

"Are you sure? It will take you awhile to do it yourself. We have a SIM card converter..."

"I'm positive. But thank you for offering." I didn't want my current SIM card or any other part of my old phone near my new phone. I handed the sales girl my debit card before she even said the price. I didn't really want to know what I had just spent.

"Okay, just give me a few minutes to get you all set up," the tech guy said. "I'll need to deactivate your current number from your phone." He held out his hand.

I handed him my phone and closely watched what he did. No parts of my old phone were transferred to the new one. Everything seemed okay.

"What's going on with you?" Eli whispered in my ear as he wrapped his arm around my waist.

"What do you mean?" I shifted slightly so that I could look up at him. He really did have kind eyes. He looked concerned about me.

"You've been acting differently ever since I started those boxing classes."

"No I haven't."

He scrunched his face to the side in the way that reminded me so much of Miles. "You have. And I'm really sorry that I've been so busy. Let me take you to dinner tonight to make up for it," he said.

"I have work."

"Call in sick."

"I can't do that. I only just started."

"Come on, Sadie. Please." He tucked a loose strand of hair behind my ear.

"If it means I can see your place." I needed to shake this feeling that he was hiding something from me. Seeing his dorm would be a good place to start. Maybe I could even do some light snooping.

Something seemed to flash across his face. But it was gone before I could register what it was.

"Yeah, sure. Dinner at my place."

"We've canceled your current plan but it's always good to double check with them to make sure they don't keep billing you," the tech guy said. "There also might be some fees for terminating your plan early."

I reluctantly tore my eyes away from Eli. "Thanks for all your help." I grabbed both phones and slid them into my backpack.

"Did you want to get the extended warranty for either device?" the sales girl asked.

I shook my head. That would be a waste of money if Liza decided to break this computer too. I was almost positive the warranty didn't cover a device being thrown out a window of a 10 story building. And even if it did, I couldn't exactly ask that question in front of Eli. He'd be suspicious of why I was asking.

"Then here you go," the sales girl said and handed me my debit card and a bag. "Thanks for shopping with us today." She had a huge smile on her face. I had probably just made her day with those sales commissions.

"Do you want me to get that?" Eli said and reached for the bag.

"No, that's okay." I held it close to my side. No one was getting anywhere near my new computer.

CHAPTER 33

Monday

I double checked that I had typed Mr. Crawford's name into my new phone correctly and pressed save. Even though I had put Kins' and Eli's numbers into my phone too, Mr. Crawford's was really the only one that mattered. The rest of the numbers were fleeting because I'd forever be a flight risk. Don would find me and I'd have to leave and start over again. Hell, maybe he already had found me.

I opened up Google on my laptop and typed in his name. There was no more new information about the case. He was still out on bail. It didn't make any sense. How had he gotten that money? I stared at the small article from the Colorado Post. They hadn't even set a trial date yet. Didn't they realize that they were making it impossible for me to move on? Just thinking about having to see him at trial made my whole body feel cold.

My fingers traced the scar on my stomach. It didn't really matter that Don was in a different state. It didn't really even matter if he ended up going to prison. I'd never truly be rid of him. The scars were a constant reminder. But at least the bruises were fading. I was finally rid of my hoodie. I looked down at the summer dress that I was wearing for my date with Eli. It almost felt strange. I was used to having the hoodie to hide behind. I suddenly felt exposed, like Eli would be able to truly see me for the first time.

There was no way I could wear this in front of him. I couldn't let him see the real me.

I stood up to change when I heard a knock on the door. Who was that? I quickly closed my computer. I was supposed to meet Eli in just a few minutes. My heartbeat quickened. Kins would have just walked right in. So, there was really only one person it could be. *Miles.* I hadn't seen him since he had wanted to walk me home. Thinking about him made me smile, even though I knew better than to let it. It didn't matter if I was head over heels for Miles or not. Sadie Davis could never be with him. And Summer Brooks had lost her chance. I ran my fingers through my hair despite the fact that I shouldn't care, and looked in the mirror. The long chain of the pendant was visible but not the pendant itself. I ran my fingers down the chain. Miles was the only piece of Summer I had left and I wasn't sure how that was supposed to make me feel. All I knew was that this pendant had given me strength, and despite what I told myself, that was mostly because of him. I took a deep breath and opened the door.

Eli was standing there with a bouquet of flowers in his hand and a huge smile on his face.

"What are you doing here?" I didn't mean to sound rude, but I was finally going to get to see his place tonight. That was the whole reason I had agreed to miss out on work.

"I wanted to surprise you." He walked into my room without waiting for me to invite him in. "You look gorgeous, Sadie." He leaned forward and kissed me on my cheek.

Fire. I awkwardly folded my arms in front of my chest. "I was just about to leave. Should we head over to your dorm now?"

"I'd rather stay here." He handed me the flowers.

They really were beautiful. I knew very little about flowers, but I recognized more daisies and some carnations. "Thank you. But I was really looking forward to spending some time at your place." I looked around for something to put the flowers in because I didn't own a vase. Finally, I settled on separating the bouquet into a few water bottles. I turned back toward him. He was smiling at me. "What?" I tucked a loose strand of hair behind my ear. His gaze was making me nervous.

"Nothing, I've just never seen you look more beautiful than you do right now."

I swallowed hard. He was changing the topic. I couldn't shake the feeling that he didn't want me to see his place because he was hiding something from me. And it shouldn't have upset me, because I was hiding something from him too. I would never be able to tell him the truth. I'd have to lie to him my whole life. I was being a hypocrite and guilt was slowly creeping into my stomach. "Are you sure you don't want to go to your place?"

"Trust me, it looks almost exactly the same as yours. Except Patrick and Kins are there right now. And I was kind of hoping to spend some time alone with you."

That was a good excuse. God, maybe it wasn't an excuse at all. He was just telling the truth. I suddenly felt even more guilty. I just wanted to go to his place to look through his stuff. I really was losing my mind. He was a good guy. A good guy that was looking at me with lust in his eyes. *He wants to be alone with me.* I wanted to reciprocate his feelings, but all I could think about was the scar on my stomach. If he saw it, it would just end in yet another fight. I was tired of fighting with him. I was just tired in general.

"Plus," he said as he pulled out a brown paper bag from behind his back, "I come bearing gifts. You didn't get a chance to see the movie showing the other night and before you left you had seemed excited to watch it."

I opened up the bag. It was a DVD of Frozen and a bottle of wine. Something seemed to constrict in my chest. Eli was the sweetest guy I had ever met. He wasn't a vigilante spying on me. He wasn't someone who could ruin my new identity. Maybe he could help me get over my hate of Disney movies. Maybe he could help me get over all of my issues. "Thank you, Eli. Let me just get the TV set up..."

"I got it. How about you just grab us some glasses and get comfortable?" He knelt down by the DVD player.

I smiled as I looked around for something to use for glasses. I settled on two mugs, poured some wine into each, and sat down on my bed. I just wanted to be in his arms. I had missed the feeling of security he had given me. There wasn't a doubt in my mind that I'd been sabotaging a good thing. A week ago I had been falling for him. My paranoia was getting in the way of me being happy. But I didn't need to be paranoid. Don was in Colorado. I was safe here. Especially if I stopped pushing Eli away. I took a sip of the wine. With each sip, it felt like my worries seemed to dissipate.

When Eli sat down next to me, I immediately rested my head on his shoulder. He wrapped his arm around my back and pulled me even closer. He definitely didn't smell like the vigilante. He smelled like citrus and sunshine, not expensive cologne. But it was Eli's familiar scent that always seemed to calm my nerves. Yes, the idea of the vigilante was exciting, but I didn't need any more excitement in my life. I wanted normalcy. I wanted to be content and safe and whole. God, I was so tired of feeling broken.

"Do I even want to know where you got this?" I asked as I lifted my mug. The last thing I needed was to get in trouble for underage drinking and draw attention to myself. But I appreciated his effort.

"I have my ways." He kissed the side of my forehead.

"Very mysterious."

He laughed. "A little mystery never hurt anyone."

"Cheers to that." I tapped my mug against his and he laughed again. I liked his laugh. It made me smile. We both watched the movie and drank the wine from our mugs. One mug turned to two and I could feel myself getting more comfortable in his arms. We seemed so normal together. I never wanted this moment to end. But it wasn't long before the parents' deaths in the movie. I waited with baited breath. No matter how hard I tried to hold them back, silent tears still fell down my cheeks as I watched the parents' boat sink in the movie. I let myself feel the heartache. I let myself remember.

But my tears weren't silent at all. Eli saw them. His fingers brushed underneath my eyes, removing any trace of my tears. "You're incredibly cute." He didn't ask what was wrong. He probably thought he knew. But he didn't know all of my demons and I didn't want him to. I wouldn't want to burden anyone with my past.

"And you're way too good for me," I said. I meant it. He should be with any other girl on campus other than me. I'd never be enough.

"Really? I was kinda thinking we were just right together." His voice was so sincere.

Just right. I exhaled slowly. "I like the sound of that."

He put his hand on the inside of my thigh.

Fire. I tried to swallow the panic rising in my chest.

His hand slid up until he was absentmindedly playing with the hem of my dress.

"I'm falling for you, Sadie."

I should have immediately said I was falling for him too. But the way he was looking at me and the sincerity in his voice just made me realize I wasn't there yet. For some reason, no matter how badly I wanted to, I couldn't say it back. I wanted to fall for him. I so badly wanted to be able to. But the truth was, I didn't think I'd ever fall in love again. I didn't think I'd ever be able to trust someone enough. Don had ruined me. No matter how many times I told myself that Eli was good and sweet, I couldn't believe it. His touch still felt like fire. It should have mattered that he was holding me while I cried. Him being there when I needed him meant a lot to me. But all I could think about were the times he wasn't there. He had left me waiting. He had left me alone.

I stared into his brown eyes and all I could see was how he'd eventually hurt me. How he'd put his hand over my mouth to stifle my screams. How he'd laugh at my pain. How he'd hold me down. How he'd break me when I was already so broken. I couldn't breathe.

"It's okay, you don't have to say it back if you're not ready," he said and gently touched the side of my face.

It burned. His fingertips were scorching. He didn't understand my silence. He'd never understand.

"I know you said you wanted to take it slow. And that was probably a little heavy so soon." He pushed his lips to the side.

It was the expression that reminded me so much of Miles. Why was I drawn more to Eli when he did that? If I wanted Miles, he was right down the hall. I could have him. Or I could have Eli. But I didn't want any of that. I didn't want someone who wanted to get to know the real me. I needed someone who wouldn't ask me questions. Someone who'd accept me the way I was. Someone who didn't care if I was broken. The vigilante.

I'm losing my mind. Or maybe I had drunk too much again. A minute ago I had thought the alcohol had calmed me down, but now my mind wouldn't stop racing. "Do you want some air? I feel like I need some air."

Eli smiled. "I'd rather stay in." His hand slid underneath the fabric of my dress.

I was being engulfed in flames. "I'm actually not feeling very well." It was the truth. I felt like I was running a temperature.

"Sadie, I consider myself a patient person, but you're driving me crazy." He leaned forward to kiss me, but I ducked out from under his arm.

If I got any closer to the flames, I'd surely burn. "I'm sorry," I said as I slid off the bed. "I need some air." I frantically searched for my flip flops.

"What's wrong? What did I do?"

I don't know. I needed to calm down. I knew how frantic I looked, but I couldn't help it. I needed to be outside. I needed the stars.

"Sadie, talk to me..."

"I just need some air." Finally, I found my flip flops under my desk. I slid my feet into them and swung the door open.

"Sadie!"

I was already walking down the hall. The flames were stealing all the oxygen from my lungs. I felt lightheaded as I began walking faster.

"Damn it, Sadie." Eli grabbed my arm and forcefully turned me to look at him.

You're hurting me.

"I don't know what you want from me. I'm doing everything I can to make you happy. And every time we hang out, you seem to push me away even more."

"I'm sorry," I whispered. *Let go of me.*

"I don't want you to apologize. I just want you to talk to me. You can't act like this and expect me to never ask another question. I'm trying, but you have to stop pushing me away." His fingers seemed to dig into my skin.

You're hurting me. My throat was constricting. "Stop." I was surprised by my own words. But I seemed to breathe a little easier after I had said it.

"Stop what? Stop caring?" His fingers were burning me. "Is that really what you want?"

Tears pooled in my eyes, but I blinked them away. *Stop hurting me.*

"She said stop."

I didn't need to look to see who it was. I'd recognize Miles' voice anywhere.

Eli didn't let go of my arm. "This isn't any of your business, man." He didn't even look at Miles. "You said you wanted to go outside, so let's go outside, Sadie." His hand gripped me even tighter.

"You're making it my business." Miles pulled Eli off of me.

I immediately grabbed my arm. I hadn't imagined it. There were red spots on my forearm where his fingers had been.

"Get the fuck off of me." Eli pushed Miles' hands away and shoved him hard.

Miles grabbed Eli's shirt and pushed him against the wall. His arm was pressed against Eli's throat.

"Please stop." I didn't want them to fight. I just need-ed the stars. I just needed to breathe.

"If I see you touch her like that again, I will end you." Miles immediately released his grip on Eli's shirt.

"Sadie, come on, let's go," Eli said a little more calmly.

I didn't want to go with him. I didn't want him to touch me.

"Get out of this dorm before I write you up," Miles said.

"We'll finish this conversation later, Sadie," Eli said. His voice didn't sound threatening. It sounded defeated.

I watched him walk away. Each step he took I seemed to breathe a little easier. And with each step, I realized that I could never love someone. I'd never be able to. If I could, I'd love Eli. I'd want him to touch me. I'd want to be with him every second of every day. That was never going to happen. He deserved better than me. I wrapped my arms around myself. It was my fault. All of this was my fault.

CHAPTER 34

Monday

"Sadie." Mile's voice was gentle. "Are you okay? Did he hurt you?"

I couldn't explain myself to him. He wouldn't understand that the emotional pain was worse than the physical pain. That all of it was in my head. No one would ever understand. "I need some air."

He didn't say anything. I could feel his eyes on me, studying me. I couldn't look at him. I couldn't bear to make eye contact with him. His scrutiny was making me feel so exposed.

"Okay," he said slowly. "Come with me." He didn't try to touch me. Instead, he just started walking toward the stairs.

I followed him. I didn't know how to not follow Miles Young. When I entered the stairwell, I was surprised to see him walking up instead of down. Where was he going? I continued to follow him until he stopped in front of a door marked, "Private Use Only."

"What is this?"

He pulled out a lanyard from his pocket and inserted a key into the lock. "Only the best view in the city." He pushed the door open.

The cool night air washed over me as I walked through the door he was holding open for me. If I wasn't already having trouble breathing, it would have taken my breath away. The city lights lit up everything as far as the eye could see. It was almost like looking at the stars in the sky. I blinked away the tears in my eyes. It was beautiful. We were on the top of the dorm complex. I walked over to the very edge and placed my hands on the concrete ledge.

"And the best part," Miles said as he leaned against the ledge beside me, "isn't even the city." He pointed to the sky.

My eyes followed his hand. *The stars.* I exhaled slowly. This was the kind of moment I had missed the most with him. He had always been so good at pointing out the stars to me. I let myself get lost in the sky.

The silence seemed to settle around us. It was like he was waiting for me to say something, but I didn't know what to say. "It's not what you think," I finally said, breaking the silence.

"You don't have to defend him. Not to me."

I swallowed hard. "He didn't mean to hurt me."

"That doesn't make it any better."

"Yes it does. He's not a bad guy. It's just me. It's my fault. Nothing is ever black and white, it's more complicated than that."

"Sadie, there is nothing complicated about what just happened. And I promise you, it was not your fault."

I gripped the ledge as I turned to face him. He looked so concerned. Where had that concern been when I truly did need him?

"You deserve better than him."

"You don't even know me, Miles. And I honestly don't understand why you care."

He put his elbow on the ledge and looked out at the city. "You remind me of her."

My heart seemed to skip a beat. "Who?"

"Summer. My..." he let his voice trail off. "The friend I told you about. I just...I couldn't help her."

I bit the inside of my lip to prevent myself from crying. "I'm not her." *I haven't been her for years.* I had stopped being Summer Brooks long before I got my new name. That part of me died as soon as Don touched me.

"I know. Because I can help you."

"I'm stronger than I look. I don't need anyone to save me."

"I don't want to save you. I'm just trying to help. You don't have to face everything alone. I'm right here, offering."

"I can take care of myself."

"I know, but I'm saying you don't have to."

I shook my head and looked back up at the stars. "Why are you talking to me instead of trying to find her?"

"Because she obviously doesn't want to be found. I don't think she ever loved me the way I loved her."

Past tense. Everything about Miles and I needed to stay past tense. "There are plenty of women at this school that are probably willing to give you whatever it is you're missing from your life. But it's not me. Just because I look like someone you used to know, it doesn't mean we're a good fit." The Sagitta pendant felt heavy around my neck.

"Sadie." He lightly touched my wrist.

Home. I saw it in a flash. Laughing in his backyard. Grass stains on our knees. Love. It had always been love in his eyes, even before he held my hand. He had cherished me once. But I didn't deserve to be cherished anymore. If he knew the truth, he'd be horrified. He wouldn't be able to meet my eyes. I could barely look at myself in the mirror. He deserved the whole world. He deserved everything I could never give him. Love. Happiness. Children. I would only be able to give him half a life. Miles Young deserved a star way brighter than me. "I have to go." My voice sounded hoarse.

"I was first attracted to you because you reminded me of Summer, yes. But it's more than that. It's not like your personalities are the same. You're reserved and deep and intriguing. I can't stop thinking about you. It has nothing to do with Summer. I like you. And it kills me that you're with someone who doesn't show you what you truly deserve. Someone that doesn't appreciate everything you are."

I didn't deserve anything but the darkness inside of me. And it made sense that I didn't have the same personality as Summer. Because she died. She died as soon as she moved in with Don. He stole everything from her. Summer was once feisty and outgoing. Summer was so full of hope. Summer had dreams. Summer had so many dreams of Miles. Tears prickled my eyes. I shook my head. "I'm sorry, I have to go." I turned away from him. I couldn't look at the smile on the corner of his mouth or his dark brown eyes. It was torture. It was too painful.

"When I see you, it's like I can breathe again," Miles said.

His words made me freeze. It was like how I felt when I looked at the stars. But wasn't that because they reminded me of him? He made it feel like I could breathe again. It was always him. He was everything good. He was everything I'd never be able to have. "Try looking at the stars." I opened up the door and went back into the stairwell. As soon as I heard the thud of the door closing, I let myself cry.

I let myself cry as I laced my Converses.

I let myself cry as I ran through the darkness.

I let myself cry until I couldn't cry anymore. Until my lungs ached. Until I couldn't catch my breath.

But I kept running. I kept running until my legs felt like jelly. I leaned against a brick wall as I tried to muster enough energy to head back home. A raindrop hit my head. I looked up. The stars were gone. I knew I had been running for a long time, but there wasn't a single star in the sky anymore. Everything was dark. More raindrops hit my face and my bare arms and legs. It felt good. Smoke rose off the pavement, giving the whole street an eerie look as I relaxed.

I shouldn't have been out so late. It was reckless. I needed to get home. But I stayed where I was. The vigilante said he followed me because I was reckless. And I needed to see him. It was like I could feel his presence. I needed to see the only other person that knew what it was like to hide behind a mask. I let the minutes tick by as the smoke from the pavement seemed to slowly encircle me. I could feel him watching me. Waiting. What was he waiting for?

A clanging noise made me turn my head just in time to see the vigilante land in the alley behind me.

"You came," I said.

He kept his hood down low as he slowly approached me. "I never left," his voice rumbled seductively. "Why do you insist on putting yourself in danger?"

"I wanted to see you."

"Why are you running?" he asked instead of responding to my confession.

I swallowed hard. Hadn't he told me to run home? I started running because of him. "I don't know," I said instead.

"You do know."

I shook my head as he took another step toward me.

"You're running away from something, Sadie, when you should be running toward something."

I shook my head. "I'm running toward something too. I'm training."

"For?" His voice rumbled.

"I want to help you."

"I didn't ask for your help."

"And I didn't ask for yours. But here we both are."

He didn't say anything, he just stepped closer toward me until I could feel his body heat. I shivered in the contrast to the cold rain.

I wanted him to kiss me. I wanted to live my dreams of him. "I can't stop thinking about you," I said. But it wasn't enough. He stayed complete still. "And you can't seem to stop thinking about me either." I realized I was holding my breath, but I couldn't seem to stop.

He shook his head. "I'm only here to warn you."

One second.

He leaned slightly closer, placing a hand on either side of my head on the brick wall.

Two seconds.

"You're running out of time."

Three seconds.

He leaned closer still. I could feel the heat of his breath. Our lips were only an inch apart.

Four seconds.

"I should be telling you to leave. But I don't want you to go."

Five seconds. "Why do you want me to stay?"

He stayed completely still. "Because you're right about me. I can't stop thinking about you. Thoughts of you consume me." His breath was hot against my lips.

I slowly exhaled. I wanted him to kiss me. I wanted to taste him.

"I'll never stop."

I swallowed hard. It was possessive. But it didn't scare me. It felt like a spark went through me. I ached for him. His lips. His touch. I watched his Adam's apple rise and then fall. I never wanted him to stop. I tilted my face up toward his.

"Sadie." His voice sounded strained.

The only thing between us was the falling rain. I stood on my tiptoes until my lips brushed against his.

A growl seemed to escape from his throat as he pushed my back against the wall. His lips met mine with a force I hadn't expected. His kiss was rough and savage as if he had been dreaming of my lips and nothing else. It wasn't comforting. It didn't feel like fire or ice. It sent an electricity through me. It made me feel like I could do anything, like his superpowers were spreading to me, like his strength was contagious. I felt alive.

He was being rough. It should have terrified me. But I felt safe in his arms. I grabbed the back of his neck to deepen the kiss and he groaned into my mouth. The noise was so carnal and raw. God, I wanted to hear it again and again.

He told me that I was everything. But he was wrong. This kiss was everything. He made me forget about Eli and Miles. He made the pain go away. I could barely breathe when he pulled away. My panting should have been embarrassing, but I didn't need to hide in front of him. He saw me. He watched my every move. He was my protector.

"If you want to help, then you can't run away from the darkness. You have to embrace it." He gently touched the side of my face with his glove, tracing the cut he had prevented from being worse. "But I don't want to see your light fade the way mine has."

"It already has. It faded a long time ago."

"It hasn't. You're stronger than you realize."

I couldn't even argue with him. The way he said it made it seem like a fact. *I am strong.* He believed in me more than I believed in myself.

"Which is why I can't accept your help. I refuse to turn you into something other than what I see in front of me. You have to go before it's too late." It sounded like it pained him to say it. Sirens wailed in the distance. His head turned toward the noise.

But I didn't want him to leave. I wanted to convince him that I could help. I wanted him to kiss me again. I wanted him to possess me. It was the only thing that seemed to keep my thoughts at bay. It was the only thing that could take away my pain. "Why can't you stop thinking about me?"

He leaned closer, and I closed my eyes, expecting another kiss. All my senses were overwhelmed. His expensive cologne seemed to consume me.

"It doesn't matter. Because I'm asking you to stop thinking about me."

I can't possibly.

"You're putting yourself in danger, because you think I'm looking out for you. But I'm not the only one watching. I know you can sense it. The way you look over your shoulder. The smile that plays on your lips. But it's not always me, Sadie. You're running out of time."

"Running out of time for what?" I opened up my eyes, but he was gone. *I'm running out of time for what?* The past few days, I had felt safe, knowing he was out there. But he was telling me that eerie feeling I got that someone was watching me was real. And that it wasn't always him.

CHAPTER 35
Tuesday

No one was coming to walk me home today. Eli and Miles probably weren't speaking to me after last night. The vigilante had kissed me but told me to stop thinking about him. He told me it wasn't always him watching. It terrified me. I had pushed everyone away, partially because my mind seemed consumed by the vigilante, and now I didn't have anyone left. It felt like he had given up on me. So, I wasn't going to walk home, I was going to run home. I was going to get stronger. I was going to figure out how to take care of myself.

I pulled my hair into a ponytail and stared at my reflection in the mirror. For some reason, my Sagitta pendant felt heavy around my neck tonight. It almost felt like a burden instead of hope. The vigilante had asked me to forget about him. I wasn't sure I knew how. And I knew that I didn't want to. I pressed my lips together, trying to remember what his felt like against mine. If he so badly wanted me to forget, then why did he kiss me?

I shook my head and stepped out of the restaurant bathroom. There was no reason to dwell on it. The only things I should be thinking about were how to get home safe and what the vigilante meant by telling me I was running out of time. The problem was, I thought I knew what he meant by the latter. Don was coming. I could feel it in my bones, like he was getting closer by the second.

"No, I've got it," Joan snapped. "Just hang up your apron and I'll mail you your paycheck."

I glanced over at the mess on the floor. A new busboy, so new that I hadn't even learned his name, had dropped a tray of dirty dishes. He almost looked like he was going to cry as he turned around. He kept his head low as he passed by me.

"Is everything okay?" I leaned down and helped Joan start picking up the broken dishes.

"Fine." She already seemed a little calmer. "He just had slippery fingers. I never should have hired him."

I thought about my first night when I had dropped a tray. Joan had been so nice to me. But it had only been one tray. The new boy had dropped one earlier tonight too. No one had even run into him, it just kind of fell out of his hands. He piled the trays too high. He really did have slippery fingers. And this tray had been piled high as well. There was broken glass everywhere. It was going to take a long time to clean up.

"I've got the rest," Joan said. "Besides, I bet you have plans with that handsome boy of yours. What did you say his name was?"

I definitely did not have plans with Miles. "Miles."

"Miles. That's a good strong name."

"Mhm," I said absentmindedly. "Tonight all I plan to do is go for a run and hang out with my roommate."

She smiled. "Plans are plans. Really, you can get going. Your shift is way over."

"Thanks, Joan."

"Have a good night, hon," she said as she wiped her hands off on her apron.

"You too." I stood up and walked toward the exit of the restaurant. Hopefully I wouldn't be dropping another tray anytime soon. I glanced at the TV monitor on the way out. The subtitles scrolled across the screen. They were talking about how crime in the city was getting worse. Apparently Mr. Crawford had sent me to the city just when it was hitting a new record for homicides. There was nothing more pessimistic than the news. There was also nothing like the news to make me feel even more scared in a city I was already terrified of. I stepped down onto the sidewalk.

"Sadie, I am so, so sorry." Eli was standing there with another bouquet of flowers.

Yes, he had hurt me. A little. I'm pretty sure it was more in my head than anything else. But I was so glad to see him. I had been dreading stepping out into the night alone. And here he was. He wasn't late. He had shown up. He really did look sorry. I didn't really know what to say. I didn't have to say anything, though, because he started talking again.

"Look, I know I fucked up. And I never meant to hurt you. It's just...you started freaking out, and you wouldn't talk to me. I just kinda flipped out. But it's because I want to help. You must see that. I care about you and I don't like to see you upset."

I had freaked out because he told me that he was falling for me. Maybe it was just because I was scared. I wanted to trust him. But there was so much doubt in my mind. "When you showed up last night, it felt like you were hiding something from me. I wanted to see your place. And for some reason, you don't want me to..."

"I really did just want to be alone with you. But you can see my place. You can come over for dinner tomorrow night, I promise. And if Patrick and Kins are there, we can all hang out together. It'll be fun."

I exhaled slowly. "That sounds really nice."

He smiled.

"Do you think maybe we could just start over? Pretend that the past few days didn't happen?" *Including when you found out about my neck.*

He sighed. "God, that sounds fantastic. Hi, I'm Eli," he said and stuck out his hand.

I laughed.

"And obviously I'm insane because I bought you flowers before I even met you." He handed me the bouquet.

"Thank you. And thank you for coming to walk me home." We started walking toward the dorms.

"I want you to be able to count on me. Let's get you home safely."

He was saying all the right things. It made me feel suspicious of him all over again. *Stop it.* "Can I come with you to your boxing class sometime?"

"Why?"

"I just want to see what it's like."

"It's just a bunch of guys beating the shit out of each other."

"Right." I waited for him to say I could come anyway, but he didn't. *He's hiding something.* And I wanted to find out what it was. "What gym did you say it was?"

"Um...Epitome. It's a small gym on the other side of town."

I nodded. He seemed worried that I was just going to show up. I didn't want to make him feel uncomfortable. *Just trust him.*

"I know we're starting over, but can I ask you a question?" Eli said.

"Mhm." I had about a million for him.

"Why did you freak out? Was it because I told you that I was falling for you?"

And the fire of your touch. "I'm having a hard time getting out of my own head," I said instead. "I think you know enough about my past to understand that." We had stopped outside my dorm. "I'm not like other girls on campus. If you want normal...you're looking at the wrong person."

"I just want you. And I'm sorry I put pressure on you. I know you weren't ready."

"It's okay, we're starting over."

"Right." He smiled. "One more question."

I nodded.

"What's going on with you and your RA?"

"Nothing."

"He's into you. You realize that, right?"

I thought about last night on the roof. Miles said when he saw me, it felt like he could breathe again. He had been pining over me, just like I had been pining over him. But it didn't take away the fact that he had made me feel abandoned. I didn't even believe him when he told me he had kept writing to me. Kins said he was a player. He was probably just playing games with my head. But I understood what it felt like to not be able to breathe. I meant what I had told him. He should be looking at the stars instead of at me. Besides, it seemed like he was more into the idea of me than he actually was into me. "I don't reciprocate his feelings."

"I don't really feel comfortable with you talking to him anymore."

I looked up at him. I had been telling myself to stay away from Miles since I first saw him at the diner. For some reason I couldn't stay away. Maybe Eli telling me to would be the push that I needed. "Then I won't talk to him anymore."

Eli smiled. "Let's be honest with each other from here on out, okay?"

I nodded.

"Sealed with a kiss?" He leaned forward before I could even respond.

Flames. Flames everywhere.

***

I opened up the door to my dorm room and turned on the lights. I was hoping that Kins would be home to hang out. For some reason, the idea of being alone with my thoughts was stifling. I was about to turn around to go on the run I had planned when I noticed a box sitting on my bed.

It definitely wasn't something I had left there. I walked over to my bed and read the mailing address. Sure enough, it said Sadie Davis and was addressed to this dorm. Who on earth would be sending Sadie Davis a package? I grabbed a pair of scissors and cut through the tape. My heart was stammering in my chest as I lifted up the cardboard flaps. There was a card with tissue paper underneath. I lifted up the card. Instead of my name on the envelope, "Turn that frown upside down," was scrawled along the front.

Tears bit at the corners of my eyes. It was the same thing my dad always used to say to me when I was upset. No one knew about that. At least, no one still living. Had I told Mr. Crawford that? I remembered being with him for days, but I barely said a word. I was terrified and exhausted. He didn't know. I had this brief sense of hope. Was it possible that my father could still be alive? I shook away the fleeting thought. *No.* I remembered the devastation I felt at their funeral. I remembered it like it was yesterday. I remembered their coffins and that feeling of ice in my veins. My parents were long gone. There must have been someone else who knew my dad saying that. A family friend I wasn't aware of? Or maybe it was a coincidence. It was a well known phrase and I was certain I had been frowning a lot recently.

The vigilante. He had been watching me. He saw my frowns. Surely he could see that I had been upset recently. That had to be it. He seemed to know me. Maybe he knew me even better than I realized. It felt like my heart was going to explode out of my chest. Did he know me when I was young? Had he known my parents? I had this sudden spark of hope. Maybe he was trying to tell me something.

I tore the card out of the envelope. There was no picture, just a plain, pristine white card. I lifted up the top and my hands started shaking. There was just one line inside.

"Let the games begin, Sadie." My name was in quotes. I threw the note back on top of the tissue paper.

I couldn't seem to make my hands stop shaking, no matter how hard I tried to steady them. What the hell was that supposed to mean? Who the hell was it from? I realized I was pacing in my small dorm room, but I couldn't seem to stop. I also couldn't seem to make myself lift up the tissue paper, because I was terrified that I knew who had sent it. *Don.*

All week I had this eerie sense that he was getting closer. It was like this ache in my bones. He was here. He was in fucking New York! And he knew my identity. He had found me.

No. He didn't know. He didn't know about my parents. I was going crazy. I never told Don a thing about my past. He never asked. He never ever asked. I pictured him putting his hand over my mouth. I couldn't swallow down the lump in my throat. I scratched at my neck, trying to rid the invisible hands from me. *I'm losing my mind.*

I squeezed my eyes shut tight. *Turn that frown upside down.* I could hear my father's voice. I wrapped my arms around my stomach. I couldn't smile through this. But I could put on a brave face. That's what that saying truly meant. *Mask your true emotions.*

I slowly lifted up the tissue paper. *Blood.* I stared down at the small bunny slippers. *My* bunny slippers. They were covered in blood. There was so much fucking blood.

I put my hand over my mouth. Whose blood was that? I had left my slippers in my yard. I remembered kicking them off so that I could run faster. There was no blood. I wrapped my arms around my stomach again. I remembered grass stains, but definitely no blood.

More memories started flooding into my mind. I remembered begging my grandmother to take me to the spot where my parents' car had crashed. It wasn't like the movies at all. It was an accident, so there was no investigation, or caution tape, or officers asking question. I had been on the street a million times on the bus to school. There was only one difference. The pavement was stained with my parents' blood.

No.

I remembered Don putting the knife to my stomach. I'd never forget the rage on his face. I remembered biting down on his fingers as the knife sliced into my skin. I tasted blood. My mouth had been filled with his blood. And I remembered looking down at my stomach as he threw me to the ground. My blood. There was so much blood. I felt nauseous.

No.

How was this a game? Don had already stolen my freedom. I put my hand on my forehead. Did he want my sanity too? I couldn't let him take the only thing I had left.

There wasn't a doubt in my mind that I was doing the right thing as I grabbed my new phone. I clicked on Mr. Crawford's name and pulled it to my ear. It went straight to voicemail.

Damn it! I called again and again and again. How could he not answer?! I needed him.

The voicemail beeped for what seemed like the hundredth time. "Mr. Crawford," I said. "It's Sadie Davis. Please call me back as soon as you get this. He found me," my voice trembled. "He's here." I hung up the phone and started pacing again. He'd call me back. He had to call me back.

The sound of the door unlocking seemed to pull me out of my haze. I couldn't let Kins see me like this. I grabbed the box and shoved it under my bed. I sat cross-legged on my bed and tried to picture anything but blood. Whose blood was it? Was it someone I knew? What if I had accidentally put someone in Don's crosshairs?

"Hey, are you okay?" Kins asked.

I shook my head and didn't look at her. "Fine, just tired. I'm going to go to bed." But I didn't move. I couldn't seem to move. Just thinking about what was under my bed made me feel like throwing up.

"You're staring at a blank space on the wall like a total psychopath."

I've already lost my mind. I tried to laugh but it came out forced. "I was just thinking." I tried to keep my voice as steady as possible, but I knew it wavered.

"About the fact that Eli came back to his dorm last night in a fit of rage?"

I didn't want to talk about last night. I didn't want to talk at all. "We got into a little fight. It was nothing." I burst out crying.

"Oh, Sadie," Kins said as she hopped onto my bed and pulled me into a hug. "It's okay. I'm sure it'll blow over." She patted my back, trying to comfort me.

"No," I croaked.

"Of course it will," she said soothingly. "It sounded like he almost got in a fight with another man. Who's the other guy? Try to get your mind off Eli for a minute."

Try to get my mind off the blood. "No one." Kins would be furious if she knew about the time I had spent with Miles.

"Oh, come on. Give me the details. You know how much I approve of you seeing more than one guy at once."

God. I needed to get a grip and change the subject. "No, it's not that. We got into a fight because I think he's been hiding things from me." The thought of Eli lying no longer seemed of any importance. I needed to get the hell out of New York. I'd never see him again anyway.

Kins continued to rub her hand up and down my back. "What kind of things?"

"He's been avoiding showing me his dorm room. And I'm not sure he's been running off to boxing classes every night like he says. He's so evasive when I ask him questions." It felt good to ramble about something else.

"Hmm."

"But he said I could come over tomorrow night for dinner." I'd be long gone before tomorrow night.

"I have an idea."

"Yeah?"

"I'm going to plan to be there tomorrow night too. It won't be a problem, Patrick always says yes to anything I suggest. But instead of actually hanging out with them, we can lead an investigation."

I shook my head.

"I'm serious. We can trick them into leaving and then ransack the place."

"Um...I don't know if that's a great idea."

"Come on, it'll be fun. You never know what you'll find under a boy's mattress."

I laughed. It sounded less forced this time. "As long as we put everything back exactly where we find it."

"But how fun would it be to totally mess everything up? Patrick would be so mad. Maybe he'd do unspeakable things to me."

It was good that her mind wasn't truly focused on the investigation. I didn't want her to get her hopes up about something that would never happen.

I must have been making a face, because Kins said, "What do you think he's hiding exactly?"

I shrugged.

"No, really. Clearly you have an idea if you want to ransack his place. Do you think he's cheating on you?"

I laughed. "No. It's just..." I let my voice trail off. Why was I keeping the fact that I had met the vigilante a secret from her? Kins would be the perfect person to talk to about my feelings for him. Or maybe she'd try to steal him away. If there was one bad boy in town worth swooning over, it was the vigilante. Did crushing on a masked stranger really make me that odd? It would probably just make me fit in even better. *What am I doing?* I was done trying to fit in. It didn't even matter if I let anything slip anymore. I was leaving. And just the thought made me start crying again. I didn't want to leave. Kins was the first real friend I had made in years.

"The suspense is literally killing me," she said and continued to rub my back. "Spit it out, Sadie!"

"I met the vigilante." It felt good to tell the truth for once in my life. It felt like a weight had been lifted off my shoulders. Or maybe I just felt better because she had been comforting me. It was nice having someone who truly cared.

She laughed. "Wait...really? Oh my God. Tell me everything."

"There isn't much to tell." *He's watching out for me. He knows me. I like him but I'm leaving.* "We did kiss."

"Shut up."

I laughed.

"Was it the best kiss ever?"

I thought about the kiss that I'd always compare to all others. *Miles.* I remembered being on the roof of my grandmother's house, staring at the sky with the boy I loved. That kiss had always been the epitome of romance to me. There was something so pure about it. Something so hopeful. Thinking about it made my chest hurt. Thinking about it now filled me with this feeling of loss. Was the kiss with the vigilante better than that? With the vigilante it wasn't just romantic. It was sexy. Just thinking about it made my whole body feel overheated.

"You don't have to say a word," Kins said. "The blush on your face says it all."

I couldn't even argue with her logic. Thinking about the kiss I shared with Miles so many years ago made me feel sad, whereas the kiss with the vigilante made me feel alive. He pulled me into the present like no one else had ever been able to. He took away the feeling of pain. Just thinking about him dulled the smell of blood in my nose and the red seared in my mind.

"Okay, so you think Eli might be the vigilante?"

It was easier to play along with him possibly being the vigilante than it was to tell her that it felt more like he was the villain in this scenario. The scorching way his fingers felt on my skin made a lump form in my throat. "I have no idea. But he's definitely hiding something." I'd just never find out what it was.

"It's okay, we'll figure it out together."

Just hearing those words made me breathe a little easier. I wasn't alone here. It wasn't like Don could just nab me from my dorm without anyone noticing. I was in the city that never sleeps. Maybe I was safer than I realized. I squeezed my eyes shut and tried to swallow down the taste of blood in my mouth.

CHAPTER 36
Wednesday

It seemed like yesterday was a terrible dream. I couldn't eat. I couldn't sleep. I pulled out my phone for what seemed like the millionth time. All day long I had waited for Mr. Crawford to call me back. I had called a few more times, but it always went straight to voicemail. I was starting to worry that something had happened to him.

I had called out sick from work again. Joan had sounded worried about me on the phone. It was nice that she cared. I was starting to notice all the things I'd miss once I left New York. Her, Kins, Miles, Eli, the vigilante... I sighed. Kins had been so worried about me that she basically pulled me out of bed after I missed my first two classes. I pretended to leave, but really I had just been sitting in the common room downstairs staring at my phone. The dorm was safe. I wasn't stepping foot outside of it.

I opened up the door to my dorm room. Kins was already getting ready for our dinner at Eli and Patrick's. I was about to tell her I wasn't up to going, when I noticed the box wasn't sitting under my bed.

"Kins?"

She smacked her lips together and smiled in the mirror. "Yeah?"

"What happened to the box under my bed?"

She turned to me. "What box?"

"The box I got in the mail yesterday?"

"I literally have no idea what you're talking about." She turned back to the mirror to apply more mascara.

"Of course you do. You left it for me on my bed last night."

"I never put a box on your bed last night. And I never saw one under it. Just your suitcase."

What? I crouched down by my bed and pushed the suitcase aside. Where the hell was it? My heart started drumming in my chest. Had I imagined it? Maybe Don didn't need to steal my sanity. Maybe I had already lost it. "Seriously, Kins, stop messing around." I stood up and started opening drawers, searching for the slippers. Fuck, what if she had seen them?

"Sadie, I never saw a box, I swear. What was in it?"

"Then how did it get in here?" I said, ignoring her. "And how did it disappear?"

"I don't know. Are you sure it wasn't a dream? Are you feeling okay?"

"It wasn't a dream." *Was it?* I remembered reliving seeing the crash site and feeling the knife in my stomach. Had I imagined it? But I wasn't crazy. *The dorm isn't safe.* The thought seemed to slam into my head in a rush. *Shit.* "We need to go."

"But I'm not ready..."

I grabbed her arm and pulled her to the door.

"Sadie, what on earth has gotten into you?"

"I need to see Eli." And I did. Even though I didn't fully trust him, he swore he'd never hurt me. He'd been taking boxing classes. For me. He could protect me from Don. He had to. God, I really was losing my mind.

"I knew you two would work it out," she said as soon as she calmed down about being dragged out of the dorm before she had finished her makeup. "Is the plan still on for tonight?"

"Yeah, sure." I wasn't even registering what she was saying. All I knew was that someone had broken into our dorm room. Twice. I needed to get as far away from it as possible.

I stared at my phone the whole way over to Eli's. "Call me back," I silently pleaded to Mr. Crawford.

"What are you doing? Put that away and stick to the plan," Kins whispered as we stopped outside Eli and Patrick's dorm building. No one was near us. She was making this way weirder than it needed to be.

"Kins, we talked about this. I'm not doing that." My heart wasn't in this at all.

"You just said it was still on a minute ago. It's too late to back out now. I'm too excited. Plus it's a great plan." She winked at me.

"I'm not..."

"But it's part of the plan."

"There doesn't need be a plan..."

"Stop talking." She slapped my arm, even though I had stopped talking as soon as I saw Eli through the glass door.

He smiled and opened it up for us.

"Hey!" Kins said, way louder than was natural.

Stop being weird! "Hey," I said and smiled up at Eli.

"It's about time you let her see your elusive dorm room," Kins said.

Eli laughed. "I wouldn't say it was elusive." He put his hand on my lower back as we walked over to the elevator. "I missed you in class today."

"I missed you too." He wanted me to be honest with him. But I couldn't tell him that his touch made me feel like I was burning. Like I was back in Don's clutches. *I'm running out of time.* I couldn't shake the vigilante's voice running through my mind. I couldn't shake the contents of the box, whether it was my imagination or not. The combination was the only reason I was here. I was scared to be alone. I was terrified and I didn't know where else to turn. And at the same time, I wanted to figure out if Eli was hiding something. What if the vigilante was warning me about him? What if he sent the box? I shook away the thought. The vigilante would have just told me to stay away from him if that was it. I tried to force myself not to think about the vigilante. He had asked me to stop. He couldn't save me from the nightmare I was living.

I noticed Kins fidgeting with her hands. Maybe I shouldn't have told her I was suspicious of Eli. She was acting so bizarrely. Or maybe she was just still upset about me yelling at her about a box that didn't exist.

"You doing okay, Kins?" Eli asked, as if he could read my thoughts.

"What? Psh. Yeah. I'm just excited to see Patrick. We've been attached at the hip recently and when his hip isn't literally next to mine I get all antsy."

Take a breath!

Eli laughed. "Yeah, I've noticed."

I didn't say a word as we exited onto his floor. I was probably acting unusual too. He opened up his door.

Kins launched herself into Patrick's arms and they started making out.

I looked up at Eli and he shrugged his shoulders.

He really was cute. But my mind wasn't on making out with him. I was solely focused on figuring out if he was telling the truth. I needed him right now, and if I couldn't trust him, who else could I turn to? I felt as antsy as Kins. "So...this is your room?" I looked around the space that was laid out exactly like my room. Very similar to my own decorations, there were no photos of his family. It made sense for me. For him, it just added to my suspicion. He had mentioned that he missed them, so why weren't there any pictures of them?

"This is it." He leaned against his dresser.

I could feel his eyes on me. Not only were there no pictures of his family, there also were barely any decorations at all. Patrick's side of the room had Rolling Stones magazine covers, posters of bands I had never heard of, and even a few of scantily clad women. Eli's...nothing. Even his comforter was just black. There was no emotion. That was suspicious all by itself. What if he was in the witness protection program too? I knew how ridiculous that was. What would be the odds of them sending two people to the same school? "You're very organized," I said.

"I like things simple."

I smiled. "Are you calling me simple?"

"You are anything but simple, Sadie."

"I'm starving," Kins said. "Did you guys order dinner yet?"

"No, we were waiting to see what you wanted, babe," Patrick said.

She beamed at him. "How about something meaty."

I tried not to roll my eyes. They really were ridiculously cute, albeit vulgar.

Eli laughed. "So...like...kielbasa?"

"Or hot dogs," Patrick suggested.

"Or sausage pizza," Eli said.

"Pigs in a blanket!" Kins shouted.

The three of them laughed. Apparently I had missed some sort of inside joke. Did the three of them always talk about phallic shaped food? I had never felt more awkward. Eli could have invited me over whenever he had wanted to. Instead, he had formed weird rituals with Kins and Patrick and left me out. If he liked me, he would have wanted me here. *What are you hiding?* I was now positive there was something here he didn't want me to see. Did he actually just like Kins? I didn't expect to feel jealous, but I did. He had fun with Kins, while all he did with me was fight.

"What were you thinking?" Eli said as he wrapped his arms around me.

"Umm...cucumbers?"

He winked at me. "Oh, I can give you that whenever you want."

Kins giggled. "Don't be gross, you perverts."

How were we being gross? She had started it. I looked up into Eli's eyes. When he looked at me, we were fine. It felt like he cared. It was the moments when we weren't together that were the worst. Mostly because I had no idea what he actually spent his time doing. I wanted to shove all those feelings aside and tell him I was in trouble. Maybe he'd know what to do. Instead I just bit the inside of my lip.

"But seriously...we want Chinese food from that place down the street," Kins said.

"Awesome, we can just get it delivered..."

"No." She swatted Patrick's hand which had already started dialing the number. "I was hoping you could pick it up. It'll be hotter that way."

"How about you two go get it, and we'll stay here?" Eli suggested.

"No." Kins gave everyone an exaggerated frown. "Sadie and I need a few minutes of girl time."

Oh my God. I had told her a million times that I wasn't going to go along with her horrible plan. "Kins," I mouthed silently at her. There had to be a better way to get them out of the room.

Eli and Patrick looked awkwardly back and forth between us.

I was not going to say the line Kins wanted me to say. I refused. We had already discussed this. All we had to do was stick with the food thing.

Kins cleared her throat. "Our periods have synced up and we've been in a mood all day."

"Sorry, babe," Patrick said. "Do you want us to get you anything while we're out?"

"No, I just need to lie down for a few minutes. We both do."

I couldn't even look up at Eli. I was mortified. Maybe Kins was fine talking about her menstrual cycle in front of Patrick, but I was not there yet with Eli.

"Yeah, we can go get the food," Patrick said. "We'll be back in a few minutes."

"Are you sure you don't want to come?" Eli whispered to me. "Doesn't walking help with, you know...cramps and stuff?"

Besides for the fact that what he was saying was extremely awkward, it was also suspicious. Why didn't he want me to be alone in his room? "I was really just hoping to lie down for a bit." I tried to sound as innocent as possible. I even batted my eyelashes at him, even though acting sexy was out of the question since Kins had just said we were both on our periods.

"Okay," Eli said. Patrick was already by the door, but Eli didn't seem eager to follow him. "We'll be back as soon as we can." He glanced at his computer and then seemed to look over my shoulder at something.

"Dude, let's go," Patrick said.

He hesitantly let go of my waist. "I'll give you the full tour once I get back."

All I heard was, "Don't go through my stuff." I held my breath until the door was closed behind them.

"Geez, I thought they'd never leave," Kins said. She was sprawled out on Patrick's bed, already rummaging through his nightstand.

"I thought we had agreed to not lie about being on our periods?"

"No, you tried to tell me it was a bad idea, but obviously I was right that it was a fabulous idea." She gestured around the empty room. "Now what are we looking for exactly? It was a little weird that he didn't want to leave you alone in here with me, right?"

I bit the inside of my lip. "A little."

"Maybe he was just worried you'd bleed all over his stuff." She laughed.

Blood. I tried to push the image of the slippers out of my mind. "Ugh. You're being disgusting." I pulled out the top drawer of his bureau. It was filled with boxers. I felt weird lifting them up to see if there was anything underneath of them. "We're looking for anything that proves he isn't who he says he is."

Kins laughed. "He's definitely who he says he is. He's just hiding the fact that he's a super hot superhero behind all those button-up shirts he wears. Don't you think if it was him you'd be able to tell, though?"

I pulled out the second drawer. I didn't have time to talk right now. I needed to find proof that I could trust Eli. I needed him to be who he said he was. Nothing interesting in the second or third drawers. I opened up the bottom one.

"I mean, you've kissed both of them. The girls in those superhero movies always seem so dumb."

"He wears a mask on his face. The hood covers his eyes. All you can really see is his lips." *His perfectly kissable lips.*

"Right. So does he kiss like Eli?"

"No, not really. It's more...raw than that."

Kins whistled. "You found a bad boy. God, I'm so jealous."

I froze when I found a dark blue hoodie at the bottom of the drawer. I lifted it up. "The vigilante wears a hoodie like this."

Kins slid off the bed and crouched down next to me. "It's a really common hoodie. You can get it at any sporting goods store. I've seen tons of people around campus wearing that."

It reminded me of the fact that I was wearing clothes right now that Mr. Crawford had picked out specifically for me to blend in. Why the hell wasn't he calling me back when he went to such meticulous planning to make me blend in? "Right." After checking the pockets, I folded it and put it back in the drawer where I had found it. "There must be something else."

"I'll look under his bed."

I moved to Eli's desk as Kins searched for dirty magazines under his mattress. His computer was password protected. After a few attempts at logging on, I knew I wouldn't be able to figure it out. Honestly, I barely knew anything about him other than where his family was from and that he was generally nice. Except for when his fingers dug into my skin. I shook away the thought and pulled open the top drawer of his desk.

His iPod was sitting in it. I lifted it up and turned it on. The screen lit up, showing that Eli truly had fixed it. I shouldn't have been concerned about what music he liked to listen to, but there was something drawing me to it. I placed one of the earbuds into my ear. *Nothing.* I scrolled through the songs, looking for one I recognized, but I hadn't heard of any of them. I clicked on one. Static blasted into my ear. *What the hell?* I picked another song. Static. Every song was static.

I pulled the earbud out of my ear. "That's weird."

"The fact that neither of them have any hidden pictures of naked women?" Kins said. "It's all too perfect if you ask me. Or maybe they've just discovered internet pornography and aren't stuck in the early 90s..."

"No." I laughed. "His iPod. I don't recognize any of the songs, and if you try to play them, static bursts through the earbuds."

"Weird." Kins walked over and picked it up. "Maybe they're like super old songs." She scrolled through his playlist. "All I can think of is that I recognize a few of the titles as street names." She shrugged her shoulders.

"Streets in New York?"

"Yeah." She pointed to one of the songs named Sussex. "Sussex street is really close to the Corner Diner actually. It's probably pretty old, maybe someone wrote a song about it."

"Which other ones do you recognize as street names?"

"Umm...Canal, Bowery, Broadway..."

"I feel like that's not a coincidence." I pulled my phone out and snapped pictures of his playlist.

"You think he like channels the radio frequencies on those streets in order to see what calls the cops are getting?"

"Maybe." I didn't know enough about technology to know the answer. But I knew someone who would. I needed to text Liza as soon as I was out of this room. I put the iPod back exactly where I had found it.

Kins was already rummaging through the other drawers.

"Do you think you know his computer password?" I asked.

She shrugged. "You probably have a better guess than I do."

"Maybe it's some kind of phallic symbol."

"I thought you might have felt weirded out by that. It's just this thing we do when we're hungry."

"I got that." I opened Eli's closet. I didn't want to talk about the fact that Kins was closer to Eli than I was. "Don't you find it weird that he doesn't having any boxing gear?"

"That is a little odd. But maybe he rents it or borrows it from the gym or something."

"Yeah, maybe." I took a deep breath. Nothing smelled like the expensive cologne of the vigilante. And there weren't any Converses anywhere that I could see. "I looked up the gym he said he goes to and it didn't even have boxing listed."

"Well, maybe it's just not a popular draw so they don't advertise it. Do you want a drink? It might help you relax a bit. They're going to be back any second and you look frantic." She pulled a bottle of vodka off of Eli's dresser. For some reason I hadn't noticed that both Eli and Patrick's dressers were covered in alcohol bottles.

"How do they have so much alcohol?"

"Eli has a fake ID. He knows a guy who makes awesome ones."

A fake identity. What if his real identity was on that fake ID? "Do you know where he keeps it?"

"His wallet, I assume."

Just then the door opened.

Shit. Eli's closet door was open. The bottom drawer of his desk was still ajar. *Shit!*

"What are you two doing?" There was hint of anger in his tone, but no one else seemed to notice. I shrunk at his words.

"We were just looking for something for my stomach," Kins said. "I'm...I'm going to vom." She put her hand over her mouth. Her eyes seemed to grow twice the size.

"Baby, tell me what you need." Patrick put his arm around her shoulders.

I tuned out the rest of their conversation, because I couldn't pull my attention away from Eli. He was staring at his desk, complete horror written all over his face. He slammed the desk drawer shut and closed his closet door. He seemed completely entranced as he put his finger down on the touchpad of his computer. His shoulders relaxed when he saw the request for a password pop up.

I had found something that he didn't want me to. But whatever he was really hiding was on that computer.

"Are you okay?" I lightly touched his arm.

He seemed to jump. "Yeah, yeah." He ran his fingers through his hair. "Everything is fine. Unless...you're not feeling well either?"

"I'm okay." It felt like I was playing with fire. I had thought Eli was a smart sensible choice. But everything about him was screaming danger now. I didn't want a bad boy. I wanted a gentleman.

He glanced once more at his desk and then back at me. "Let's eat." There was a smile on his face, but I knew it was hiding a frown.

I didn't feel safe here either.

CHAPTER 37
Wednesday

Liza didn't answer my text. Or my phone call. Or my other text. I had too much pent-up energy and I was too scared to go back to my dorm, so I went for a run. The city was full of people. If I stayed on crowded streets, I'd be fine. It was safer than anywhere else, that's why Mr. Crawford had sent me here. Why wasn't he answering my fucking calls? I started to run faster, trying to rid myself of my anger and fear.

It seemed like I finally had a breakthrough with Eli, and it was driving me crazy that I didn't know what it meant. I was so close. I could feel it. I needed my phone to ring. If it was Liza, hopefully I could figure out what was going on with her help. If it was Mr. Crawford, I'd hightail it out of the city.

I picked up my pace. Every day it got easier to run faster and farther. As soon as the thought ran through my head, I got a terrible cramp. *Damn it.* I stopped and crouched over. I had just made a turn onto a street that was less crowded. I should have sucked it up and kept running until I hit a more popular street again, but the pain was searing. I placed my hand on my stomach and felt something hard. I looked down. There was a vial sticking into my t-shirt. What the hell? I pulled it out and felt a pinch in my skin. I teetered to the side, my shoulder slammed against the brick wall. *Fuck.* I heard footsteps approaching.

No. I tried to run, but I toppled over my feet and landed hard on my shoulder. The pain in my arm was even worse than the one in my stomach. *He's here.* The sound that escaped from my mouth was even more horrifying than the pain. I sounded like a wounded animal. I sounded strangled. My windpipe was constricting.

I pulled my phone out of my pocket, but it was immediately knocked out of my hand. Who was I going to call anyway? A blurry face appeared in front of mine. I recognized him. Gavin Moore. He was a friend of Don's. He used to be around the house all the time. He knew what Don had done to me. He saw the way I was treated and he stayed silent, watching me with his dead eyes. But he wasn't looking at me like that right now. He was smiling. My whole body felt cold.

He reached out and ran his thumb along my cheek. "He wants your pretty little face back, sweetheart. And he doesn't care how he gets it."

My face. I thought about the knife sliding under the skin on my jaw. *He wants my face.* I saw my phone on the ground a few feet behind Gavin. I needed to get to it. I could call the police. If Mr. Crawford couldn't help me, maybe they could. But my body refused to move.

Gavin's hand slid down to my neck. "I've always wanted to know what it felt like to completely own your body." His fingers tightened slightly around my throat. "I know what you like." His fingers tightened even more. "Don said he didn't care whether I brought you in dead or alive. He doesn't care about you anymore, sweetheart. But maybe we can make a deal. I can keep you safe." His hand slid to my breast.

No. Tears bit at my eyes. Everything was so blurry. I couldn't move. But it wasn't from fear this time. I felt stronger than I ever had. It was from whatever was in the vial. I was frozen. I wanted to break every finger he touched me with. I wanted to punch the smile off his face. Anger seared through me, closely followed by fear. I might as well be back with Don. He was going to take me. I couldn't be a prisoner again. I'd rather be dead.

Gavin ripped my shirt open. "I can take care of you, sweetheart. I'll keep you safe." His fingers slid down my stomach.

This isn't real. This can't be real. But the gunshot sounded real. It echoed in my ears. The blood splattering on my face felt real. It was hot and sticky and I could feel it sliding down my cheeks. The sickening thud of Gavin's body falling on the pavement sounded real. I could see it. He wasn't touching me anymore.

I couldn't move. My body was paralyzed.

"I've got you." The vigilante's voice rumbled as he lifted me into his arms.

My blurry vision was focused on his face. His lips. His perfectly kissable lips. I was falling asleep. But I wanted my eyes to stay open. My protector had saved me. I tried to speak but nothing came out of my mouth. *You saved me from reliving hell itself.*

"You're going to be okay."

You were almost too late. I breathed in his cologne. I was okay now. The pain in my shoulder seemed less sharp when I was in his arms. I tried to blink the sleepiness away.

I wanted to remember him holding me. His gloved hand brushed against my skin. Maybe I imagined it, but it felt like his fingers hesitated as he covered me back up.

"Stay with me, Sadie."

I could feel him walking.

"Keep your eyes open."

I couldn't. Maybe he was running now. My only sense was his overwhelming good smell. I sighed into his strong chest.

"Stay with me, Summer."

Summer? My name echoed around in my head. *He does know.* Did I imagine that? All I could hear was my name.

Summer. I could hear my grandmother's voice

Summer. I could hear my mother's voice.

Summer. I could hear my father's voice.

Everything was black.

CHAPTER 38
Thursday

"Given the circumstances, I'm not sure it was a random attack," said a hushed voice.

I closed my eyes tight. My whole body hurt. Where was I?

"You think someone is trying to hurt her?"

Miles? I'd recognize his voice anywhere. Why was he here? Where was here?

"It would be consistent with the evidence of physical abuse, yes," the man I didn't know whispered.

No. You can't tell Miles.

"We tried to call her parents but there was no response," the unfamiliar voice said.

They're dead. Summer. Summer. Their voices seemed to echo in my head. It was all I could hear. My eyelids flew open. I wasn't dead. And I was ashamed that a small part of me wished that I was. I missed them. I let the tears fall down my cheeks. I missed them every day of my life. For some reason I felt close to them last night, closer than I had in years. I groaned.

"Sadie?" Miles said.

My vision slowly came into focus. I immediately wanted to close my eyes when I saw the look of sympathy in his. But then I felt the warmth of his hand in mine. *He's holding my hand.* I had been trying my hardest to avoid us touching. And this was why. Because I felt whole when our skin touched. He had always made me feel whole. He gently ran his thumb along my palm, keeping me calm as I slowly registered the fact that I was in a hospital room.

Ow. I looked down at my arm. It was in a sling. "What happened?" My voice sounded hoarse and my head was pounding.

"We were hoping you could tell us," the doctor said. He was no longer whispering and he had a concerned look on his face.

"I was mugged." Lying about things like this was second nature to me.

"Sadie," Miles said gently. "You were given a heavy dose of sedatives, it wasn't just a random mugging."

I couldn't look at him. I couldn't look at the doctor.

"We've set your dislocated shoulder, but it will hurt for a few days," the doctor said. "You're lucky it wasn't worse. There are a few police officers that want a statement from you. I recommend telling them the truth. They're just trying to help."

I nodded my head. I couldn't deny that I needed their help. Mr. Crawford had abandoned me here and I was in danger. I remembered Gavin putting his hands on me, telling me that Don wanted me dead or alive. And I remembered the bullet piercing his skull. I remembered the blood. God, there was so much blood. The heart rate monitor I was attached to started beeping rapidly, but I couldn't seem to calm down. The vigilante was a murderer. *But he saved me.*

"I'm going to give you two a minute while I let them know you're ready to give your statement."

I waited until the doctor was out of the room before turning back to Miles. "Why did they call you?" I tried to ignore the hurt look on his face.

"They didn't call me. They tried to call your parents, but no one answered. And then they called Kins. She had texted you because she was worried that you weren't back to the dorm yet and she was one of the only numbers in your phone. She stopped by my room freaking out and I offered to come with her."

Right. "Where is she?"

"Asleep in the waiting room."

Light wasn't pouring in through the window, but it didn't seem like it was quite nighttime. Was it morning? Or had more time than that passed? "What time is it?"

"Almost 8 p.m. Kins and I have been here since last night. I was so worried."

A whole day had passed then. My head was pounding. I realized he was still holding my hand. There were tubes sticking out the back of it. Maybe someone else would have been upset in this situation, but it wasn't exactly the first time I had wound up in the hospital. For some reason, I couldn't stop looking at my hand though. It almost felt like he was an extension of me. "I'm sorry."

"What are you sorry for?"

I'm sorry that I can't tell you the truth. I'm sorry that I have to push you away when all I really want is to keep holding your hand. "Waking you up in the middle of the night. You don't have to stay."

His chair squeaked as he shifted closer to me. "I wouldn't be here if I didn't want to be."

"I'm okay now. Really, you should go get some sleep."

"I don't think I could sleep even if I wanted to."

I swallowed hard. "Why?"

"Because of everything the doctor told me."

"What happened to doctor-patient confidentiality?" My heart was hammering in my chest. How much did he know?

"You were unconscious. I told them I was your brother."

"They shouldn't have told you anything." My mind still felt hazy but I remembered the doctor whispering. *Physical abuse.*

"He didn't even have to tell me, I already knew. I see the way that your boyfriend treats you. I see the way you freeze when he gets angry. Sadie, you don't have to defend him."

"It wasn't him."

"Then who was it?"

I didn't have an answer for him. He couldn't know.

He placed his other hand on top of mine, cradling my hand between his. "The doctor said that you've broken almost every bone in your body. He said there are marks on your back that are consistent with burns and knife wounds. And that there's a pretty nasty scar on your stomach. And he said he had reason to believe that it wasn't just physical abuse either."

"He doesn't know me. He couldn't possibly know any of that. And it isn't true."

"He thought you broke your arm. He did an x-ray and when he saw that your bones weren't aligned properly he got concerned..." his voice trailed off.

The doctor did x-rays on my whole body? Without my consent? And told someone the results without asking me? I could sue this hospital to oblivion. I had the money to hire the best attorneys in New York. I shook away the thought. I didn't even understand my reaction. Who had I become? It felt like I had completely lost any resemblance of Summer. And I didn't like who Sadie had become. The doctor was just concerned. And Miles was just concerned. The problem was that I didn't have any answers. "I don't know what you want me to say."

"I should have fucking written him up when I caught him drinking." He dropped my hand.

"Who? Eli? It wasn't him."

"Then who was it, Sadie?"

"I don't know. It was just some scary looking guy." *Terrifyingly scary.*

He grabbed my hand again. "You can talk to me. If you're scared of something, I promise that I won't tell anyone. It can stay between us. Just tell me who did this. Let me help you."

I pulled my hand away. I wasn't dragging Miles into this mess. "I don't need your help. Why do you keep offering to help me?" Want and need were two very different things. I wanted him desperately. I wanted him to hold my hand and make me feel safe for the rest of my life. It's what I had always wanted. I let the feeling of loss he had given me all those years ago take over my mind. It was the only way I knew how to push him away. To keep him safe. I didn't need him. I didn't need anyone. And if he offered to help me one more time, I was going to lose it.

"Because I care about you."

"Sadie!" Kins barreled into the room. "Thank God you're awake." She embraced me in a hug.

"Ow," I mumbled.

"Geez, sorry. What the hell happened to you?"

I stole a glance at Miles. He shook his head, as if he could hear my silent question. I was glad that Kins didn't know. Her finding out would ruin everything. It would be the tipping point. And I wasn't ready to leave. I tried to keep my face blank. *God, what the hell was I thinking?* I needed to leave. No matter how much I cared about them, I didn't belong here. I was putting them both in danger by staying. But I still didn't want to scare them. "Some guy tried to mug me."

"Welcome to, New York, I guess." She gave me a small smile.

"I'm fine though, really." Hopefully Miles would accept my excuse too, but I had a feeling he wouldn't.

"Good. You scared me half to death." She gave me a much more gentle hug. "I know there were a few cops that wanted to talk to you about it." She turned to Miles. "We should probably get going. She needs her rest."

"I think I'll stay," Miles said.

"Don't be ridiculous. You haven't slept since I woke you up in the middle of the night. You need some rest before classes tomorrow. Right, Sadie?" She gave me a crazy looking smile and nodded not at all subtly toward Miles.

Was she seriously using this moment to take advantage of them being alone? I didn't want them to be together. But I also needed Miles to leave before I confessed all my worries and fears. I felt too comfortable around him. I didn't want to do something that I'd regret.

"Kins is right," I said. "You should get going. Thanks for coming though."

Kins walked around the bed and grabbed his arm.

He lowered his eyebrows slightly and just stared at me.

I dropped his gaze. He wasn't mine. Out of the corner of my eye, I watched him stand up. Kins' hand was still wrapped around his arm as they walked toward the door.

They weren't together already, were they? I held my breath. For one second. *No.* For two seconds. They couldn't be together. For three seconds. Of course I wanted them both to be happy. For four seconds. But not together. It hurt even more than I expected it to. For five seconds.

Miles lowered his shoulder slightly and stepped away from her to open the door.

I exhaled slowly. He didn't like her.

"Feel better, Sadie." His gaze seemed to bore into mine. "I'll be back after class tomorrow, okay?"

I didn't say a word, mostly because I knew I wouldn't still be here after class. I needed to get the hell out of this city. I watched them disappear and it felt like my heart crushed into a million pieces. Would that be the last time I ever saw him? There was no reason to assume the worst. The police were going to help. I pushed myself into a sitting position as I waited for the cops. But could they really help me? Would they think I was crazy like Kins had when I mentioned the box?

I scratched my arm nervously and completely froze. It was wet and sticky. The smell of blood seemed to completely fill my nose. I looked down at the inside of my forearm and almost vomited.

There were red words smeared across my skin. "Your move."

Blood. What the fuck? I clasped my hand over my arm. Who's blood was that? Who had been in my room? The doctor, Miles, Kins, the cops...*God.* Had I really expected them to help me? They'd think I was insane. They'd think I did this to myself. They'd think I made up the box. I need-ed to help myself for once in my life. I pulled the IV out of my hand. *Fuck that hurts.* I winced as I climbed out of the bed. My clothes were folded on a chair. I quickly pulled on my shorts and tattered t-shirt and laced my shoes. There was a dark blue hoodie draped across the back of the chair. It wasn't mine, but I definitely recognized it. I lifted it up and held it against my chest. The vigilante's cologne seemed to waft around me. He left me his hoodie? A noise outside my door interrupted my thoughts.

There was no way I could talk to the police. I needed to disappear. I ripped my sling off, ignoring the searing pain in my arm, and zipped on the hoodie. It was huge on me, but I didn't even care. It made me feel safe, despite the fact that I was in terrible danger. I lifted the hood over my head and slipped out the door. As far as I could tell, no one followed me.

There wasn't a doubt in my mind that if I stayed here any longer, one of Don's hit men would kill me or worse. The more time I spent with anyone, the more I was put-ting them in danger as well. I had to go. I pulled my phone out of my pocket. I pressed on Mr. Crawford's name and held the phone to my ear. *Please answer this time.*

There was a terrible screeching noise. "This number is no longer in service," said a computerized female voice. "This number is no longer in service," it repeated. The screeching noise resumed.

I pulled my phone away from my ear. How could his number no longer be in service? He was my only way out of this mess. He told me he'd always answer my calls. He was supposed to be there, waiting for me when I needed him. And I fucking needed him right now. My heart started racing even faster as I crossed the street. Had something really happened to him? Was it because of me? What the hell was I supposed to do now? Why hadn't I called Mr. Crawford right after I recognized Miles? I waited until it was too late. The city felt claustrophobic. It felt like the buildings were crashing down on me.

Your move. The bloody message on my skin made me shiver. Don was turning my life into some kind of sick game. I stopped on the sidewalk and ignored the people rudely telling me I was in the way. *Stupid New York.* I scrolled through my missed messages until I found a response from Liza. She hadn't really answered any of my texts, all the response had in it was an address. But that would do.

"I'm on my way," I typed and pressed send. She'd help me. Out of everyone I had met here, I probably knew her the least. For some reason, though, I just knew she'd help me figure this mess out. She had to.

I followed the directions on my GPS until I came to an apartment building in a much nicer part of town than the last one. I found the intercom and pressed the number for the address Liza had given me.

"You woke me up," Liza said groggily through the call box.

"I think I found something."

"If there isn't a cup of coffee in your hand for me, I'd really reconsider coming up. I get grumpy when I haven't gotten enough sleep."

"I have coffee for you," I lied.

"You know I can see you, right?"

Of course she had a camera down here.

"This better be good." The door buzzed open and I quickly grabbed the handle.

I took the elevator up and wandered down the hall to her door. Before I even knocked, I heard a bunch of bolts being unlocked.

The door swung open. I had thought her hair was unruly before, but it looked like a rat's nest piled on top of her head tonight.

She pushed her glasses up the bridge of her nose. "You're dressing like the vigilante now too?"

"It's his, actually." I pushed past her and into the apartment. It was definitely nicer than the last one, but the set up was virtually the same. There were computer and TV monitors everywhere.

"You talked to him again? Did you figure out anything that might point to who he is?"

I turned back to her. "Not exactly. I need your help."

She pursed her lips. "Last time you came, you promised you had information on the vigilante. Everything you told me I already knew. So now you're telling me you don't have anything else, you just want me to fix your computer again or something?"

"I wouldn't say throwing my computer out the window was fixing it. And this is related. You agreed that the vigilante is here because of me. And I'm in trouble."

"I was up late last night chasing down a lead. I haven't slept in over 24 hours. I need some coffee." She turned away from me and walked into the small kitchen. There was already a pot brewing.

Did she really have no reaction to me being in trouble? Maybe she was the wrong person to confide in. Unfortunately, she was the only one that could make any sense of what I had found on Eli's iPod. And I knew it was all related. It had to be. It was the only lead I had. I stood awkwardly in the hallway until she rejoined me.

"Does this have anything to do with the vigilante breaking his MO again?" She walked past me toward her computers.

I followed her. "How do you know about that?"

"The dead body that showed up in the dumpster on 9th avenue? The guy's rap sheet goes further back than my birth. And the bullet that pierced his skull was registered to his own gun. I'm pretty sure he didn't shoot himself in the back of the head, so I'm assuming it has something to do with what you're not telling me."

"I don't know what you're talking about."

"I'm talking about the fact that your name isn't really Sadie Davis. Who are you?" She wasn't kidding, she really did get bitchy when she was tired.

"That's not why I'm here." I just needed help tracing Don. I needed to know if he was really here. I needed to know if he was the one messing with my head.

"I know. You just need my help again. Well, until you start talking, I'm not helping you. I'm not an idiot. You being here puts me in danger too. So if you want my help, you better start talking."

It didn't seem like she was bluffing. Mr. Crawford was missing as far as I could tell. There was a bounty on my head, or my face more literally. I was caught in the middle of some twisted game I didn't understand. Despite how much I wanted to believe I could handle all this on my own, I couldn't. And it seemed like Liza was pretty good at hiding. Maybe she wouldn't get hurt in the crossfire. "My real name is Summer Brooks and I..."

"I *knew* it."

"What?"

She turned back to her computers and pulled up an article about my case. "As soon as I saw Gavin Moore's body turn up, I saw the pattern. He's a hit man for Don Roberts. And so was the other guy that made the vigilante break his MO. It was easy to put the pieces together. Your disguise is good, but it doesn't really fool anyone who's known you recently."

She brought up a picture of me, one from the report filed against Don. It was supposed to be in evidence. How did she even find it? There was a bruise on my eye and a cut on my lip. I looked terrified. I probably looked the same way right now, minus the red hair and blue eyes.

"I should have put it together as soon as crime started to increase," Liza said. "Not just petty crimes either. Shoot outs, rapes, homicides, it's a cesspool. You singlehandedly brought the Helspet Mafia to New York City."

It felt like cold water was running through my veins. "What are you talking about?"

"Did you really not know?"

I didn't know. "I thought he was a drug dealer." God, I was such an idiot. Of course it was more than that. The parts of town we always lived in seemed fine when we moved, but turned south shortly after. He destroyed everything in his path.

"Drugs are a part of it, but it's bigger than that." She pulled up a picture of Don Roberts. "And he's the head of all of it. You were living under his roof for six years. How could you not have known?"

"I thought crime lords were...older."

"You watch too many movies. They have to be young and strong enough to defend their territory. It's not a game for the weak. And Don Roberts certainly fits the bill." She clicked on another computer and a video of him appeared. He was walking down the street. There were tall buildings all around him.

A chill ran down my spine. "He's here?" It's what I had feared.

"He's been here ever since he was released on bail."

"He's not supposed to leave Colorado." My body felt like ice. "He's not allowed to leave."

"But he's Don Roberts. He has connections. Hell, his connections have got connections. And not necessarily legal ones. Crime has increased ten-fold since he stepped foot in this city."

This was the darkness that the vigilante was talking about. It was all my fault. What was I supposed to do? Go back to him to fix it? I couldn't go back. Gavin said he didn't even want me back. He just wanted me dead. "This is all my fault."

"Yeah, it is."

I wasn't sure why I thought she'd comfort me. We weren't exactly friends. "What am I supposed to do? I can't go back. He'll kill me. I got him arrested." *I burned his face.* "I was in the witness protection program for a reason. You have to help me. He's been sending me these weird messages about some twisted game he wants to play. He's messing with my head." I could tell how frantic I sounded, but I couldn't seem to stop. "There's a bounty on my head. And my witness protection handler isn't answering his phone. I don't know what to do."

She looked disgusted by my outburst. "Easy. You just have to find his weakness."

"He doesn't have any."

"Everyone has weaknesses. For example, you're the vigilante's. He's putting himself in danger to save you. He can't take on the whole mafia by himself. It's only a matter of time before he's the one that ends up in some dumpster."

I wouldn't let anyone die because of me. She was right. I had already been leaning toward the decision to disappear again. This was the final push. "I'll leave."

"Then you better hope that you're Don's weakness too. If he doesn't follow you, he's going to destroy this city."

I knew that better than anyone. He destroyed everything he touched. His fingertips were like fire on my skin. The thought of Eli came back to me. "I did have something for you. I don't know if it's related to this or the vigilante or what..."

"All of this is related to the vigilante."

Right. "Well, I was thinking about my computer being bugged. And at first I thought it was my handler from the witness protection program, but now I'm not so sure. I think it was this guy I've been seeing. He has this iPod that is clearly not for music." I pulled up the picture of Eli's iPod on my phone and handed it to her. "Can you make any sense of that?"

"They're all street names. Maybe they're handoff spots?"

"But why was there static when I listened to them?"

"Static?" She pushed her glasses up her nose. "Why didn't you say so? It's probably radio frequencies then."

I gave her an empty stare. "Like, to monitor phone calls to cops to see if he can help?"

She laughed. "You think he's the vigilante? This is way too complex for him. No offense to your knight in shining armor, but like I said, he's not great with computers." She shook her head like I was the dumbest person she had ever met. "It's probably how he gets instructions from his boss. There must be a different frequency on each of these streets. Check points kind of."

"His boss? So you think he's working for Don?"

"How the hell should I know? I haven't spent any time with any of them. All I'm saying is that this is some next level stuff. I don't even know where he'd get this technology. But I wouldn't put it past Don for having it. Like I said, his connections have connections."

Eli's working for Don. It shouldn't have been surprising. I already knew that he was bad news. My gut had been absolutely right about him. He wasn't safe at all. But now he was more dangerous than I had ever realized. He'd been spying on me this whole time, pretending to care. Just the thought made my blood boil.

"Look, don't chase this."

"What if it could lead me to Don? What if..."

"Are you seriously going to try take down the Helspet Mafia all by yourself? Just because you're wearing a pair of Converses and a hoodie doesn't make you a superhero. You need to get the hell out of New York City before you get us both killed."

Liza wasn't my friend. She wanted me to leave the city and take the darkness with me. I wondered if the vigilante would stay once I had left. Had he really started all this because of me? It had to be something more than that. He had to have a reason greater than my safety. I thought about the money he had been giving to the poor. I had put a great guy in danger for no other reason than my attraction to him.

I nodded. She was right. I wasn't a superhero. I was terrified of Don, and whenever I was in his presence I completely froze. "Thank you for everything," I said.

"And thank you for leaving."

No, she definitely wasn't my friend. Or maybe she just had social issues. I walked over to the door and opened it. She didn't even glance over her shoulder or wish me good luck. I closed the door behind me and shoved my hands into the pockets of the vigilante's hoodie.

That's when I felt the piece of paper. I pulled it out of my pocket as I stepped onto the elevator.

Sadie,

If you refuse to stop putting yourself in danger, at least make it a little easier on me. I added myself to your speed dial.

-V

V. Did that stand for vigilante? Or did his name actually begin with a V? I studied the handwriting until the elevator door dinged open. Even his manly scrawl was sexy. But none of that mattered. I was his weakness. If anything, this note proved that. I had to leave. Besides, he had asked me to stop thinking about him. I slid the note back into my pocket. Maybe once I was safely out of New York, I could text him. I'd tell him I was okay and that he didn't have to worry, even if it wasn't the truth. The only thing I seemed capable of was lies.

CHAPTER 39
Thursday

"Jesus, Sadie. I've been looking all over for you."

I hadn't expected Eli to be standing outside of my dorm building. But there he was, with more flowers, and more looks of apology on his face. He should have looked apologetic. He had been spying on me this whole time.

"I was busy." I stayed a few feet away from him. I didn't want him anywhere near me.

"Busy? Kins told me you were in the hospital. Are you okay? What happened?" He took a step closer.

Stay the hell away from me. "It was just a random mugging. But I'm fine. They didn't even steal anything."

The concerned look on his face seemed to falter. "You think I can't tell when you're lying to me, but I can. Look, let's go inside and we can talk about what happened." He took another step toward me.

"No." If I was going to start saving myself, now seemed as good a time as ever.

"Come on, we need to get inside." He didn't look like he cared about me at all. He looked pissed.

"I'm not going anywhere with you."

He exhaled slowly. "I'm not messing around. We need to go. Now." He grabbed my wrist.

"I'm not messing around either." I pulled my arm away from him. "I'm not going anywhere with you. You've been lying to me ever since we've met."

"Me? You're joking, right? I'm the one that's lying? You won't even tell me who hurt you." He was raising his voice. People on the sidewalk were starting to stare. He was just like Don, his temper seeming to rise without his control.

"Because I don't feel comfortable talking about it. You keep pushing an issue that I'm trying to get over. I can't talk about it because I don't want to. And this isn't about me, it's about you."

"Seriously? Because the list goes on and on for you. I specifically asked you to stop talking to Miles." He was yelling at me now. "And I had to find out from Kins that he spent all night and day by your side at the hospital. How do you think that made me feel?"

"Are you seriously jealous? It doesn't even seem like you like me. Why did you really ask me to stay away from him?" I was certain he had a whole different reason than whatever lie he was about to say.

"Because I like you. Of course I like you."

"All you do is lie to me! You wanted me to stay away from him because you thought he'd ruin everything."

"Ruin everything between us? Yeah, I was fucking worried about that and obviously I had a right to be. And just for the record, I haven't lied to you. You're losing your mind."

That's what Don wanted. He wanted me to think I was completely crazy. "Oh yeah? That gym you've been going to doesn't even have boxing classes."

"You've been following me?"

"No. I just looked it up online because you've been acting so evasive."

He laughed. It sounded strained. "I haven't lied to you. All I've done is tried to help you." He grabbed my wrist more forcefully this time. "And I'm asking you to trust me when I say that we need to get inside."

I pulled away from him again. "I listened to your iPod."

"What the hell? I knew you went through my stuff."

"How else was I supposed to learn anything about you?"

"You could have asked me. Unlike you, I would have loved to have a conversation. I was never constantly pushing you away."

Maybe he was right. But I didn't have time to regret anything else. "I don't have to explain myself. You've been the one spying on me."

"Fuck." He ran his hands through his hair. "Look," he said dropping his voice. "It's not what you think."

That was the only confession I needed. "Why, because I think you're trying to hurt me? This was never about us, I'm just a job to you."

"You have no idea what you're talking about."

"Stay the hell away from me, Eli." It was true. It was all true. The fire from his touch. I should have followed my gut. He was bad news. I didn't even need to know the specifics. He was part of the darkness that I had brought here.

"You know what? Fine. I've done everything I could to help you. I'm fucking done." He grabbed my arm once more. "Some people can't be saved."

I pushed his chest so that he'd get off me. "You're right. People like you can't be saved."

"You've just made a terrible mistake." He looked incredulous.

I turned away from him. His threats meant nothing to me. Yes, he was working for Don, but I wasn't scared of him. The only person I truly feared was his boss.

"Sadie, wait. Sadie." He grabbed my shoulder hard.

Fire. And it wasn't just because he had grabbed my hurt shoulder.

"I'm sorry. I shouldn't have said what I did. I'm just trying to help you."

It's like he was at a war with himself in his head. Maybe he didn't want to hurt me, but ultimately that wasn't his decision. He'd burn everything in his path. "Let go of me."

"We have to go inside. I'm serious. If you'd just hear me out..."

I stomped on his foot. Hard.

"Fuck." He released my shoulder and grabbed his foot. "Sadie!" he called after me, but the door to my dorm building was already closing.

I heard his fists pounding on the glass door.

"Sadie!"

CHAPTER 40
Thursday

I ran up the stairs. Hit men were after me. Don was after me. Eli was somehow involved with them. I couldn't trust anyone. It was exactly what the vigilante had warned me about. I had to get out of here.

I burst through the door to my floor. As soon as I grabbed a few things, I'd disappear. It was better that way. But my feet slowed when I saw Miles' door. And then they stopped completely when I was standing right outside of it. I knew he was sleeping. He had left the hospital to do just that.

My hand seemed to lift and knock on his door without me telling it to. My feet stayed firmly planted, even though I was trying to make them walk away. This was a bad idea. Seeing him would make it so much harder to leave. How was I supposed to say goodbye to him again? Did I even want to?

His door opened. "It's the middle of the night, what..." his voice trailed off when he saw me. He was wearing a tight t-shirt and boxers. That was it. He wasn't the same boy that had abandoned me. He was a man. So why did my heart still feel the same way about him?

I stepped forward and wrapped my arms around him. I breathed in his scent. He still smelled like the grass we used to roll around in. God, he smelled perfectly the same. *Home.* Miles would forever be home to me.

He didn't hesitate to wrap his arms around me too. "What are you doing out of the hospital?"

I kept the side of my face pressed against his chest. *I've always loved you. I'll always love you.* I clung to him with full knowledge that I'd never see him again. My heart seemed to break all over again. "I'm sorry that I pushed you away." I couldn't answer his question. All I could do was apologize for causing him any pain.

His lips brushed against my ear. "You don't have to apologize, Sadie."

"And I'm sorry that I threw your pain in your face."

"I was just thankful that you listened."

He was so good. He was way too good for me. I had to say goodbye. I just didn't know how. "Can you just hold me for a few more seconds?"

"Do you want to come in?" His lips brushed against my ear again.

He was offering to hold me for longer than a few seconds. Hell, maybe he was offering to hold me forever. Time was supposed to heal everything. But time had never healed my wounds from Miles Young. And if I stayed in his room tonight, if I let our relationship grow any more, this time it would kill me.

I'm so sorry. Please forgive me for disappearing again. "One day you're going to find someone so good. So perfect. And so worthy of you. Promise me you'll keep your heart open?"

He put his fingers under my chin and lifted my face so that I'd meet his eyes. "Why do you not see how truly extraordinary you are?"

His words brought tears to my eyes. Extraordinary? That wasn't a word that anyone would use if they knew the real me. I was broken. I was weak. I was running away from my problems because it was the only thing I knew how to do. "Just promise me."

He lowered his eyebrows slightly. "I've already found everything I want."

I swallowed hard. God, I wanted him to kiss me. I wanted a new kiss that I'd compare everything to for the rest of my life. I wanted to stay in his arms for eternity. *I'm in trouble.* All I had to do was say it out loud. He'd help me. Our lips were only a fraction of an inch apart now.

"Sadie?"

Shit. I turned my head just in time to see Kins staring at us.

"How could you?" She sounded devastated. She shook her head as she retreated back to our room.

Maybe I was wrong about everything. Maybe I was the one that burned everything in my path. "I have to go."

"Sadie." His fingers on my wrist were gentle, loving. "I can't make a promise I don't intend to keep."

That was our goodbye? A guarantee that we'd both be miserable for the rest of our lives? Maybe he'd feel differently once he realized I was gone. But I couldn't live with that chance. He deserved the world. My eyes met his one last time. For the first time, I realized how exhausted he looked. It may have just been because I had awakened him, but I felt like it was deeper than that. He claimed he still missed Summer. Maybe I was finally helping him move on. And it killed me. It killed me to know that I was going to hurt him all over again. I wished that I could tell him everything I never got to the first time around. How he always meant so much more to me than the stars. How I loved him since the first moment I saw him. "You've always been better off without me, Miles."

He lowered his eyebrows slightly.

I wasn't sure why I had said that. I realized my mistake as soon as the words fell out of my mouth. *Always.* Why would I say always when we had only just met? What had I just done?

His lips parted slightly like he was about to say something, but he closed them again.

I couldn't stand there and let the pieces slowly fall together. *Goodbye, Miles Young.* I stood on my tiptoes and kissed his cheek. The warmth of his cheek made my lips tingle. I could hold on to that feeling of warmth. I'd need it. I turned around without another word and walked as fast as I could to my room.

All I could feel was pain. Not the pain in my shoulder though. The pain in my heart. I would never see Miles again. That was it. I had always wanted to know if he was well. This had to be closure for me. He'd find someone wonderful because he was so fantastic.

I opened up my door and walked into my room. Kins was sitting on her bed crying.

"Kins..." I didn't really know what to say.

"You knew I liked him." She wiped her tears away with her hands. "How could you?"

"I'm so sorry." Everyone was better off without me. I wanted to comfort her. I wanted to apologize a million times. But I didn't have time. The longer I stayed, the more danger she was in. I grabbed my backpack and shoved a few articles of clothing inside.

"Are you even listening to me?" She threw her pillow at me. "I want to talk about this. You said you weren't even attracted to him. What did I ever do to you?"

"I'm sorry," I said again. I threw more things into my backpack.

"I'm gonna sleep with Eli." Her words were icy.

That was harsh. The threat would have stung more a few days ago, but now I couldn't care less who Eli slept with. "If that'll make you feel better, then do it." It was good that she was making me upset. It made it even easier to walk away.

"Why won't you even look at me?"

I looked over at her sitting on the bed. Her mascara was streaked down her cheeks. I immediately felt bad again. "I'm sorry, Kins. I'm just going to go. I know I haven't been the best roommate, and I am sorry." I pulled out my worn copy of Harry Potter and the Sorcerer's Stone, the one with my father's inscription, and stuffed it into my backpack.

"You're leaving? You can't just leave. I want to talk about this."

"I just think it's better if I go home." I tried to keep my voice even on the word "home."

"What do you mean home?" She sniffled. "It's the middle of the week. You have classes."

"I'm dropping out." It was extreme, but what did it matter? She'd have wondered why I never came back. This would make her understand.

"What are you talking about? I don't want you to do that. I just...it hurt to see him with you like that. I don't want you to leave me."

She was my first friend in a long time. And it hurt to lie to her. "I'm sorry." It seemed to be the only thing I knew how to say.

"What's going on?" She wiped away the rest of her tears. Even though she was upset, she looked more concerned about me now.

I bit the inside of my lip. "Eli broke up with me and I hate this city, so I'm leaving." Heartache always made people do stupid things. It was a good excuse.

She nodded as if she understood my sudden interest in Miles and my reason for wanting to leave. "There are so many guys in this city. You don't need Eli."

"I know." I pulled my backpack onto my shoulders. "But that doesn't mean I want to stay."

"Does this have something to do with that box?"

Why did she bring that up? Had she lied to me? I felt compelled to throw everyone under the bus tonight. Kins was the only one that had access to our dorm room. I had thought someone broke in. But there hadn't been any signs of forced entry. It was almost like they had a key. Could she be involved in this?

She just stared at me, waiting for my answer. She looked almost too innocent. Like Eli had been too nice.

"No, not at all, I just have to go."

"Just stay, we can talk about this." She slid off her bed. "You can't leave because some guy broke your heart. That's so crazy."

Crazy. It's exactly what Don wanted. My hand grabbed the handle of my door.

She took another step closer to me. "Seriously, don't go. Everything's going to be okay."

Her reassurance terrified me. It sounded fake. It sounded rehearsed. I opened up the door and ran out before she could get any closer to me.

"Sadie, stop!"

I ran down the hall and flung the doorway to the stairwell open. Was she really involved too? Or was I just losing my mind? My whole world had just come crashing down on me again. The only difference was that this time I wasn't sure I would make it out alive.

CHAPTER 41
Thursday

My bus wouldn't be coming for another hour. I walked into Central Park. It was the only place that really felt like home in this city. I had told myself I felt comfortable in my dorm and with the new people in my life, but it was all a lie. All I knew were lies. Which made the decision about where to go even easier. For ten years, all I had wanted was to go home. Now I was actually allowed to. Hopefully Don would follow me out west and then I'd work harder to disappear. I had to draw him out of the city. It shouldn't be that hard, darkness always had a way of following me.

I walked off the path and sat down in the grass. I leaned against the rock behind me and stared up at the dim stars. If I looked really hard, I could see Sagitta. Maybe the arrow was pointing me home. Maybe I could finally get some peace if I went back there. Maybe I could let some of this pain go. I lightly touched the center of my chest.

"You can't leave," a voice rumbled behind me.

I wasn't surprised that he had figured out my plans. He was always watching. "It's what you wanted." I continued to look up at the stars. There had already been so many goodbyes. I wasn't sure I had another one in me. Besides, it would just end up with me not trusting him either, leaving me with nothing.

"Not now." He stood in front of me, blocking my view of the stars.

"Nothing's changed. You don't even know me. I'm putting everyone in danger by staying, including you." I stood up and started to walk away from him.

"Some risks are worth taking."

His words made me freeze in my tracks. *I'm not worth it. I'm not worth any of this.* "You killed someone."

"I didn't have a choice."

"You always have a choice." I hadn't even realized it, but I was mad at him. How could he take someone's life so easily? Mine had been taken from me. No one had given that a second thought.

"He was hurting you." He took a step closer to me.

I could smell his cologne. It made me feel slightly dizzy. "I'm used to being hurt."

"And I refuse to let anything else happen to you."

"Which is exactly why I have to go. I'm not going to let you get hurt when I'm the one being targeted. I already have my bus ticket. It's too late, I'm not changing my mind."

"I know you feel it too," he said, ignoring me. "I know that you're conflicted." He placed his gloved hand on the center of my chest.

I did feel it. It was like he could feel my pain. It almost felt like he was taking it away, putting it on himself. I was suddenly able to breathe a little easier. But it was way more than that. I felt this undeniable connection between us. I didn't understand it. I didn't even know him. I shook my head. "You told me to stop thinking about you."

"It'll kill me if you leave," his voice rumbled.

"Why? Why do you care so much about me?"

"Because I see the real you, the you that you try so hard to hide. But you can't hide from me. I've always seen you. Your beauty, inside and out, captivates my soul. There's a goodness in you that I crave. I can feel the pain in your heart. It cripples me. I'm tormented by your frowns. I'm only at peace when I see you smile. You're everything to me. You're the calm to my chaos. The silence to all the noise. You're the air that I breathe. And I know you understand me, the way no one else possibly could. Because you know what it's like to hide behind a mask too," he whispered.

He knows? He could have meant anything by that. Maybe he thought I was hiding something else from him. But it didn't seem like it. *He knows that I'm Summer.* "Let me see your face."

He stepped closer to me until I could feel his body heat. "You don't need to see me. I'm the one you dream about. I'm the only one you need."

"You can't stalk my dreams like you stalk me in real life."

"Your words may push others away, but not me. Tell me that I'm wrong." He put his hand on the side of my face. "Tell me that you don't shiver at my touch. Tell me that you don't dream of my lips. Tell me you don't want to know what it feels like to have me inside of you." His breath was hot in my ear.

Jesus. I swallowed hard.

"You don't understand. It's more complicated than that." I tilted my head back so that our lips were only an inch apart. My body did shiver under his touch. I had dreamt of his touch so many nights. And I had dreamt of so much more.

"I do understand. You told me you were strong enough to face your fears here. You told me you wanted to help. So stay." He pushed the hoodie off my head and let his fingers tangle in my hair as he pressed himself against me. "Please stay."

"I was wrong." I let the tears fall down my cheeks. "I'm in trouble and I don't know what to do."

"I know. But I won't let anything happen to you."

I shook my head. I'd get him killed. "I'm so tired of living in pain. But I'm not strong enough to fight it."

He wiped my tears away with his thumbs. "Yes you are. You're made of steel, Sadie."

Sadie. He didn't know. No one would ever know. I wanted to forget the pain. I wanted to become the person he saw. And it had been far too fucking long since I hadn't felt scared when I heard my name affectionately spoken on someone's lips. It was like I had no control over my body. I grabbed the back of his hood and pulled his face to mine.

He didn't hesitate to kiss me back. His mouth completely possessed me as his hands pulled me even tighter against his chest. It wasn't just a kiss. I could feel it. He wanted more. And I wanted him to make me forget about my pain. I wanted to overcome my fears.

His lips wandered to my neck as his fingers found the zipper of my hoodie. "This looks much better on you."

Just the sound of it unzipping made me want him even more. What was I doing? I didn't know him. How could I feel safe doing this if he didn't let me see him? "Let me see your face."

"You won't like what you see," he growled.

"I don't think that's true." I grabbed the bottom of his mask and rolled it up his neck until I felt the scruff on his chin.

He pushed me backwards until my back hit the cold rock. It sent a shiver down my spine.

I could have told him to stop, but I didn't want to. His fingers trailed up the insides of my thighs. Maybe I was losing my mind. But I knew he could take the pain away. I knew he was stronger than I was. "Please let me see your face." My voice was less demanding this time.

He knew he had me right where he wanted me.

He hooked his fingers in the waistband of my shorts and pulled them and my thong down my thighs.

"We can't..." We were in the middle of Central Park. Yes, we were off the path, but that didn't mean people couldn't see us. My words were completely meaningless. I wanted him and he knew it.

He pulled my face back to his. "We can." His lips found mine again as his hands wandered to my ass.

Fuck. I could feel his hardness pressed against me. It was almost like I needed him. I couldn't remember the last time I had felt truly needed. Wanted, yes, but needed? I could hear it in his voice. He didn't just want me, he needed me. Could I make his pain go away like he could mine? Is that what this was? For some crazy reason, we needed each other because no one else could want us with our masks on?

He grabbed my ass and I immediately lifted my thighs around him.

I couldn't even think straight when his hands were on me. Maybe I didn't feel the fire because of his gloves. But I didn't care. All I knew was that I felt safe. And I hadn't felt truly safe in ten years.

I had also never been more excited by anyone's touch before. Maybe I had just walked away from the love of my life. Maybe a part of me would always regret turning down Miles. But I didn't have to live forever in pain. I couldn't do that. I was already holding on to so much. *Help me forget. Help me move on.*

I was panting when I pulled my lips away from his. I put my hands on both sides of his masked face. There was no doubt that he had a strong jaw line. And his lips were heaven. But I wanted to truly see him. "Let me see you," I whispered against his lips.

He pulled my hands from his face and pressed the backs of them against the cold rock. "Feel me instead," his voice rumbled as he thrust himself deep inside of me.

Oh God. My fingers tightened around his.

"Fuck," he groaned into my mouth.

He was huge. All I could feel was the pressure of him pushing against all my walls. I thought the first time I did this on my own accord would be gentle and loving. But I knew deep down I could never have that. And maybe this was what I wanted. Raw. Rough. Passionate. Savage. Each thrust of his hips felt better than the last. I wrapped my legs tighter around his waist.

It could have been naive, but I did feel love. He watched me. He protected me. That was love in its own twisted way. All I really knew was twisted. Because the first time I had truly given myself to someone, I wanted to fuck instead of make love. What was wrong with me?

But God, it felt so right. And each time he thrust into me, I felt the pain slipping away and bliss taking its place. He made me feel whole. He made me feel like my demons were smaller than they actually were. He made me feel so fucking alive.

"I can't stop thinking about you." His breath was hot against my neck.

"I don't want you to stop."

He groaned at my words. "Say you'll stay." He pulled out of me and pressed the tip of his erection against me.

I watched his Adam's apple rise and then fall. I wanted to touch it. I wanted to taste it. I wanted all he'd give me. "I'll stay."

He thrust himself inside of me again, even harder.

Fuck. My lips found the skin on his neck. He tasted as good as he smelled. If this was all he felt comfortable with me seeing, I'd take it. I'd revel in it. I kissed underneath his jaw and relished the rough feeling of his 5 o'clock shadow on my lips. I was lost in him. I was lost and I never wanted to be found again.

He tilted his hips slightly and I swore I saw the stars. Nothing had ever felt so good.

"Please don't stop," I moaned.

I felt his smile against my neck. "I'm not the one threatening to go anywhere." His lips traveled down my clavicle.

"I'll stay. I promise I'll stay."

His pushed aside my tattered shirt with his nose as his lips found my breast. His tongue slowly encircled my nipple.

What was he trying to do to me?

"You're perfect," he said.

My body arched toward him and he lightly bit down on my nipple.

I couldn't even help the moan that escaped from my lips. I was so close. His mouth. His cock. His hands. He was the perfect one.

He lifted his face to look up at me. And from the angle, it was the first time I had ever seen his eyes. They were a deep brown. I felt like I stopped breathing when our eyes met. He was staring at me like no one ever had before. Complete smolder. I could feel the heat from his gaze. He let me see him. He trusted me. And that trust made me lose control. I could feel myself clenching around him.

He immediately closed his eyes and groaned. His eyelashes were long. For some reason I found them irresistible. I wanted to kiss every inch of his face. I so badly wanted to see him.

I felt his warmth spread up inside of me. It was the best feeling in the world. I had never felt so whole before.

"Look at me," I whispered as soon as I was able to speak again.

He squeezed his eyes shut tighter as he released my hands.

I grabbed both sides of his face. "Please."

He lowered his head, hiding his eyes underneath his hood again, and slowly pulled out of me.

I felt empty. How could I feel so lost when he had just made me feel so completely full?

He had taken away the pain, emotional and physical. But as soon as he placed me back down on my feet, it returned. My chest ached. I put my hand on my hurt shoulder.

He knelt down in front of me and pulled my shorts back up. He kissed my hipbone and then pushed the hoodie farther up my stomach. He kissed the jagged scar along the side of my bellybutton. Somehow that was even more intimate than what we had just done. How did he even know that I had it? *He's been watching me.* But for how long? I gulped as he slowly lifted his head.

He seemed to wince when his eyes landed on my shoulder. He released the baggy hoodie. "I hurt you." He quickly stood up and took a step away from me.

"What? No." I removed my hand from my shoulder. "No. You made me forget about the pain. I couldn't feel it," I said softly.

"You were just in a hospital. You should still be there."

"I'm okay."

He clenched his hands into fists.

It was like I could truly see him for the first time. He was tormented. How could two souls so destroyed possibly feel complete with each other? He told me that I wouldn't like what I saw if he took off his mask. I'd probably see a reflection of myself.

He took another step away from me.

"Where are you going?"

"You're safe here. That's all that matters. Call me if you're in trouble." He pulled his hood down even more over his eyes.

"And what if I'm not in trouble?" *What if I want more of you?*

He pressed his lips together. "I don't know how to stay away from you."

I didn't say a word as I watched him disappear into the darkness. *I can't stop thinking about you. I don't know how to stay away from you.* I was his weakness. It was just like Liza had said.

CHAPTER 42
Thursday

It felt like my chest was going to explode. He saw my scars and he kissed them. He saw my pain and he took it away by putting it on himself. He understood me better than anyone. And if I kept my promise to him and stayed, it would kill him. If I left, he claimed it would kill him. I had doomed him either way. I shook away the thought. He'd be hurt if I left, but it wouldn't physically kill him. I needed to get Don to follow me out of the city. I needed to take the darkness with me.

I started pacing at the bus stop terminal. Saying good-bye to Miles seemed like the right choice. I felt like he was better off without me. I felt strong for being able to say goodbye. I felt good about my decision. Selfless. Saying goodbye to Kins was an easy choice. I was just putting her in danger. And I cared about her. She was my best friend. I didn't want anything bad to happen to her. Or maybe she was trying to hurt me. I felt crazy.

I put my forehead in my hand. But the vigilante? I couldn't feel good about that decision. Wasn't he in danger either way? What if Don didn't follow me? *He'll follow me. He wants my life.* I had to go.

My heart was torn. No matter how much I told myself I was making the right choice, it killed me. All of it. Miles, Kins, the vigilante. I'd miss them. I had somehow made roots in a city where the stars were barely visible. I had felt more free here than I had in the past five years. I forced myself to sit down on the bench, but then my knee started bouncing uncontrollably.

If I stayed, what was the worst that could happen, really? I closed my eyes and took a deep breath to try to help clear my mind. *Blood.* I immediately opened my eyes. That's what I had brought here. I needed to rid the city of darkness. I needed to be as strong as the vigilante thought I was. *Made of steel.* I nodded to myself. I could be that for him. Yes, we had both given into desire, but that wasn't what he truly wanted. What he wanted was for me to stop thinking about him. He had even told me so.

I thought giving myself completely to someone would ease my fears, but for some reason it made them stronger. It was easy for me to put myself in his shoes. I looked down at my Converses. What if he left me like I was about to leave him? I knew what it felt like to be abandoned. I thought about the way he had put his hand on the center of my chest, absorbing my pain. I placed my hand where his had been.

And my heart stopped. Where was my Sagitta pendant? It felt like my throat was constricting. I checked the pockets of my hoodie and shorts. Had I been wearing it in Central Park? Or the hospital? Jesus, had Miles seen it when I was wearing the hospital gown? I couldn't remember the last time I had felt it around my neck. Had it slipped off before my run last night? Was I wearing it when I went to Eli's? What about when I was at the restaurant last?

The bus pulled into the terminal. I couldn't leave this city with a part of me missing. *Shit!* I had to leave. I stood up and watched as other people climbed up the bus steps. My feet, however, stayed firmly planted. I had to go.

But my gut was demanding that I stay. I shook away the thought. I'd just stay to find the pendant. It wasn't like I didn't have enough money to buy another bus ticket. I'd just get one once I found it. I nodded to myself, like that plan made perfect sense.

I was supposed to be forgetting my past. But my past was exactly what made me watch the bus pull away. I touched the center of my chest. I needed the pendant. I couldn't explain it. It wasn't just Miles or my parents or my youth. It meant everything to me. It meant as much to me as the stars in the sky. It had been with me through everything. I had to find it. And then I'd leave.

Don's here. Just thinking about him made me want to run after the bus. But I had already made up my mind. I'd just have to retrace my steps. Where was the last place I had seen it? I knew it had been around my neck in the bathroom at the restaurant when I had changed into running clothes. Had I lost it on my run? It could be anywhere by now.

But I'd find it. I didn't have a doubt in my mind that I could find it. If I looked hard enough, I could always see the constellations. Besides, it wasn't like it was an expensive diamond. It meant a lot to me, but in reality it was just an old keychain from a vending machine at a grocery store. I just hoped that no one had thrown it out. There was a lost and found at the restaurant. I could check there first.

It only took me a few minutes to run to the Corner Diner. The door was marked with a closed sign, but I could see Joan sitting inside the diner going over the books. I knocked on the door.

She immediately looked up. She seemed surprised to see me. And she should have. It was almost midnight.

"Hon, what on earth are you doing here so late?" she asked as she opened the door.

"Hey, Joan, I'm sorry to bother you. I just, I lost my necklace and this was one of the last places that I remembered having it..."

"Come in, come in. Why are you up so late?" She looked at my backpack.

Could she tell I was fleeing the city? "I was just studying at the library."

She nodded kindly. "Okay, hon. You look a little pale, though. Let me get you something to drink. Sit down."

"Oh, no, that's not necessary. I really need to get back home. I'm exhausted."

"Well, at least sit down for a moment. I'll go grab the lost and found." She disappeared into the kitchen.

I sat down and started nervously drumming my fingers on the table. *Please let it be in that box.*

She came back out with a glass of water and the lost and found box. "Drink. You look dehydrated."

In a lot of ways, she reminded me of my grandmother. She was a little rough around the edges, but had such a good heart. I took a sip of the water. Why was I lying to her? She was one of the nicest people I had met. I didn't want to leave her in the lurch. "Actually, Joan, I need to give you my notice. I'm sorry it's not more time, but I'm dreadfully homesick..." I let my voice trail off.

"You're leaving?"

"I'm sorry, I know you require two weeks, but I can't stay here any longer."

"Are you sure? Is there something I can do, hon? I know moving to the city is a big adjustment. Maybe you just didn't give it enough time?"

"No, I'm sure. I really am sorry."

"That's really too bad. I loved having you here. Honestly, you were the best help we've gotten in a long time." She pushed the box toward me. "I can't remember finding any necklaces recently, but maybe someone else put one in here."

I sifted through the contents. My necklace wasn't here. *Damn it.* Maybe I had lost it on my run? I bit the inside of my lip as I pushed a few more things around. At the bottom of the box there was a blank white card, almost identical to the one I had gotten with the slippers. I lifted up the top flap.

"You're terrible at this game, Sadie." My name was in quotes again.

It felt like all the air had been knocked out of my lungs. I lifted my eyes to Joan.

"Sorry, hon." She looked over my shoulder.

Before I could turn my head to see what she was looking at, I felt the barrel of a gun press into the back of my skull. I swallowed hard when I heard the person behind me cock it.

"Joan?" I hated how desperate my voice was. I wasn't going to beg her for my life. If she wanted me dead, there was nothing I could do. All I knew was that it wasn't Don behind me. If it was, I wouldn't still be breathing.

A smile curled over her lips. "You think I would normally hire someone with no references at my establishment? You think I'd give someone with slippery fingers a second chance? There are no second chances in the real world. My great grandfather built this business from nothing. I would never jeopardize his legacy."

I thought Eli was the bad guy. I put so much of my energy into proving he was out to get me, that I hadn't seen the signs pointing to Joan. She was right in front of me the whole time and I had been completely blind. I trusted her. "Why?"

"Don's a friend. I promised to keep an eye on you."

"If you knew what he did to me..."

She laughed. "You think your pain makes you special? It just makes you human."

I swallowed hard. The things he did to me weren't human. "But he wants me dead. Why didn't you just kill me?"

The barrel of the gun seemed to press more firmly against my skull.

"Change of plans, hon. He's setting up shop here. But your friend seems to be messing up all of his plans."

I started to shake my head but immediately stopped as the gun nestled down to my neck. "I don't know what you're talking about."

"The only person Don wants dead more than you is that pesky vigilante."

No. "I don't know him."

"We'll see if you change your mind about that once you see our leverage."

"You can do whatever you want to me. But I don't know the vigilante."

"There's three reasons why that isn't true. Eli." She put one finger up. "Miles." She put up a second. "And Kins." She put up a third.

My roots. I had finally made friends and she was going to kill them. *Please, no.* I tried to put on my best poker face. "You're lying."

The smile returned to her lips. "Where's the fun in that?"

I held my breath. For one second. I had brought darkness here.

For two seconds.

And I was too late.

For three seconds.

I was the fire that destroyed everything in my path.

For four seconds.

I wasn't made of steel at all.

For five seconds.

She nodded to the person behind her.

It took me five seconds to finally realize that the present was more precious than the past. Five seconds to realize that the people I had here meant more to me than I ever realized. Five seconds to realize that I had just broken everything. I was five fucking seconds too late.

My head slammed against the table as the butt of the gun hit the back of my skull.

LETTERS FROM MILES

Want to read more about what Miles was up to while Summer was in foster care?

Letters from Miles contains the letters he sent Summer over the years they were apart. The letters that she never received…

To get your free copy of *Letters From Miles*, go to:

www.ivysmoak.com/mos-amz

FORGED IN FLAMES

Can V save Summer?

Find out in book 2 of the Made of Steel Series, *Forged in Flames*…available now!

A NOTE FROM IVY

I was inspired to write a superhero story because I've always loved shows like Arrow and The Flash. And who doesn't love a sexy superhero? There's just something about that mask...

But this story was always more than just sexy superheroes to me. I put my heart and soul into Summer Brooks. I channeled every bad thing that's happened to me and became an emotional wreck while writing this novel. I don't think I've ever cried so hard while writing a character. And I hope that emotion showed in these words. I hope that you cried with me and loved with me.

Ivy Smoak

Ivy Smoak
Wilmington, DE
www.ivysmoak.com

ABOUT THE AUTHOR

Ivy Smoak is the international bestselling author of the
Made of Steel Series and *The Hunted Series*. When she's not
writing, you can find her binge watching too many TV
shows, taking long walks, playing outside, and generally
refusing to act like an adult. She lives with her husband in
Delaware.

Twitter: @IvySmoakAuthor
Facebook: IvySmoakAuthor
Goodreads: IvySmoak

Recommend *Made of Steel* for your next book club!

Book club questions available at:
www.ivysmoak.com/bookclub

Made in the USA
Las Vegas, NV
09 October 2021